the
California Roll

Books by **John Vorhaus**

*   *   *

The Comic Toolbox: How to Be Funny Even If You're Not

Creativity Rules! A Writer's Workbook

The Pro Poker Playbook: 223 Ways to Win More Money Playing Poker

Killer Poker: Strategy and Tactics for Winning Poker Play

Killer Poker Online: Crushing the Internet Game

The Killer Poker Hold'em Handbook

Poker Night: Winning at Home, at the Casino and Beyond

The Strip Poker Kit

Killer Poker Online 2: Advanced Strategies for Crushing the Internet Game

Killer Poker No Limit

Killer Poker Shorthanded (with Tony Guerrera)

Under the Gun (novel)

the

California

Roll

a novel

John Vorhaus

Shaye Areheart Books
NEW YORK

Published in the United States by Shaye Areheart Books, an imprint of the Crown Publishing Group, a division of Random House, Inc., New York.
www.crownpublishing.com

Shaye Areheart Books with colophon is a registered trademark of Random House, Inc.

Library of Congress Cataloging-in-Publication Data is available upon request

ISBN 978-0-307-46317-3

Printed in the United States of America

Design by Lynne Amft

10 9 8 7 6 5 4 3 2 1

First Edition

To Dan, David, Sarah, Jen, and Tom—
I trust I've been a good bad example

The best offense is a good pretense.

on the snuke

The first person I ever scammed was my grandmother, who had Alzheimer's disease and could never remember from one minute to the next whether she'd just given me ice cream or not. I'd polish off a bowl, drop it in the sink, walk out, walk back in, ask for another, and get it. Boom. They say you can get sick of ice cream if you eat too much. I found that was not the case.

They also say you can't cheat an honest man, but I say you can. The honest ones never see it coming.

In first grade, I cooked up the Golden Recess, which was a Ponzi scheme, though I didn't know to call it that then. I got my classmates to pool their allowances for me to invest in something. Action figures? Baseball card futures? I really don't remember. By the time the pyramid collapsed, I'd netted twenty bucks—huge money for first grade—and I didn't even do time because, though of course I got caught, no one believed a little kid could have such larceny in his soul.

Honest people. Like I said, they never see it coming.

And snukes—scams or the people who perform them—may have a bad name, but it's not always the case that someone gets burned. In fact, when you think about it, the best cons are the ones that leave people feeling like they got something for their money. And you know what? Sometimes they even do.

Consider the Doolally shorthair.

I'm like nine, ten, something like that, and I find this stray dog. He was a real mess, with matted, gunked-up fur and scarry evidence of many fights. I knew if I took him to the pound, they'd kack him for sure, and I couldn't stand to see a dog go down. So what I did, I shaved him and sold him to unsuspecting yuppies as an exotic purebred: the extremely rare and fairly expensive Doolally shorthair terrier. I charged a ton because, again, with honest people, they definitely think the more you pay, the more it's worth. Of course, it wouldn't do to have his hair grow out on them—who ever heard of a longhaired short-hair?—so before I sold him, I trained him to pigeon home. Which, at the first opportunity, he does. I shave him again and take him back again, and oh, the happy couple, they can't believe I found their pre-cious pooch! I explain how the Doolally is so valuable and rare that they all get GPS microchipped at birth, and these yuppies are so grateful, they give me a reward, which I protest taking but take just the same.

So the dog bolts again, and I return him again, this time spinning a yarn about how the chip only has a limited number of resets, whatever the hell that means, and had to be replaced—at cost, of course. This they totally buy, and why not? I mean, just look at me, such a choirboy. Beatle bangs, cherry cheeks, scout's-honor smile. That's always been a strength of my game: I look so straight, you'd never believe I'd try to sell you your wallet out of your own back pocket.

Anyway, the dog jets again, and I trot him back again and get paid again. I'm definitely thinking, *good times.*

But it can't last forever, right? Even the dullest dull normal will eventually catch on, so after the Doolally's last scamper, I show up with another mutt, some additional stray I rescued. I suggest that the

Doolally is a little more peripatetic—at that age I was all about the SAT words—wandery, yeah, than they can handle, but this other dog is a real homebody and won't go nomad like the Doolally. A schnuffle-hund, I called it. Very rare.

Sadly, the schnuffle costs a bit more, and would they mind making up the difference?

I kept that one dog, the original Doolally, and placed him in about five different homes before he had the bad luck to get run down by a rototiller (how does *that* happen?), and in the meantime, that's the lives of five other strays I saved, plus five other families who got the loyalty and love of a worthy woofer, even if they sort of overpaid for it. So you see, it was like the Haiphong phone book—a Nguyen-Nguyen situation.

Which is not to say that every day is Sunday in the park with George with me. Having been a grifter now for about twenty years (if you count the ice cream thing as the start, which I do), I recognize the big pitfall, and no, I'm not talking about getting (A) arrested or (2) the crap kicked out of you. (Both I have, and neither's a big deal.) I'm not even talking about what they call grift drift, where you have to make rootlessness your root and homelessness your home because it doesn't pay to set a stationary target, not in this line of work. No, the real problem with life on the snuke is how it makes you cynical. Once you know how easy it is to pull wool—and it seems like I knew it neonatally— you start to expect the worst, or at least the least, of people. It's not fair and it's not fun. So I work hard to keep up my pointillist perspective— make every day indeed Sunday in the park with George if I can—and I always try to give my victims the metaphorical reacharound, so they can feel like crossing paths with me wasn't the worst thing that could've happened to them in life.

According to me, I'm moral.

Plus, according to me, I'm normal, which is not at all abnormal when you think about it, because everybody's default view is the view from inside their own skin. Though I appreciate that I strike some as strange. First, there's my career, my chosen line of work, which few would choose. Next there's my inexpressive expressiveness. I learn like a sponge, and like a sponge I hold everything without judgment and sort without order. I'm equal parts lunch bucket, pop culture, and string theory, and this can make me appear quite random at times, though I find that people find that part of my charm. Of course, what they call charm I call a tool, but that's a subject for a different time.

Then there's my name: Radar Hoverlander. Seriously, who's got a name like that? People assume it's a *fabricat,*[*] possibly something I cooked up between when I entered Harvard at the age of fifteen and when I got expelled for celebrating my eighteenth birthday in the apse of the Appleton Chapel with a bottle of absinthe and the underage-yet-in-my-defense-wildly-precocious daughter of a Radcliffe provost. That's a reasonable supposition. Certainly if I'd been cursed with a Doe-value name, my first order of business would have been to tart it up to suit the grift. Zakaz Kouření, Vietato Fumare, something like that. But Radar Hoverlander I was born, and I have the birth certificate to prove it. Which assertion, of course, might not be all that assuasive, since when it comes to birth certificates I had six at last count. What can I tell you? Documents of identity are to my line of work what bromine and xylene neutralizers are to an EPA cleanup crew. You like to have choices. Anyway, for my given name I can thank my father's whimsical bent toward palindromics. Which, when you think about it, thank God for Radar, for I could just as easily have been Otto. Or Gro-gorg. Milton Notlim. Lysander A. Rednasyl. All of this, by the way, according to my mother, for by the time I was old enough to ask such questions, the old man was long since coopgeflonnen. North to Alaska.

---

[*]An invention. Like this word.

South to Ixtapa. Or just into the vapor where grifters go when grift drift takes them too far too fast.

Hoverlander, they say, is a family name. German or Dutch, they say. Fabricat, say I. Pure Ellis Island improv. Probably the original was something with an unspeakable number of consonants, or an unsightly and un-American -ilych or -iliescu suffix, which would never do for this conniving bloodline of mine. From what I know of my family—on both sides, because like attracts like—we've followed the main chance for a thousand years, with moving on and blending in our ancestral stock-in-trade. Find a place, stay till you wear the welcome mat flat, then scat. That's how we ended up in California. We just kept heading west till we ran out of west. The earliest memory I have of my mother is her standing on the end of the Santa Monica pier, saying, "Guam. I wonder what *that's* like."

Shortly thereafter, my mother discovered that while a deftly batted eyelash can cadge a drink or liplock a landlord, no amount of coquettish demur can deter the clammy hands of cancer. So with Dad in the wind and Mom in the ground, it was just me and my mentis non compos nana through all the years of my childhood. I perpetrated the fiction that she was taking care of me, though of course it was the other way around. In the end, I had to forge some papers, reinvent her as a navy nurse (with Antarctica Service Medal, because if you're going to lie, lie big) and park her in a VA hospital where liberal applications of morphine derivatives eased her transition from this life to the next.

And by the way, if you want to know why I got kicked out of Harvard, really the apse and the absinthe were just the tip of the icebag. I always said that the thing with the provost's daughter was an affair of the heart, but in the wake of that myocardial infraction they went back and exhumed my application, cut through the Gordian knot of its lies—so I made up the Finnemore World Prize for Teen Excellence and awarded myself one, so sue me—and gave me the boot. I think they should have given me a scholarship. Doesn't imagination count for anything in this world?

Still, Harvard at fifteen, that was something. I've always had a restless mind.

But a real problem with honesty.

It gets me into trouble sometimes.

the noochis of
this world

Look at this flapdoodle. I mean, just look at it.

My name is Patrick Noochi, the Fund/Property Manager to Mr. Kim Woo Koo, Daewong Group founder. Last November, my client Mr. Kim come to South Amfrica and made a fixed deposit valued at US$55.5M with Rand Bank South Africa. Howsomever, Mr. Kim has been sentenced to ten year's in prison for fruad and embezzelment relating to the collapes of the firm under $8.2 billion dollars of debt. I am contacting you to asist in repatriating the money and will renumerate your effort to the some of 20per:Cent of the gross.

Ignoring for the moment all the heinous crimes against syntax, is this not the weakest, most obvious sort of scam spam you've ever seen in your life? You wouldn't fall for it. I wouldn't fall for it. No soul in his right mind would fall for it. Which means that the Patrick Noochis of this world, if they expect to make a living, must find souls in their wrong minds. While these are not exactly plentiful, lesser life forms do rise to a Noochi's bait every day. And I suppose you could argue that the Noochis of this world are doing us all a service by systematically financially culling the ignorant herd. But that argument is a slippery slope for a grifter, one that slides straight downhill into a big, steaming pile of smug. Because if you figure that the dense deserve to be punished for density, you soon become an avenging angel for stamping out stupidity, which can never happen because they'll always have more stupidity than you have stamp. So you end up just wasting your time, plus ignoring the manifest difference between moral and morally superior. I will tell you this much: I never hold my marks in contempt. I respect them as people. I do. Which is why I cherish my wins.

It's not easy. Do you know what the failure rate is in my line of work? For every ten scams you try, nine won't work. The mook is either too clueless or timid to catch your pitch or, at the other end of the spectrum, too wary or chary to buy in. Really, the population of possible marks exists on the narrowest bulb curve between too dim and too bright. That's why these days so many use the Noochi method, casting a worldwide net on the web. *You've won the lottery! Lose weight by osmosis! Mr. Kim needs your help! Be a secret shopper! Have a ten-inch johnson!* Yeah, their win rate is micrometric, but they make it up in volume. Like tossing dynamite in a stock pond—you're bound to kill *something.* Me, I prefer a more sporting approach. Hook a big fish, see if you can land him. You want to work for your get. That's how you earn your sense of self.

And by the way, being a good con artist takes much more than knowing how to copy and paste the text of someone else's snuke: *Make thousands at home stuffing envelopes!* Even the gift of gab is not enough; hell, any fast talker can sell you a car or a condo. Or even nothing. Do you know how many scut-level grifters are working door-to-door at this very moment selling services they never intend to deliver? Home repair, driveway paves, window work—if someone offers you a deal on aluminum siding that sounds too good to be true, trust me, it is. They'll take your deposit and be three states over before the check clears.

Or maybe not. Maybe they'll loiter a while to strip-mine your bank account. After all, you've just given them a piece of paper with your name, address and phone, account number, and signature. A license to rob you at pen point, Merry Christmas.

But bunco at the highest levels requires a complex package of skills. I can read lips, pick pockets, pick locks, run a six-minute mile, hot-wire a car or disable its engine, field-strip an M16, throw a pot, and build a working computer from scratch. I know biology, geology, and half a dozen other ologies, including theology, which is more useful than you might imagine in this God-fearing world. I can preach a sermon, hit a baseball, bake a cake, splint a broken bone, jam on electric guitar. None of it's wasted. None of it. You never know when you're going to need to come off as an expert. Or jump off a roof and know how to land. When I was a kid, they called me a polymath and imagined that I didn't know what that meant. That's really the key to a grifter's skill set: knowing what they don't know you know. Like languages. I'm fluent in German, Russian, and Portuguese, and could get conversational in, say, Ελληνικά σε μια εβδομάδα (Greek in a week).

This one time I was working unlicensed salvage from a NATO base in Baden-Württemberg, selling, I don't know, missile parts or something to some random Hans *und* Franz. They were *sprech*ing between themselves, and guess what? They're undercover oink. If it weren't for me knowing German and them not knowing I knew, I'd be stewing in a Stuttgart hoosegow now.

I can operate a forklift, make brandy, read a blueprint, and do fairly heavy math in my head. I shoot scratch golf, which is just bedrock useful, because golf hustles, like pool hustles, are insurance, something you fall back on in slim times. The one I like best is where I let the mook play best ball. Taking three drives, chips, and putts per hole, and playing the one he likes most, he thinks he's getting a huge edge—so huge that he'll often give odds—but what he doesn't realize is that all those extra swings add up. He's playing like fifty-four holes of golf while I'm playing only eighteen, so by the back nine, his ass is dragging, while I'm still as peppy as a preppy on Red Bull. Even playing best ball, he doesn't stand a chance. Plus, people can't putt for money. Not if they're not used to it. Pressure is leverage. A good grifter eats pressure for lunch.

But pressure is a double-edged sword—for the truth is revealed under such, for snuke and mook alike. Truth about your essential nature. Truth about what you want out of life. Sometimes a truth you didn't even know was out there. Like maybe the control you thought you had was just the illusion of control all along.

Which brings us by roundabout means to the start of our tale.

It was Halloween. I had crashed a party in the Hollywood Hills by putting on no costume whatsoever and walking in the first open door I saw. When they asked what I was supposed to be, I said, "Party crasher," and this struck them as so charming and conceptual that they just pointed me to the bar and said have a good time.

I had nothing in mind so crass as a petty boost. Not that I couldn't. Infiltrating a host's bedroom is easy as getting lost on the way to the can, and the things people think are hiding places . . . really aren't. But that's not what I'm about, not on Halloween.[*] See, for most people, Halloween is their one night a year to sell an imaginative lie, while for me it's just the opposite, my one day of the year for me to be me, should I so choose. After all, tell people on Halloween that you're a con artist and what's the chance they'll believe you? You're just all charming and conceptual, that's all. So—literally—a busman's holiday.

---

[*] Or even ever. The day I'm sniffing through panty drawers for loose change is the day my big toe starts itching for the trigger.

Even so, one thing I was doing—the thing you never ever stop doing on the grift—was prospecting for leads. At any party, anyway, you'll find me chasing the main chance, seeking that sweet harmonic convergence of deep pockets and weak mental defense. Defenses drop on Halloween, as a function of altered identity but mostly as a function of booze. Plus, I have some lovely Christmas cons that take about six weeks to put the partridge in the pear tree, which makes Halloween sort of the kickoff to the Christmas scamming season.

So there I was, panning for grift in a stilt-level Mulholland Drive mansionette with a stunning view of the San Fernando Valley, the magic of its twinkling lights alchemized out of dust, grit, and imperfectly combusted hydrocarbons. This was a Hollywood producer's party, as I gleaned from context: the framed signed movie posters in the front hall and the swarm of urgent actorlings costumed in disguises sufficiently elaborate to impress but not so elaborate as to hide the identities of people whose need to be recognized is, let's face it, pathological. I disqualify these struggling artisans from con consideration, for they generally prove to have no money, plus, their interpersonal answering machines are so relentlessly set on Announce Only that you can't get your pitch in edgewise.

At Hollywood parties, even Halloween ones, actors and others are always working the room. Unlike me, they're not trying to steal an honest buck; rather, they carry this myth inside them, the Myth of the Perfect Party. They believe that they're always just one party (or industry softball game or even AA meeting) away from encountering that one producer or casting director or studio executive who'll change everything for them forever. With this flawed thought in mind, they relentlessly parse everyone they meet into two groups: Those Who Can Help My Career and Those Who Don't Exist. To be "nonpro" at a Hollywood party is to be a wallflower perforce.

I noticed this one older couple, clearly nonpro and therefore fully marginalized, completely ill at ease in their homemade Raggedy Ann and Andy drag. Hopelessly adrift on this surging sea of ego, they had eddied to a corner of the living room and stood isolated in their own private backwater. I had it in mind to join them there, pitching myself as a socially awkward inventor of medical devices—in search of investors, of course—as out of place as they in this clove-cigarettes-and-appletinis crowd. First, though, a quick spin to the bar to collect some sparkling water, for we socially awkward inventor types are notoriously teetotal.

As I waited at the bar, the woman beside me said, "Couldn't find a costume?" I looked left and absorbed at a glance the parts of the whole: Nordic nose, slightly seventies cinnamon shag, big silver hoop earrings, bas relief collarbones, and the rounded curve of breast beneath a creamy satin vest that missed exactly matching her teal blue eyes by about 5 percent of spectrum tilt toward true green.

"You either, it seems."

"No," she said, looking herself down and up. "I misunderstood. I thought it was come as you are."

"On Halloween?"

"Like I said, I misunderstood. What are you drinking?"

A good grifter adapts quickly to changing circumstances, so ... good-bye, socially awkward inventor, hello, bourbon connoisseur. "Fighting Cock," I said, fully expecting a nervous, entendre-engendered laugh.

Instead I got a haughty, "Here? You're lucky if they pour Four Roses."

"Four Roses, then," I said with a shrug. "You?"

"GMDQ," she said.

"Not familiar with that libation," I said.

"Libation." She snorted a laugh. "Like, 'Let's all get libated tonight?' "

"I'm not sure *libated* is a word."

"Oh, it's a word," she said. "Not that you care."

"What's that supposed to mean?"

"Nothing," she said. "You just don't strike me as a slave to orthodoxy."

"I admit I've never been accused of that," I said. "And GMDQ?"

"Get Me Drunk Quick. Two parts vodka, one part attitude."

"Might want to cut back on the attitude," I said. "I think you've had a little too much already."

This also created a hole where a laugh should have been. Nevertheless, she extended her hand, offered her name—"Allie Quinn"—and waited for me to offer mine back. This was not as simple a matter as you might think, for I had many to choose from, and your name, let's face it, defines you. Kent Winston makes you a bowling buddy; Raleigh Newport is an investment counselor. Who did I want to be?

It was Halloween. I chose to be me. "Radar Hoverlander," I said.

"Radar?" she asked. "Like that guy in *M*A*S*H*?"

"No, but I get that a lot."

By now the bartender was waiting to serve us. Allie pointed to two bottles and said, "That and that." We got our drinks and moved away from the bar. "Now," she said, "what's up with the mufti?"

"I assume you mean the word in the sense of civilian clothing, not interpreter of Muslim law."

"Now you're just showing off," she said. I shrugged. "So. The costume?"

"I'm a party crasher."

She gave me a long, blank look before saying, "Oh, I get it."

You ever get that feeling like you just farted in church?

With four simple words—"Oh, I get it"—Allie ruled my noncostume not charming and not conceptual but merely self-conscious and lame. This would have bothered me were it not for the known true truth that women seduce men precisely by making them feel self-conscious and lame. It's the first move of an elegant and time-tested three-act play.

Act one: Steal status. Like it or not, in the world of women and men, men hold the high ground. True, women man the sex valve and can shut it off at will, but as long as man has hand, this problem is not irresolvable. Meantime, whether in negotiation, sales, or seduction, it's difficult to win uphill battles against status, so job one is to level the playing field. Women can do this to a man just by judging. Mock his haircut. Laugh at his ignorance. Look down your nose at his nose. Dis his supposedly clever costume concept.

Belittle a man and he will be little. This is a known true truth.

Once he's weak and vulnerable, it's time for act two: Initiate intimacy. To make a man covet your opinion (and therefore covet you), you need to create a bond, and the best way to do this is to touch. Brush a hand along a shoulder. Stand too close. Push a random strand of hair out of his eyes. Pluck lint, even. Your tender touch renders him like a dog in submission position.

Now comes the third act in this little passion play: Extend validation.

Validation (and this is an absolutely historically verified known true truth) is a mighty aphrodisiac. Let a man feel good about himself, and he will adore you out of gratitude. Tell me I'm wrong, guys. Tell me you haven't ever thought, "I like her because she likes me." You can't help it. It's human nature.

This is why hospitalized soldiers fall in love with their nurses, and not just in movies but in real life. First they experience this steep status drop from *warrior* to *patient,* and they're forced to surrender control, which they hate. Next, it's meet the new boss—this nurse who initiates intimacy in all sorts of sponge-bath and bedpanny ways. Finally, the intravenous validation drip: *You're a good man, soldier, and a good patient; you're going to be okay.*

So there you have it. Steal status with a mock or a smugly held opinion. Slice through defenses with the stiletto of intimacy. Then make 'im feel good. After that, you can write your own ticket.

So when Allie absently reached behind my neck to flip down the label on my shirt, I had to believe she was on script.

And when she suddenly started liking my jokes, I knew I was being played.

dilated in

When you lie for a living like I do, you become pretty sensitive to the lies of others. This isn't telepathy, telemetry, or tele- any-thing else. It's just looking for the bedrock rationale. It didn't take a particularly large leap of insight for me to realize that by plan and design, Allie had laid siege to my company. I couldn't help wondering why. You might think she just liked the cut of my jib, but I've seen my jib and I'm here to tell you it's not cut that cute.

So I decided to do a drunk check, because drunks will make choices that only make sense by way of drunk logic. This is useful to men, who often have no card of seduction to play, save a woman's impaired judgment. What you do is, you hold up your hand, fingers spread, really close to her face, and ask how many hands you're holding up. If she says one, she's sober. If she says five, she's drunk. If she says, "Five . . . wait . . . one," and then falls out laughing, the pump is, shall we say, primed. The element of surprise is critical for a fair reading, so I sprang it on Allie without warning.

She looked past my hand and eyelocked me with the knowingest wry smile. "The drunk test?" she said. "Really?"

And turned and walked away.

Okay, so maybe she wasn't hitting on me after all.

I shrugged it off. In this business you shrug off a lot of false starts. I set down my drink and went looking for the misplaced displaced rag dolls. They had departed, but I noticed a clean-cut kid in hospital scrubs, wearing a stethoscope made of pens and a surgical cap fashioned from a Writers Guild of America bandanna. He carried a computer keyboard and a copy of *Screenwriter* magazine.

None of which caught my eye like his shoes.

I slid over and struck up a conversation—never hard at Halloween parties, because every conversation begins with *Let me guess*. "Let me guess," I said. "Script doctor?"

"Got it in one," he said. "Most people don't."

"Well," I replied, "with all due false modesty, I'm smarter than everyone." I filled in the space of his chuckle with the selection of an appropriate name. "Nick Rauchen," I said. We shook hands. He introduced himself as Jason Dickson. "But you're not really a writer, right?" He shook his head. "I think you're . . ."

I love the look on people's faces when you guess right. It's not that hard, really. You just read the facts at hand. For starters, he had that Myth of the Perfect Party look in his eye, and even as he talked to me he was looking past me, as if there might be a better conversation, a hotter lead, a more compellingly life-changing contact waiting for him somewhere out there among the swarm of sexy kitten costumes and knights in aluminum armor. Thus this: not a writer—because writers know better than to buy into that myth—but interested in writers. And a white guy name. Not just white but deep-pockets and prep-school white. Harvard white. I recognized the vibe. But it was the shoes, really, that told the tale, for this Jason couldn't resist wearing his status shoes to a costume party. Peeking out from under his scrubs, a pair of Tod's Monk Straps, the exact kind you wear if you're an earnest young striver at a first- or second-tier Hollywood talent agency where appearance is as important as competence or ability. For confirmation, I had checked out his fingernails, and, yep, they were manicured. *Manicured*. So then, in sum . . .

"An agent."

He blinked. "How did you know?"

"I read minds."

"What, you mean like professionally?"

Man, talk about a soft opening. Now I started to grind the grift in earnest, spinning a colorful yarn about my brief stint as a stage hypnotist and my board certification in something I invented on the spot called witness therapy. Eventually I worked around to my putative current profession, playwright and performance artist. I riffed on this theme for a while, and by the time I was done, he'd paid cash up front for VIP seats to the premiere of my utterly nonexistent one-man show, *Come Up Pants,* at the equally nonexistent NoHo Playhouse. He gave me his business card so I could mail him the tickets.

I don't even consider this working.

It's all about the want. Everyone has one. Identify the want of your fish and he's halfway in your boat. Poor Jason the Agent Boy was clearly treasure hunting; I just had to convince him I was treasure, an undiscovered talent he could ride to high heights in his agency. And here's the beauty part: Since he was looking for treasure in the first place, it was easy for him to see it in me.

People see what they want to see, and sometimes they hand you their money.

But after the snuke, I started to feel a little detached. I wandered around the party, not really measuring marks or anything, just floating. I caught a glimpse of Allie engaged in animated conversation with some guy in a bear suit. She was smoothing the nap of his fur. I felt an odd irk at that, quasi-queasy almost. We were the only two people at the party not in costume. Were we not made for each other, or each other's company, at least? Meanwhile, everyone else at the party began to look quite transparent to me, their costumes no longer concealing them at all. I could tell who was drunk, horny, angry, resentful, frustrated, or bored, as if they wore their emotions like subtitles. I was familiar with this heightened awareness. It often comes after a score: a lingering presence in the zone, still dilated in.[*] Yet there was this dispassion, too, something also common in the wake of a scam, even a workaday one like this. First I get high, then I get low. The little voice inside my head is saying, "Yeah! Score!" but then, after a pause, "Now what?" In this business, it's always about the now what, and after the what, there's just more what and more what after that. In the grift, we call it the disconnect, and actually you have to have the disconnect, or otherwise you start having sympathy for your marks, and then you play them soft. Not good.

But this party, past its peak, had passed its pique. True, there were still some targets about, getting drunker and more vulnerable by the moment. At minimum, I could lay pipe for snukes down the road. Yet suddenly I couldn't be bothered. I thanked my host (who pretended to know who I was) and headed out.

I walked downhill to my car, but loitered at it and didn't get in. There was something bothering me about me, a mental splinter of sorts, or a toothache I couldn't help probing with my tongue. Where did I and the party part company? It wasn't like me to ride a bummer. I like parties. I like me. I like my job. I like how every single situation I'm in is an opportunity to hone my craft. I mean, I could be getting my television hooked up and find some way to con the cable guy. That's a gift. I love that gift. I use it every chance I get and I never, ever get tired of it. "All manic all the time," that's the tag line for Radio Radar. But just then I felt flat as a piece of paper. What had sucked all the joie from my vivre?

---

[*]Why not? Can't one be on target and wide open, too?

And here came the answer, dancing barefoot down the street, holding her strappy heels in her left hand. Balance appeared to be a problem, for the street was steep and all those GMDQs seemed to have gone to her head.

"Well," she said, "if it isn't Hoover Loverhandler, master of the mufti." She came up and stood quite close to me, and pronounced each next word like a sentence: "I. Want. A. Cigarette."

"Sorry," I said. "Fresh out."

"That's okay. I don't really smoke." She smiled. "Like you don't really drink. I saw you ditch your bourbon." *Really?* She was watching me? I'm not used to that, and couldn't decide whether I liked it or not. "But still, you seem like a knowing guy." She twirled her shoes by their straps. "Do you know what these are?"

"I believe they're called come-fuck-me pumps."

"Ooh," she said to the universe, "this is a smart one." Then, to me, "Drive me home, smart one. I'm smashed." To prove the point, as if it needed proving, she waggled her fingers in front of her face, said, "Five, no, one!" and fell out laughing. Though it was less like being drunk and more like a staged reading from the Book of Drunk.

"What about your car?" I asked.

"No car. I teleported."

"Really? In this neighborhood?" I archly arched an eyebrow, pushing it doubly ironically high.

"Of course not," she said. "Who teleports in this neighborhood? My friend drove. She split with some guy." Allie put her hands on her hips, framing her waist with her shoes. "So? Ride home or what?"

So I drove her home. Or no, not exactly home. At her instruction, we switchbacked along Mulholland to Outpost, then downhill into Hollywood. But when I got into the grid, somewhere near Gower and Fountain, she said, "This'll do," and was out of the car before it even stopped.

She'd left behind one of her shoes. "Hey," I said, bending to pick it up, "You . . ."

But she was gone. Nowhere to be seen. For a drunk chick with one shoe, she sure moved fast.

Maybe she teleports after all.

java man closest 2 u

If you Google "Radar Hoverlander," you'll get a bunch of hits on thrust vector control systems—radar-guided surface deployment mechanisms for off-planet rovers. Most of it is blue-sky development shit: "As soon as the rover is ready to roll, the tether connection will be severed and the Sky Crane will fly off and crash-land a short distance away." Which certainly sounds like a party, but anyway it amuses me to think that my quirky name has such an oddball double meaning. Like Johnny Ben Wa Balls must feel every day.

If you Google harder, eventually you'll find your way to a little website called www.radarenterprizes.com. There you will be persuaded that yours most humbly truly is the proud proprietor of a company selling embossed items for promotional use. Need a pen with your company's name? I'm your guy. Giveaway cameras for your wedding? No problem. "Compliments of" calendars or mouse pads? Just click to order. No job too small. Now this, I'm sure you'll agree, is a boring-ass business, but it provides cover, something I can file taxes on. A shell of a shill, then, my flag planted in cyberspace to provide evidence—well, fabricat evidence—that little Radar is legit. If you click on <u>Contact us</u>, you can send a message to info@radarenterprizes.com, a mailbox I check only infrequently because the bulk of what I receive is bulk nonsense—come-ons for Vilagra or Vinagra, and *You've received an e-card from a friend!*—and nothing annoys a scammer more than someone else's lame attempts at spivery. But I do check it. You never know what will wash up on your beach, and fulfilling a legitimate order takes no more effort on my part than forwarding it to my liaison at a certain factory in Shenzhen. I never leave money lying on the table. That's just not good practice. So I periodically sift through the spam; anyway, it tickles me to see what the lesser minds of the snuke cook up.

The morning of November 1 found me sitting out on the tiny deck of my duplex, feet up on an empty crate of military-surplus gas masks (yard-sale score—can't resist a dumb bargain), poaching wireless on my laptop. The view from up there was spectacular: a steep drop down to Silver Lake Boulevard; lush, overwatered hills on the far side, reeking with bougainvillea and overpriced homes; and the downtown skyline in the distance, a towering picket fence of glass, corruption, and chrome. I'm not much for aesthetics, but on certain of these clear L.A. days, when the wind blows warm off the desert and sends all the smog to Catalina, you can almost pretend the place is pretty.

Usually to get online I just piggyback the wireless router of Rita and Cecilia, the pair-bonded ovarians who live in the downstairs half of my duplex. Today for some reason it wasn't kicking a strong signal, so instead I jumped the WiFi from Java Man, the coffee joint at the base of the hill below. Good ol' Java Man. You like to see a coffee chain giving Starbucks a run for their money.

Checking a week's worth of e-mail, I found the predictable ballyhoo of online casinos, penny stocks, and university degrees. Amid the spasm of spams, there was one I actually liked, from an outfit calling itself Charity Clearinghouse. They proposed to have you donate, through them, to charities of your choice—which donations are, of course, fully tax deductible. Now here came the pitch, a tangy twofer of money laundering and tax fraud. For every dollar you donate, they promise, you get half a buck back, deposited into an offshore online bank, whence you can online-shop or ATM back to cash or whatever, with ol' Uncle Sammy ever none the wiser. Of course there's no such thing as a free lunch, so Charity Clearinghouse admits to holding back a certain percentage of your donation for administrative services. But you're okay with that; considering your prospective tax break, you still come out way ahead, as does your charity, with the IRS footing the bill, and when you think about it, isn't that what damn big government should really be doing with your money anyhow? Hell, yeah!

So, it's the Haiphong phone book all over again, right? Unless you're dumb enough not to realize that you'll never see a buck back to your off-shore online bank. And, depending on how you make your contribution (credit card is easiest, you are informed), your financials will be thoroughly harvested after the fact. But I liked this scam. I did. It preyed on cupidity, stupidity, munificence, and our national passion for screwing the IRS. In my neck of the weeds, that's a perfect storm.

I was thinking I might even arrogate the structure of the yak for myself, maybe dress it up in Santa clothes for Christmas. Did I feel guilty about stealing the intellectual property of some fellow *artiste trompeur*? Come on. There's nothing new under the sun. You think Patrick Noochi invented the Spanish Prisoner? You think anyone did? It was probably around for centuries before it first popped up in print in 1910. Hell, I've run the game a dozen times myself, usually where I'm the title character, live and in person, on the lam from the law and desperate for you to take this here $20,000 certified check, in exchange, if you will, for just a little getaway green.

Saying you can't jack another snuke's yak is like saying a writer can't use Boy Meets Girl because Shakespeare (that old thief) got there first.

Not that there wasn't room for improvement. Something like . . .

oh, I don't know . . . a cover letter from a phantom CPA validating the dodge and urging you to lock up your deductions by year's end. Nothing like a little "time is of the essence" urgency to light a fire under a mark. But even as I game-planned the gag, I knew I'd never take it out for a spin. And why? The same mental splinter as last night. For some reason, the idea just didn't appeal. I told myself it had nothing to do with ripping off folks during the Santa season, but I think it probably did, a little. Every now and then my conscience pops up out of its burrow like a meerkat on the scout, and this was one of those times. So I mentally set it aside and went back to browsing my mail.

I came across this, from one bricabrac@resender.com: "*Hey, bourbon guy. What time is vespers? What do Adam Ant and Charles Bronson have in common? Put them all together, they spell Java Man closest 2 u. Bring shoe. Love, Cinderfuckingella.*"

Huh.

Interesting.

Well, bourbon guy was obviously me, the smartass who wanted Fighting Cock, the sour mash pride of Bardstown, Kentucky. Cinderfuckingrella was equally obviously Allie, if you're willing to grant a come-fuck-me pump as analogous to a glass slipper, which I was. Vespers is Catholic evening prayers, so that'd be basically sunset. And the link between Ant and Bronson? Turns out they share the same birthday, November 3. Right around the corner, and why was I not surprised?

I wondered how Allie could be sure that she'd e-mailed the right address, but then I realized it was probably a blanket blast, with nothing in the text to aught but puzzle a wrong recipient. Weirdass spam, they'd think as they junk-drawered it. The only one it would mean something to was me.

But . . . "Java Man closest 2 u"? How did she know which Java Man was closest to me? (The one I could hit with a rock from here.) Had I mentioned it in passing? I replayed our conversation from the night before. One thing I'm good at is remembering what I've said, a somewhat indispensable skill to a professional who must keep the leashes of his lies untangled. Had I told Allie I lived in Silver Lake? No, I was sure not. Besides, what would that tell her? Java Mans abound here, six alone within the radius of the next dead cat. No, she had to know exactly where I lived. And she had to not mind that I knew she knew.

This disturbed me. I'm used to looking over other people's shoulders, gathering the data that makes me look so casually magic on the job. I don't like it the other way around. With the enemies you make in this game, you don't want them knowing where you live.

Sometimes their poison-pen letters explode.

So I keep my tracks well covered; someone who could uncover them was a bit of a concern just on general principle.

And then telling me she's doing it. That was just brazen. Brazen enough, of course, to set my alarm clock for Tuesday, which is what she wanted, no doubt. But I'd be busy till then. When I met Cinderfuckingella again, I'd know a thing or two about her, too.

For starters, I did a web search, using the same ham-fisted Google tool she'd probably used. I hate Google. It returns such vague and random results. Allie H. Quinn lives in Rosedale, Manitoba, and plays province-level field hockey. Alyson ("call me Allie!") Quinn has 346 friends on her MySpace page. There are 19,734 people in the United States with the first name of Allie. As for my particular Allie: nothing at first blush. So I dug a little deeper.

The grift in the modern age ably employs the internet as another trick up its voluminous and fluttery sleeve. Especially useful are certain backdoor database search engines you can buy if you know where to look, or hack if you know how to hack. No point in taking down a bereaved widow, for instance, till you gauge the breadth, depth, and liquidity of her husband's life insurance. Properly equipped, you can weevil into company records, university archives, any state's DMV. You're your own personal Freedom of Information Act. So I used available tools to apply a more rapier touch to my search for the increasingly mysterious Allie Quinn.

Nothing. Nothing I couldn't immediately dismiss as a false positive, anyway; I'm reasonably certain that Aileen O'Quinn was not my gal, less for the distant agnation of the name match and more for the fact that the octogenarian stroked out and died last week. Of course, there was no reason to believe that "Allie Quinn" was even remotely close to her real name, and growing evidence to suggest it was pure marzipan. But the fact that she'd phony up to me made her more vexing still. At this point, I had to assume she was working my same side of the street. But why was she working *me*?

I attacked the info underground from a slightly different angle, accessing a national bunco photo database. It's a fact of the grift that sooner or later you will get popped, which translates into fingerprints and mug shots. For the sake of protecting innocents from the predations of guys like me, law enforcement creates and circulates our profiles, including a list of our favorite snadoodles—check kite, parallel marriage, what have you. Say someone turns up in your Walmart parking lot working a hijacked-appliance dodge, where you think you're buying a stolen stereo but all you're actually buying is a box of rocks, which you'd have to be dumb as to go for that gaff, but whatever. In that case, your local Jake can sneak a perp snap and try to make a match. So you see, the internet not only works for us but against us. It's a cat-and-mouse game. Jake thinks he's the cat.

Since men on the razzle outnumber women ten to one, my search task was easier than if I'd been looking for, say, me. I'm in there, of course, with three known aliases, Milad Majid, Bo Nada, and Sretan Božić, all of which happen to mean Merry Christmas in one language or another. They list my specialty as long con securities fraud, which I think is a little misleading. I short con, too.

So sorting by gender was a given. I could have sorted also by age, but I didn't. Though I thought Allie was contemporaneous to me—north of twenty-five—I couldn't swear that she wasn't ten years older. Or younger: I've known some precocious girls in the game.

Their daddies teach them. It's cute.

Likewise, I didn't filter for, say, geographic tendency or hair color, because quality mooks know to how keep moving and dye. And Allie Quinn, by her sheer absence from the realm of usual suspects, was starting to impress me as a quality mook. The more I virtually paged through the virtual pages, the more I became convinced I wasn't going to find her there. An hour later, search complete, I knew: If Allie Quinn was on the razzle, she had yet to make the database.

Two immediate questions came to mind. How did Allie know where I lived, and why did she want to meet? I mulled the second question first. It didn't seem likely that her only interest was in getting her shoe back. Just to be sure, I inspected it closely, to see if it was a particularly pricey brand or had a secret compartment or was made of drugs or something. Nope. Just your run-of-the-mill Payless pump. So then what?

In my experience, human motivation can be broken down to the four broad strokes of sex, love, money, and revenge. Everything else we chase—power, glory, information, exultation, stimulation—is just a subset of these. Like the sign says, "Money can't buy happiness, but it can rent sex." So was sex what she wanted? Was Allie on the make? We've already discussed the disangular cut of my jib. I'm not "boyfriend cute," not even "sidekick cute," really. Yes, I watch what I eat and stupidly believe that regular aerobic exercise will extend the span of my life, for what that's worth. But I don't kid myself—as catches go, I'm strictly catch and release.

So then, not sex.

Love, then? Love?

Lovely.

But not likely.

Look, I believe in love. I understand that my father loved my mother, though ultimately the two of them were so the same that they repelled each other like like magnetic poles. At that, I'd have to say he loved the grift far better than he ever loved her, or me, for that matter. He loved being in the wind, and that was a love that took a lifetime to wean and nurture and grow. So love, real love, isn't sudden. Or if it is sudden, it's perverse, like when you meet someone you think can fix your broken parts or fill some hole in your life, and your defective brain misinterprets this as "love at first sight." Was Allie capable of this kind of malformed stalker love? Could she have spotted me across a crowded room and said, "That's the man to undamage me"? Unlikely. I had to credit her with more common sense and self-awareness, and certainly more cynicism, than that.

So: not sex, not love, then money. But what money? How? You meet someone at a party, even a Hollywood Hills party where people have a loose enough grip on their cash, how do you know this random stranger has a sufficiently deep and accessible pocket? Well, you don't know. You prospect. But what would Allie have seen at first glance that made her think of sinking an exploratory well in me? I'm what you call a hard mark, sufficiently chary to see the grift coming and get out of its way. And it shows. At least I think it shows. Around here we have a saying, "Only victims get victimized." No way do I come off as a victim, unless that's part of my grift, which at a Hollywood Hills Halloween party it definitely is not. If Allie's in the game, she knows this. If she's not in the game . . . well, what the fuck?

Oh then, let's say revenge. Let's say she's the sister of someone I mooked, and now she's playing back at me. That had a certain logic, but it didn't pass the sniff test for a couple of reasons. First, dumb runs in tight circles, and if you're dumb enough to fall into a conhole, no one you know—not your sister, your best friend, your coworker, priest, or dog—is smart enough to play you back out. Second, someone on a revenge tip just wouldn't be that open with her play. No, "Java Man closest 2 u" was either a big semaphore or a casual mistake, and it didn't feel like a mistake. She's on to me, wants me to know it, and knows I'll figure that out.

Bottom line: I'm being grift-wrapped for something I cannot yet see. But why?

Why being a dry hole, I took a whack at how, or rather two hows. How did she know where I lived, and how did she arrange to meet me at a party that even I didn't know I was going to crash? The connect-the-dots answer had to be: She's been following me, looking for an opportunity to "meet cute." (She *was* cute; and it crossed my mind to wonder whether I was spending all this psychic energy on her because she presented a threat or just because I liked thinking about her. I liked how she smelled. Vanilla.)

I went to the living-room window and looked out. The view from my deck is spectacular, but the view out front, not so much. Just a pot-holed asphalt street, some jacarandas, and the flat facade of the garage across the way, with stairs going up along its side. A cat sunned himself on the bottom step. Apart from that, nothing. What did I expect? To see her casing me from some parked car, Garbo cigarette hanging from her lip?

She doesn't smoke.

And she knows I don't drink.

But wait . . . something else. I replayed a part of our party conversation, the part where I said "libated" and she said it wasn't a word, not that I cared. That was it. That "not that you care." The sort of thing you'd say about someone only if you knew it was true. And she'd just met me.

But she knew me.

She'd made a study.

The hairs on the back of my neck stood up.

Grifters are hunters.

We don't like to be prey.

the original mirplo

At a quarter to Vespers on Tuesday, I was just heading out to Java Man when my cell phone rang. I half entertained the fantasy that it would be Allie, coming clean, 'fessing up, solving the big mystery for me before I had to suffer the actual indignity of sloping downhill to the cafe. Or maybe just calling to remind me to bring the shoe. (Though how she'd have my phone number would be another mystery yet to be solved.) But a glance at caller ID revealed what I should have known: It was Vic Mirplo. The original Mirplo. Truly one of a kind.

Mirplo is the worst sort of mook: careless, rash, sloppy, lazy, ignorant, reckless, feckless, dense, and disrespectful of the mark. Classically opinionated and ill informed, he has no tangible gift for the grift, yet fancies himself a master—or as he's put it on more than one occasion, "an ascended Stairmaster"—of the craft. He vaguely understands that cons call for misdirection, but his idea of this is on a par with pointing and shouting, "Look, Halley's Comet!" while he snatches an apple from a fruit stand. Nor is sophistication his strong suit: I've actually seen him try to pass photocopied and hand-scissored $20 bills on the daft logic that "the Treasury's regular printer is on strike." Thanks to this moronic convergence of ill-chosen career vector and sad lack of skills,

Vic has been in and out of jail more times than is healthy for a grifter, but his scams are always so laughably low-rent that he's never done hard time, which was good, because hard time would've cracked his fragile being like an egg.

Vic was working a crude scalper scam outside Dodger Stadium when our paths first crossed. Lamely passing himself off as stadium security, he'd try to finesse tickets or cash or both—as "evidence"—out of unsuspecting sellers or buyers, and then basically just run like hell. Inept at selecting his victims (as he was inept at any decision more complex than paper or plastic), he had tried to put the touch on a pair of USC linebackers, who'd chased him down, roughed him up, and tossed him in a trash can. I saw the whole thing happen. I thought it was pretty funny.

"What are you laughing at?" he asked as he hauled himself out and wiped mustard stains from his already amply stained mulberry wind-breaker.

"You," I said. "What the hell was that?"

"A con," he replied. "You wouldn't understand." I offered to buy him a beer and have him explain it. I just couldn't resist learning about the grift from his nescient perspective.

But it turns out that buying a Mirplo a beer is like feeding a stray cat. Unfortunately, you've made a friend for life.

To befriend a Mirplo is to subject yourself to a never-ending cas-cade of need. He'd need money, food, booze, or dope. Or bail. Or a ride. A place to watch the big game. A place to crash. Or a present for his mother. And even when he'd try to return the favor, it would invari-ably go wrong. Once, he borrowed my car—"borrowed," as in "took without asking"—so he could work the gas station con and get me a fill-up. In this snuke, you dress like a businessman and persuade the mark that you've been robbed and now must panhandle gas money or else—dire need—you'll miss a vital sales call, lose the sale, have your wife's dialysis cut off, whatnot. Only, Vic neglected to dress the part or convincingly play it, and one gas station attendant held him at bay with a baseball bat while the other called the cops. It cost me $256 to get my car out of impound.

So why did I adopt him? I don't know. An uncharacteristic fit of charity, perhaps. Though in fairness, he did occasionally prove useful, in a blunt-instrument sort of way. If you need, for example, someone to deliver an utterly unconvincing lie to a mark, or a bag of money to the wrong address, Vic is your man. And he does have a certain cataleptic charm, a sunny membrane of optimism utterly impermeable to reality—and equally oblique to critique: There aren't too many people who will smile while you call them stupid to their face. And if they adore you, as Mirplo adores me with all the dopey loyalty of an Irish setter, you bask in their devotion. Approval, as noted, is a heady drug.

So the phone rang, and it was Vic, and I answered, mentally girding myself for the inevitable onslaught of Mirplovian white noise. Nor was I disappointed.

"Radar!" he shouted, "Guess where I am!" As I could hear a recorded voice in the background announcing the departure of the Border Flyer for San Diego, I guessed Union Station. "Damn, you're good," he said. "Hey, what are you doing right now?"

"Wishing I hadn't answered the phone."

"Yeah, great, fine, terrific. Listen, what do you think about this? I'm a passenger on a train, right? And I've got this bag, like a doctor's bag, or maybe a briefcase, and I leave it on my seat, unattended. Go for a drink in the club car."

"Who'd buy?"

"Ha fucking ha. Do you want to hear the grift or not?"

"Go on."

"So okay, so when I come back, I look inside and, *Whoa!* My money's all gone. Where did it go? Who stole it? And it was for my sister! Who's a *nun*!"

"Your sister the sister?"

"That's right. It was for orphans. *Blind* ones. Or no, not blind. What do you call it when the mouth's all screwed up? Cliffed palate?"

"Cleft."

"That's the one. So anyway, I sob it up for a while, till the other passengers all pitch in to make me feel better."

"Or maybe just to shut you up."

"That works, too. What do you think? Class A con?"

"But nobody messed with your bag."

"Yeah? So?"

"People will have seen that. They'll know you're lying." Like everybody always knows a Mirplo is lying because that's all a Mirplo ever does.

"Oh. Oh, yeah, you're right. Damn, I thought that one was foolproof."

"Depends on the fool."

"Shit. Damn. Where am I gonna get some money?"

I suddenly had an idea. Probably a bad one, but when you can't fight fire with fire, you fight it with fools. "I know where you can get some coffee," I said.

I waited for Vic on a side street around the corner from Java Man, and it wasn't too long before he drove up in his forlorn Song Serenade, an exhausted Chinese beater he called Shirley Temple and loved with all the passion a man can have for a sedan as fundamentally flawed as he is. The driver's door squealed a pained protest as he opened it and clambered out. With his greasy hair pulled back in a lank ponytail and a flannel shirt hanging from his bony chest, he had the look of a grunge junkie, Seattle, circa 1990. "What's the gaff?" he asked, his eyes almost wet with excitement. "Who are we taking down?"

"No gaff," I said. "I just need you to check something out." I gave him a description of Allie—cinnamon shag and those teal eyes being the key signifiers—and sent him in to see if she was there and who she was with. "Take your time," I said. "Look around. Her team'll be spread. See who she makes eye contact with."

"Got it," said Vic. He started off, then turned back. "Uhm . . ." He rubbed his thumb against his fingers.

I forked over a five spot. Vic cocked a brow. "What?" I said. "Not enough?"

"Lattes don't grow on trees, man." I handed him a ten. He "forgot" to give back the five. Say this for a Mirplo: they work every inch of the grift.

He sidled off. A few minutes later he returned, holding a cup the size of a tub. "Does this feel light to you?" he asked, hefting the drink. "It feels light to me. Why can't they foam it all the way up?"

"Hey, Vic, how heavy is foam?"

"Oh," he said. "Oh, yeah. I see your point." He took a sip, and recoiled in pain, sloshing some of the drink on the ground, and some on his ratty jeans and bad sneakers. "Ow! Shit! I burned myself." He eyed the cup speculatively. "Think I can sue?"

"Later," I said. "Did you see the girl?"

"Yeah, no, she's not there."

"Are you sure?"

"Dude. You send me in to check out a notable rack of lamb, and you don't think I'll spot her? She's not there." He got a faraway look in his eye as he mentally called up the scene inside Java Man. "There's . . . let's see . . . two goth-looking counterettes, one with bad acne, the other with a lip ring which I'm here to tell you does *not* do a thing for her look, some sad pud pounding away on his laptop, a Brian Dennehy–looking motherfucker by the door, and a creepy wedge with a sex offender goatee reading the *New York Times*."

"Did you check the bathroom?"

"Does a dog fart? I'm not stupid, Radar."

"That's debatable."

"And that's beneath you. Who is she, anyway?"

"Nobody. Just this chick I met."

"Well, she stood you up. Wanna go shoot stick? We could hustle."

"Vic, . . ." I was about to point out that you had to have some kind of skill to make the back end of a pool hustle work, but then I thought, *Why bother?* Talking to a Mirplo about strategy is like talking to two-year-old about sharing. "You go," I said. "I'm gonna wait this out."

"I gotta say, man, it's not like you to get hooked on trim." *Hooked on trim?* Who talks like that? "But I'm not gonna leave you, buddy. I'll be your wingman."

"Thanks anyway. I'll be fine."

"Yeah, huh? But I've got no place else to go, and besides . . ." again the thumb-and-forefinger gesture. ". . . no scratch."

I sighed heavily. "Will twenty get you in the wind?"

"You kidding? Twenty'll get me half a hooker." I paid Vic to leave, and I have to tell you, it didn't feel half bad. Like taking care of a retarded brother. He drove off, his perilous Serenade coughing the blue smoke of an engine badly in need of a ring job. I went back to watching the Java Man, but no one of note came or went. Eventually I decided to go in and check it out for myself.

I had to credit Vic's observational skill. He'd nailed everyone in the place (except for the girl with the lip ring—I actually thought it worked). I ordered a coffee and read the inspirational quote on the cup: "*The truth speaks with a trumpet voice.*" That had some logic, but grift logic: If you can't be right, be loud; if you're loud enough long enough, you will appear to be right. I settled in at a wobbly round table by the window and occupied myself with someone's cast-off crossword puzzle. This nimrod had arrived at *naked* as a synonym for *succulent* (it's *juicy*), which made Alaska's capital *Nuneau.*

Okay, then.

At first I kept half an eye on the door, but I soon became absorbed in the puzzle. I'm like a dog with a bone with these things. Once I get my teeth into one, I can't let go. I was just figuring out that 23 across, *linguistic keystone,* was *Rosetta,* when I noticed the guy Vic had identified as a Brian Dennehy–looking motherfucker bending down beside me.

He did bear a resemblance. The barrel chest, the jutting jaw, the close-cropped hair all gone to gray. I made him to be in his sixties but had to give or take a decade, for though he looked hale enough, there was a weary or distracted air about him, like he was feeling, I don't know, maybe old before his time.

"You dropped this," he said, picking up a thick wallet from the floor and holding it in his beefy hand. It was a counterfeit Calvin Klein, which you could tell at a glance because the embossed lettering on the front read Calvin Klien. I knew where it came from. They sell them downtown in Santee Alley, along with $20 Bolex watches, Barbee dolls and Narlboro cigarettes.

"That's not mine," I said.

"Really? Because it was right under your chair." He dropped it on the table. We made eye contact. This was unusual, for most strangers won't look you in the eye, not even over a found wallet fat with cash.

As for the wallet . . .

"It's really not mine," I said. I reinforced the point by patting the bulge in my back pocket. "Turn it in at the counter. Maybe someone will claim it."

"Okay," he said. He picked up the wallet, but awkwardly, so that it fell out of his hand and splayed open on the table. (I had to admire the deft clumsiness of the move.) We could both see that the credit card slots all were empty. "Strange," he said. "There doesn't appear to be any identification." He picked up the wallet again and gave it a good going over—making a point, I thought, of showing me the sizable number of sizable bills inside. "Nothing," he said after his inspection. "Just cash. Oh, and this."

I knew what "this" would be before he handed it to me: evidence of some kind that the money in the wallet was tainted or criminal and therefore not traceable or returnable. Sure enough, he passed me a creased and folded piece of paper, which bore columns of figures, including dollar amounts and numbers expressed as odds. "What do you think it is?" he asked.

I played along. "Looks like a betting slip," I said. "Whosever wallet this is, the guy makes book."

"Book?"

"He takes bets illegally."

"Really?" The man's eyes grew wide, as if I'd just fingered a white slaver or serial killer. "Well, I wouldn't know anything about that."

Lay it on a little thicker, why don't you? I thought. But I let the man make his pitch. It had been a long time since I'd seen someone try to pull off a pigeon drop. I was interested to see how he'd set the hook.

He played the guileless angle to the hilt, which isn't typically how the pigeon drop goes down. Usually the wise guy leans heavily on cynicism and outrage, noting how he and the mark have an almost moral responsibility to keep the ill-gotten cash they've found. Still, even draped in innocence, he managed to hit all the classic pigeon-drop beats. Having verified that the money was both dirty and anonymous, he then phoned "a lawyer friend" for advice on how to proceed. The friend apparently suggested that we rathole the cash while we took the necessary legal steps to ratify our claim. Then came the bit about how both of us should put up some earnest money to demonstrate our good faith. At this point, his faux naïveté played particularly well, for my new best pal simply couldn't see "any reason in the world" not to trust me—but his lawyer friend said to approach it this way, and in matters such as this, lawyers generally know best, right? I matched him innocence for innocence, and enthusiastically assured him that I had no problem fronting as much cash as necessary, but I hoped it wouldn't be more than five hundred bucks, because that's all I had on me. I looked to see if his eyes would give away his greed on this, but to his credit, he kept his "concerned citizen, slightly out of depth" mask firmly locked in place.

All that remained at this point was for us to divvy the loot. He'd hold my earnest money and, "because I seemed trustworthy," I could hold the wallet and its much larger sum. First, though, did we really feel comfortable with the wallet in plain sight? He asked one of the counter girls for a paper bag, which, of course, sets up the ol' switcheroo, where a wallet full of cash becomes a wallet full of Yellow Pages pages.

But we weren't going to get that far. It was time to blow the guy's cover.

Because here's the thing about coincidences: Generally, they aren't. If I was waiting in a random Java Man for someone who knew suspiciously too much about me, and I "just happened" to get hit with a chestnut like the pigeon drop, the chances were vanishingly small that these two events were unconnected. So when the citizen returned from the counter, I took a stumbly step into him—and picked his pocket. A moment later, he was staring at two Calvin Klien wallets, lying side by side on the tabletop. One contained cash, though of course a grifter's roll, with a few big bills for show and the rest just a whole bunch of ones. The other wallet contained money-cut pages from a Bible. Or no, not the Bible, the Book of Mormon, which I thought was an interesting touch.

"Well," he said with sheepish frankness, "that didn't take you long."

"Nor would it," said a voice by the door. Allie's, of course. She crossed to us and cast a casual arm around the old man's shoulder. "You have to remember, Grandpa: This is Radar Hoverlander, the brightest bulb on the bush." Then she turned to me and said, "Hello, Radar. And where's my goddamn shoe?"

dishonest honesty

I gave her the shoe. She stuffed it in a dilapidated Hello Kitty back-pack, and patted my cheek. By way of thanks, I suppose. "Want some coffee?" she asked. "I'm buying."

"I'm good," I said.

"Oh, that you are, sweetie. Why do you think I tracked you down?"

"The question," I admitted, "has crossed my mind."

"Of course it has. Well, don't worry. All will be made clear just as soon as I get my hands on a hammerhead."

"Hammerhead?"

"Black coffee, extra shot."

"Won't that keep you awake?"

"Honey, nothing keeps me awake. When I want to sleep, . . ." She shot me a wink. ". . . I sleep."

She ordered her drink from one of the goth counterettes, while I and the man she'd identified as Grandpa stood on either side of an awkward silence. I sized him up a second time, in light of the new information. Grandpa? He looked old enough, but then again not. I wondered if *grandpa* was code for *sugar daddy*. After a moment, he said, "I'm Hines, by the way. Milval Hines."

"What kind of name is Milval?"

"Family," he said with the laconic shrug of a man who's been asked that question many, many times before. It made me feel self-conscious. After all, it's not like I've ever won the John Doe Prize for Everyday Names; I guess people who live in Radar-shaped houses shouldn't throw stones. But Hines was already past it, on to other subjects. He asked with self-deprecation, "What gave away my play?"

I didn't know where to begin. To the trained eye, everything about his approach—the overly overt pigeon drop, the all-text-no-subtext betting slip, the call to the alleged lawyer—shrieked amateur antic. Even Vic would've done a better job; at least he'd have put some spin on the gaff, colored it up with distracting noise. Hines's pitch had the wide, flat feel of a curveball that didn't break. Truly it had been doomed from the start. But I didn't feel like busting his chops, for who holds an amateur to pro standards? So instead I said, "You did fine. I'm just hard to mark. Like that one said," I hooked a thumb in Allie's direction, "I'm the brightest bulb on the bush." This seemed to satisfy Hines, and the bubble of silence formed around us again.

After a moment, Allie sauntered over, and when I say she sauntered, I mean she moved through space like she owned it, every bit of it, from the racks of vacuum-sealed coffee bags and Java Man T-shirts pinned up on the wall for sale all the way down to the atoms that comprised these things and the quarks and neutrinos that passed through them, and us, on their infinite voyage from wherever to fuckall.

To put it more prosaically, she had that look of someone holding all the cards.

She shivered theatrically. "It's cold in here," she said, though it was not, particularly. "Let's go to your place." A gesture with her cup, up and through the back wall of the Java Man, pointed roughly in the direction of my duplex.

This could have been a bluff. It was possible that she knew

approximately, like to the nearest Java Man, where I lived, without actually knowing the street address. So I prevaricated. "My place is a mess," I said. "The maid hasn't come since . . ."

"The maid comes on Thursdays," she said most matter-of-factly. "She's with a service, the Damsels of Dirt, and if she cleaned in the nude, I wouldn't be surprised—*perv*—but in any case, she spends three hours at your place." Allie fired out the address like pellets from a paint gun, "2323 Silver Sedge Road. From there she goes to Eagle Rock, to the condo of a day trader who, I know for a fact, has her clean in the nude." She smiled at me sweetly. "Her name is Carmen. Strawberry margaritas loosen her lips."

I closed my eyes, then opened them again. I could feel muons and leptons passing through my body. "It's a bit of a climb," I said at last.

"We don't mind," said Allie. "We're fit."

And fit they were. I took them the back way, the hard way, up a flight of steep, crumbly steps that ended about thirty feet below my back deck, and gave way there to a narrow path where it's almost hands-and-knees time. You can get dirty; if you're not careful, you can lose your footing and slide all the way downhill till the Dumpster behind the Java Man breaks your fall or, possibly, neck. But Allie took the ascent with the placid alacrity of an alpaca, not even breaking a sweat. Hines was less nimble but more stoic. I walked them around to the front of my place and let them in. It seemed weird, and not altogether comfortable, having guests in my home.

I'm a terrible host. Are you supposed to offer people drinks? Snacks? What? The sort of characters who come to my place—Mirplo, his low-rent friends, random other bit players in the grift—usually bring their own, and it's usually Steel Reserve and pork rinds. In fact, looking at my joint through strangers' eyes, I suddenly became quite self-conscious. Damsels of Dirt notwithstanding, the place was congenitally unkempt, with books and magazines scattered about, naked

CDs pining for their cases, and piles and piles of unopened mail. Dust motes dancing in the last red rays of sunset gave the very air a shabby feel. I pointed the pair to a couch and hoped nothing would crunch when they sat. Then, to regain some semblance of cool, I grabbed a chair from the dining table, flipped it around backward, and straddled it, resting my head on my crossed arms and affecting the most convincingly who-gives-a-damn mien I could muster.

"First things first," I said. "Tell me how you found me. This conversation goes nowhere till you do."

Allie shrugged prettily. It occurred to me that she did most everything prettily. It should have occurred to me that this would be a problem. "I met a friend of yours," she said. "Not long on social graces or, you know, brains. But he does sing your praises."

Of course. Mirplo. If it were a snake, it would've bit me.

"He should keep his opinions to himself," I said.

"Maybe. But . . ." Again the shrug. This time I took it to mean that whatever Allie wanted out of Vic—information, money, maybe a foot rub—he'd have been powerless to resist. Doubtless, she was right. You recognize people with personal power, and Allie oozed charisma from every pore. I shot her a nod to acknowledge her manifest mastery over the weak mind of a Mirplo. She continued, "I told him I needed someone with a specialized set of skills. Your name came up."

"I'm surprised he didn't promote himself for the gig."

"Oh, he did, but . . ."

"I know, last float on the clueless parade."

"I gave him a finder's fee. The thing is, I need someone with some actual ability here. Just because Vic calls himself an oven doesn't mean he can bake bread. Besides," she said, "your reputation precedes you." This sent a chill through me. In my business, reputations that precede you also often haunt you. Sometimes they chase you down and knock you in the head with a brick.

"Where, exactly, did this precedent take place?"

"In my office," offered Hines. "I'm an investment counselor. Well, semiretired. Apparently one of my clients took your advice over mine." *Oh, man.* I could think of ten different ways that had gone wrong: pump and dump, insider-trading fake, phantom gold mine; classic pyramid, death-benefit buys, financial-planning seminars, affinity fraud, trapdoor hedge fund. When I get my hands on loose money, I'm not the kind to let go.

The picture, in any case, was starting to come clear. "So you think I ripped somebody off, and tracked me down to exact your revenge." I decided to play the bravado card. "So what's the riff now? One of you holds me down while the other beats me up?"

Allie laughed, trumping the bravado card with the formidable Ace of Ridicule. "Radar," she said, "does this look like a revenge tip? Honestly, if I wanted revenge on someone I'd be thinking more along the lines of available fuels, incendiary triggers, and a good benzene accelerant." *Huh?* I gotta tell you, it's not every day a dead-bang cute girl of unknown provenance sits across from you on your own couch and spins out the practical aspects of an arson fire. "Plus, pay attention," she said. "I already told you we need you for work."

"What kind of work?" I asked.

Said Milval, "I want you to teach me to grift."

Sure, that's a good idea. Right up there with teaching the art of medieval trebuchet construction to a blind amputee with Bell's palsy. Grifters are a breed apart. To be good at it, you have to have a taste for danger, a heightened sense of self-preservation, and, at the end of the day, a certain dishonest honesty, the unsentimental knowledge that you fly through life solo. Sometimes, in my dark moments, I feel a little like a remora, clinging to the tiger shark of humanity, feeding on its crumbs or, as the case may be, feces. Other times, I feel like the shark. At no time do I feel like the things I know could be authentically conveyed to someone not born and bred in the grift. It's in the blood, like peanut allergy.

So my first reaction was to reject the proposal out of hand, send these two packing, and go on about my business—top of the to-do list being to track down Vic Mirplo and kick his flat white ass for telling tales out of school. But the grift isn't about first reactions, it's about measured responses. And the fact that Allie had been clever enough to climb into my life and chill enough to talk about arson made me think that my disengagement, however I chose to effect it, should be gracefully staged. No sense in leaving a trail of tears. So I just nodded and said, "Go on."

Allie looked me up and down. I got the icy feeling that she had accurately registered both my mental rejection of the proposition and my decision to play cozy with that choice. Nevertheless, she appeared to take my answer at face value. "It's kind of a Make-A-Wish Foundation thing."

"Oh, God," I said, looking at Milval, "don't tell me I'm on your daisy chain." (Where daisy chain is the sum of things you want to do before you push up those eponymous perennials.)

"Nothing so dramatic," he said. "So far as I know, my health is as good as the next man's, provided the next man is sixty-three with no history of smoking or excessive drink. Why, just last month, a doctor shoved his finger up my ass and pronounced—"

"You know," I said, "I'm almost positive I don't need to know about the state of your prostate, no matter how robust. Why don't we keep this on the bare-bones track if we can?" Milval nodded his acquiescence, and looked to Allie to continue.

"My grandfather," she said, "is what in his day they called a square. All his life he's played by the rules, and while he can't say that this strategy hasn't borne certain fruits—"

"—By which she means I'm rich."

"—he now feels that the time has come to let loose a little. You know, try something new."

Milval felt constrained to amplify. "My wife dragged me to church every Sunday from the day we wed to the day she died. And do you know what I thought about every damn Sunday?"

I couldn't begin to guess. Were I in church, I'd be pining for an iPod.

"Mostly, I thought. *If this is the only life I have, why am I wasting it here?* Lately, that question has come to assume a somewhat greater state of urgency."

"Healthy prostate notwithstanding?"

"Healthy prostate notwithstanding. Mr. Hoverlander—may I call you Radar?" I shrugged a nod. "I've been good all my life. Textbook good. Ticket to heaven good. Good to my friends, good to my wife, good to my kids, . . ." a nod toward Allie, ". . . my grandkids. I never cheated on my taxes; hell, I don't even cheat at golf. Can you imagine?" He paused—for effect, I felt—and then continued. "I'm not sick, and I'm not that old, but I am tired. Tired of all those rules, you know? What were they for? What good did they do me? What good do they do me now? All my life, I've never been bad. Just for once and just for real, I want to know what that's like."

"I understand the impulse," I said, "but why the grift? I can think of lots of ways to be bad. Have you considered shoplifting? Buying pharmaceuticals from Canada? Or how about this: Find yourself an adventuress about Allie's age and pursue that prostate investigation on a more, you know, recreational basis."

"Radar, don't be gross," said Allie tartly. It was absolutely the first crack in her cool and I wondered whether it represented a deeper emotional fault line. I made a mental note to explore the fissure later. One thing you always need in the grift is to know where someone's buttons are and how they can be pushed.

"The issue is not sex," added Milval. "I've lived a long time. I've had all the sex I need." I tried to wrap my brain around that concept and failed by a fairly wide margin. "It's a matter of the life of the mind. I want a problem I can sink my teeth into, one that carries real risk and real reward." He rose to his feet and strode around my apartment in a state of unsuspended animation. "You're young," he continued. "You can't imagine what it's like to be my age. To see the end of the line lurking, if not exactly around the corner then somewhere down the street or in the next block. And from what Allie tells me, your life hasn't been burdened by an excess of conventionality. However, mine has. And I don't want to die saying, 'Mine *was.*' Do you understand?"

"Why don't you let Allie be your guide?" I asked. "She seems to have a natural bent for this sort of thing." Yeah, she did. Tracking techniques. Contrived encounters. Cryptic e-mails. Cinderfuckingella shoes. Allie was no more innocent of the grift than I was. Which meant that her gift of me to gramps was just an attempt to hold him at arm's length from her own true nature, or agenda.

"But you're the, er, professional," said Hines.

I know what you're thinking. I was thinking the same thing. This whole setup had, well, setup written all over it. But what was I going to do? Bust Allie for trying to play me? Then hope she'd lose interest and go find some other mook to mook? I couldn't see that happening. But nor could I see me willingly drinking the Kool-Aid of the first chick slick enough to squeeze a Mirplo till he popped.

So: Let's assume that Milval Hines saw his clever granddaughter as nothing more than someone who could track down other clever people like me. Let's also assume that Allie's gift of a bad-boy adventure for her beloved grandpa was so much smoke concealing . . . well, whatever lay behind the smoke. And while we're at it, let's further assume that Allie's smart enough to know I'm smart enough to know all this, so that if I say, "Okay, sure, I'll train the dude," I'm really saying, "Okay, sure, I'll see the next card." And the peculiar nature of this thing is that each of us knows the absolute truth about the other and absolutely can't speak it. Grifters are many things, but frank and open and honest do not head the list. They don't even crack the top ten.

So what you end up with is wheels within wheels, right? Wheels within wheels within wheels. An "I know that she knows that I know that *she* knows" Ouroboran serpent that eventually swallows its own tale. I don't know about you, but I find this shit interesting.

Still, I could have walked away, either with sufficiently face-saving "my dance card is full right now" excuses or just the common grifter's vanishing act, no explanation, no forwarding address. But it was a measure of Allie's skill of assessment that she either intuited or deduced two irresistible fixatives gluing me in.

One was a puzzle. We know I'm a dog with a bone with those.

The other was Allie herself, coming off like a ballsy, no-shit schoolmarm who treated me with all the respect due a slow learner in the back of the class. I'm a huge sucker for that.

Or just a sucker, full stop.

So now we're reading from a mutually arrived-upon script, and it's my line, and what I come up with comes out in my huskiest tough-guy voice of concern. "The grift's not easy," I say, running my fingers theatrically through my hair. "And it's sure as hell not cheap."

"I spent ten thousand dollars once," said Hines, "learning to appraise heirloom jewelry. I know the price of a quality education."

"Fine," I said. "Where would you like to begin? Maybe a few pointers on how to make the pigeon drop less lame?"

"If that's what you suggest, but don't you even want to discuss your fee?"

I thought about this for a moment. Of course, one classic way of moving the mark in your direction is just to push him away. *The more you pay, the more it's worth,* right? And someone who went ten dimes into jewelry appraisal was likely to go very deep pocket indeed. But that didn't feel like the right angle here. After all, if Hines was prepared to pay for the mystery, it seemed like the mystery should start right here at the price tag. Besides, any good negotiator will tell you that naming the first price is the first step to getting screwed. "Don't worry about that," I said. "I'll get my taste. If I'm good at what I do, it won't even come out of your end."

I looked over at Allie. She was beaming. Like she knew exactly how good I was at what I do, and what a fun little Disneyland ride this would be for gramps. But what about her ride? Where was *it* headed, and who was the passenger? That needed thinking about, so I decided to bring this little conclave to a close, take some distance, and start sorting the players from the scorecard. "Okay," I said, "I'll need some time to map out a snuke. You cool with that?" Allie hit me with her best doe-eyed look, a look so convincing that at that point she seemed not a mistress of the grift but, indeed, the last true innocent.

Have you played much poker? A certain situation occurs in the game where you get so confused that you don't know whether to raise, fold, or screw the waitress. It's called getting lost in the hand, and that's where I was just then. I honestly didn't know whether Allie was on the straight or so pretzeled out that I couldn't tell where the ingenue left off and the femme fatale began.

I decided to track down Vic Mirplo and get his input.

While also, of course, not neglecting to kick his flat white ass.

twenty-five cents a tit

L ike a comet leaves a trail of stardust across the night sky, Mirplo inevitably leaves a clumsy mess in his wake. Set out to track him down and you'll hear comments like, "Oh, yeah, he was in here last night bowling for beers. He stank out the joint." Or, "Tried to run a shell game in front of an LAPD substation. Can you imagine?" Or— and this one I love—"He was selling parking places outside the Hollywood Bowl." This last gag was a Mirplo favorite, possibly the lowest low-rent snadoodle the human mind has yet devised. What he does, he finds a parking place near a crowded sports or cultural event, pulls his shitbox Song Serenade half out of it and waits there till someone comes along and asks, "Are you leaving?" "Sure am," he says, "for five bucks." Then he and Shirley Temple go troll for another open space and start the gaff all over. He's been known to net literally tens of dollars an evening. Seriously, what a mook, huh?

In this case, of course, I didn't have to track him down. All I had to do was text him:

        biz prop big $$ RU n?

This brought him running faster than a cat to a can opener.

We met at Broadview, a topless joint in Atwater Village that I love for its name and Mirplo loves for its liberal no-cover, one-drink-minimum policy. The girls in Broadview are skanky in the extreme—their needle tracks practically glow in the blacklight. But if you sit in back and look like you don't have any money, no stretch for Vic, they never hassle you and you never have to tip anybody anything. And they have the requisite body parts to meet all your ogling needs, at a price anyone can afford. According to Vic's twisted math, since he could nurse a single watery beer through roughly a dozen floor shows, this works out to something on the order of twenty-five cents per nipple, not at all bad value if you're horny, borderline broke, and unlikely to get laid in any circumstance short of lying on your back with a hard-on when a nymphomaniac alien drops out of the sky, legs spread.

I was sitting at the bar drinking tonic water when Vic shambled in looking like the drop-off bag at a Salvation Army thrift store. Happy to see me, he extended his hand for a manly fist bump. I took my tonic and tonic and dumped it on his head. He barely had time to sputter, "What the fuck?" before a bouncer was among us, a hyperinflated poster child for Winstrol with the word *killre* tattooed on his thigh-size biceps. I wondered if *killre* was intended as the British spelling, like *theatre,* or just a dermal typo.

"Is there a problem here?" asked the bouncer in a voice that cut through the lowest registers of the Broadview's PA system, just then cranking Boston's "More Than a Feeling," stripper Kimi's signature tune for your viewing pleasure.

"I'll leave that up to him," I said, fixing Vic with a stare so clearly hard and meaningful that it actually managed to penetrate to the deeper recesses of his brain.

"We're fine," Vic decided at last. "I could use a towel." The bouncer reached over the bar and brought out a limp, brown rag rank with mildew. Vic wanly thanked the bouncer, who went off to look large somewhere else. Then, tossing the rag back behind the bar, Vic ran the sleeve of his ratty sweatshirt over his head and asked, "Okay, how did I fuck up?" Say this for a Mirplo: They never think the indignities they suffer are undeserved.

I told him about my run-in with Allie Quinn, and tore him a metaphorical new one for leading her to me.

"That bothered you?" he said, genuinely surprised. "But why? You already know her. You've met her before."

"The fuck I have."

"Yeah, you did. Last time, though, she had orange plastic hair."

As Vic Mirplo is the clumsiest liar who ever drew breath, I had to believe that he at least *thought* he was telling the truth. So I had him run it down.

"It was the car show," he said. "Don't you remember? Last year at the convention center. We were working the test-drive scam."

"*You* were working the test-drive scam," I corrected. This was another low-rent Mirplo venture, where he set up a booth (okay, a box on a card table) outside the convention center, offering car fans a free shot at test driving the hot new whatever out of Tokyo or Detroit. His "display" consisted of crudely cut photos from magazines, and his entry forms were a stack of bad Xeroxes, but nobody seemed to mind too much; nor did they balk, terribly, at giving up their e-mail addresses, phone numbers, and other useful digits. The promised drawing, of course, never took place, but Vic banked a dollar per entry form from data consolidators who would later phish contest entrants with the chance to learn race-car driving from blissfully unaware NASCAR pros. All *that* took was valid plastic and, well, the rest was garden-variety credit rape. Meanwhile, back at the car show, Vic was more bird dog than scam artist, but among his limited gifts is that of gab—he had no trouble getting the punters to fill out a form. To sweeten the deal, he gave out free Dodge Stealth pens to everyone who filled out a form. And where did he get the pens? By the handful from the Dodge Stealth booth when the booth babes were otherwise occupied. Swear to God, plunk a Mirplo down on a desert island without food or shelter, and his native resourcefulness could easily keep him alive till the end of the day.

I, meanwhile, had been stalking somewhat weightier game, from actual leased space on the convention floor, where my fabricat high-end import enterprise discreetly offered gray-market luxury sedans to quote-unquote discerning individuals who didn't mind skirting California's clean-air or safety standards. The cars in question, I claimed, had been manufactured overseas to bullet- and kidnapping-proof standards, for sale to African dictators or South American drug lords. Geopolitical flux being what it was, some of these cars now needed backup buyers, the intended customers having apparently been deposed or murdered, but it's an ill wind that blows no good, right?

I faced some hard questions. If such a car wasn't imported through normal channels, they asked, how could it possibly be street legal in California, or indeed anywhere in the United States? And if it were imported through normal channels, how could it be so cheap?

Skeptics, huh? Honestly.

I explained at painstaking length that there are two ways to bring cars into the United States without bothering with the niceties of smog, safety, and so forth. First, you can call them museum pieces, and show paperwork intending them for either private collection or public display. The other approach is to call them movie props. Thus they come into the country as art or tools, not cars, so you're home free. Once the vehicles are on American soil, it's no problem and (relatively) minimal cost to street-legal them through certain bureaucratic backdoors. Backdoors which, naturally, I knew how to pry open—else why would I offer such cars for sale in the first place? So I took some down payments, generated ironclad escrows, and told the buyers to see me next week in my Long Beach showroom. I "warned" them that the showroom was none too elegant—more like a warehouse, really—which seemed to feed both their something-for-nothing avarice and their vicarious sense of outlaw adventure. Arriving at the address in question, they would find only a Church's Fried Chicken, but oh well. The wings there can be quite tasty.

The thing is, did I not vaguely recall meeting some Shibuya cutie at my booth? Was she not tricked out in the latest Tokyo toygirl fashion: teeter-tower platform boots, pleated go-go skirt, virginal blouse in irony white, and, yes, a wig of orange plastic hair? Did she not question me at surprisingly knowledgeable length about the chances of acquiring a fully armored CLS55 AMG Mercedes for her (doubtlessly fictive) Yakuza benefactor, while her friend, another geisha bonbon, stood by, fending off Mirplovian advances? Could it really have been Allie in Ginza drag?

Mirplo seemed to think so. "Trust me," he said. "I have a pornographic memory." To drive home the point, he called my attention to a dancer just coming onstage as the DJ said, "Let's give a big hand for Chastity," with all the enthusiasm of a grocery store clerk announcing, "Clean up on aisle four."

"Wait'll she thongs down," said Vic. "You'll see: She's got a tattoo of a Krugerrand on her left butt cheek. I guess she thinks her ass is gold." He paused to chuckle in anticipation of his own lame joke. "And if gold is cellulite, I guess she's right."

I realized I couldn't blame Vic after all for giving me up to Allie. He probably thought she and I were old chums by now.

As for Allie, this seemed to prove she was in the game, if not as a full-time player then at least a weekend warrior. But why was she subcontracting out such a cushy gig as this? Did she so not want to look fallen in Grandpa's eyes? Why would he care? He was a Ready Teddy, too.

Sometimes when there's a problem I'm trying to solve, I find it helps to talk it through out loud. Mirplo's not the best interlocutor for this because his observations are either off-point or just flat inane. But he had helped me put Allie in context, so I thought I owed him a glimpse of the big picture. Which I gave him. When I was done, all he said was, "Dude, you should beat cheeks."

"What?"

"Get out of town. Dislocate. Go to Vegas. That town's easy. I used to rip it up."

"Really?" I couldn't help asking. "Then why are you here?"

He didn't miss a beat. "Sinusitis," he said. "That desert air kills."

"Yeah, well, I'm not blowing town. So far all I've got is an innocent offer to turn teacher. Why should I say no?"

"Orange hair," said Vic, simply.

"What do you mean?"

"A girl capable of orange plastic hair is capable of anything. Besides, you like her."

"Oh, bullshit."

"Then you just want to get your wick wet. Those are the only two choices."

"You're nuts," I said.

But was he really? I couldn't be sure. And the thing you have to remember in the grift is that money is money and sex is sex, and many a deal slides sideways when the line between the two gets blurred. Which gave me all the more reason to make the smart play and just disappear into the distance. It wouldn't be that hard. I'm a master of the fast transition. In a week's time, I could be Aghvan Aghajanian of Glendale, Arizona, unlicensed trader in desperation gold, priced low because bought from motivated sellers (and also because mostly tin).

But damn if I'd give her the satisfaction! Here she'd been in my life less than a week and she already had me jumping through all sorts of unintended and unanticipated hoops. What did she have over me?

Why did I want more?

In the end, then, the smart play and the play you make are not necessarily the same. Out of sheer cussed-mindedness, I decided to see the thing at least to the next level. After all, I'd told Hines that I'd cook up a con for him, and it's a function of my restless mind that even while I was thinking of a dozen different reasons to pull the rip cord, I also happened to think of one cool way to work Milval's former profession into a reasonably tasty snuke.

I could, if I worked it right, even make a nice chunk of change.

Maybe I'd take Allie to Cabo.

the merlin game

Picture this: You've got a shiny quarter in your hand, and 160 people are watching you flip it, via webcam. On the screens of half the 160, you flash a prediction: This coin will land heads. The other half gets the other prediction: This coin will land tails. If the coin lands heads, you disconnect the 80 people who saw you guess tails, and with the remaining 80 you run the same drill. Half see you call heads, half see you call tails. Once again, you boot the ones who see you guess wrong. The remaining 40, notice, have now seen you guess right twice in a row. No big deal, right? But then you do it again and again and again, culling the numbers as you go, from 40 down to 20 to 10 to 5. Now you have 5 people who have seen you make correct predictions not once or twice but five times in a row. Still not that impressive, right? After all, it's only a coin flip, and the odds of nailing five straight coin flips are a mere 31 to 1 against. Hardly a number from the Nostradamosphere. So even if a guy has seen you guess right a few times in a row, he's not a believer, and even if he's a believer, with how much hard cash would he be likely to back his belief?

Coin flips. It's hard to get rich one quarter at a time. And let's not forget that some people will consider that the quarter was gaffed all along, and, hey, they might not even be wrong.

But what if instead of a hundred-and-a-half initial observers you had thousands? And what if instead of five trials you had a dozen? And instead of a cheesy (potentially two-headed) quarter, suppose you had something much, much harder to gaff, at least in most people's minds. Let's say your declared area of predictive expertise was the hoodoo voodoo of the stock market. Or not even the stock market. Maybe something more exotic. Derivatives. Hedges. Futures. Commodities. Exchange-traded funds. Mutual discount accruals. Or perhaps investment vehicles that no one's ever heard of, for the simple reason that no one has crawled around inside the part of your brain where your lies are born. Suppose you found yourself trumpeting your knack at forecasting market movement in highly volatile CCAs (currency core aggregates) (the latest thing) (which you just made up). If you started with 200,000 onlookers, you'd have roughly 199,999 doubters (and one drunk). Enough correct predictions later, by the reverse mitosis of reducing the cell body by half, and half again, and again, you'd have only a couple dozen observers left, but each and every one would swear on a stack of prospectus disclosures that you, my friend, have the true gift for picking winners. Their pumps thus primed, they're now ready to put their money where your mouth is. Pig widgets. Silicon communion wafers. Asteroid shields. And why not? If you can be religiously right in the notoriously fickle CCA market, whatever that is, you're bound to bank big wherever you decide to invest next. And since you're the kind of guy who likes to share the wealth, you invite those whose trust you've absolutely earned to come along for the ride. And who wants to be left off that gravy train? It's leaving the station now, folks. All aboard. *Woo-wooo!*

This scam has been known by many names in many times. Choose Not to Lose. Magic Mirror. Orders of Magnitude. I call it the Merlin

Game, since that legendary necromancer was said to have aged back-ward, and who couldn't pick winners if all he had to do was watch them flash past in his rearview mirror?

The Merlin Game's limitation has always been just getting your initial guesses in front of enough eyes so that by the time you've sliced the sucker cake in halves, quarters, eighths, sixteenths, and thirty-seconds, a large enough pond of confidence remains to be profitably drained. Thanks to the internet, that problem has vanished: Leads abound.

Qualified leads, though, those are another matter.

Which brings us to Milval Hines and his preretirement career as an investment counselor. He probably knew thousands of people who had faith in him. These are what the straight world calls "clients."[*] They didn't trust him implicitly, mind you. They listened to what he had to say and then made their own judgments. He likely never represented himself to be anything other than someone who analyzed trends and passed along what he learned. He flimmed no flams, in other words, but simply did his homework and demonstrated through diligence that he could turn modest risk into reasonable gain.

Now Hines has a problem. In the midst of his existential melt-down, he wants to start having fun, the kind of fun that violates federal law. But it's not so easy. The inertia of his reputation holds him back. His former clients all know him to be a straight shooter with an ade-quate market sense and a respectable ROI, so how can he suddenly reinvent himself in their eyes as an investment savant who's gone from pretty good trend spotter to lock-solid win picker? Can't. Obviously. In the words of the grift (Texas branch), "That dog don't hunt."

Bottom line, he couldn't be a Merlin.

---

[*] Though in a broader sense there's no real difference between a client and a mark. Just ask anyone who thought he got a great deal on a new car.

But he might have just *met* one.

This was the pitch I laid out for him a few days later in his Pasadena office-park office. The place was about what you'd expect for a semiretired investment counselor: a pretty-but-not-too-pretty receptionist, comfortable but not ostentatious leather couches, copies of *Inc.* and *Forbes* in the lobby. The mahogany walls of his inner sanctum, heavily punctuated with degrees and diplomas, had built-in shelves laden with what we call "appreciation hardware," trophies for everything from serving as your organization's treasurer to donating uniforms to the local Little League team. To me it all just looked like credit for time served and reminded me that if the one thing I had to do every day was the same thing every day, my career would likely be cut short by the precipitous slitting of my own wrists. But that's just me. Some people crave boredom.

Hines did not seem to be one of them just then. His eyes shone with delight when I walked in, and he welcomed me like a lodge brother. I half expected a secret grifters' handshake, and if he had found one on the internet, I'm sure he would have laid it on me. As it was, he'd clearly been registering hits on websites like fraudreka.com and hoaxandjokes.org, for his mind was alive with the possibilities of the grift.

"Wishing wells," said Hines after we'd batted a few pleasantries back and forth like shuttlecocks. "Did you know you can invest in wishing wells? I've been in finance all my life and I've never even imagined such a thing!"

Of course I knew all about wishing well franchises. They come in a spectrum of snadoodles, from relatively clean charity funnels to outright skim machines. After all, practically every shopping mall, amusement park, and roadside attraction in the land has some sort of standing body of water into which people feel a gut compulsion to throw their loose change. Who collects that coin?—some street bum scrounging for the price of paint thinner? Don't kid yourself. Small change is big business, and if the shopping mall isn't gleaning the take itself, it's subcontracting the work to some brothers with an Italian (or in this modern world, Serbian) surname, who may hire the bum and equip him with hip waders but are definitely keeping the fat end for themselves.

Well, with that much money in wishing wells, it wouldn't take long for someone to rate it as an attractive investment vehicle, right? When I worked the gaff, I leaned heavily on the fact that there were many more wishing wells than could adequately be serviced without appropriate capitalization, and of course those who capitalize deserve to be compensated. This was nothing short of bald-faced bafflegab, but I succeeded well enough to actually list and trade a named security on a smallish regional exchange. To this day, thousands of investors, mostly in the mid-South, have extensive holdings in Wishing Best, Inc., along with lavishly printed stock certificates that show a barefoot, straw-hatted Huck Finn casting a fishing line into a money pool. They're worth the paper they're printed on. Maybe more to collectors.

Hines thought that coin harvesting was a play we should definitely investigate. He knew a lot of hard-core givers in the Prius-proud crowd who would happily dive into charity wishing wells. I asked him how he'd manage the situation if he wasn't able to meet his projected and promised returns. He said he'd just use the money from those who came along later.

"Congratulations, Milval," I said, dryly. "You've just invented the Ponzi scheme."

He looked completely crestfallen. I guess his research had taken him far enough into the grift to realize that every Ponzi scheme contains the seeds of its own destruction. It's worse than a castle built on sand. It's a castle made *of* sand *on* sand on a beach in a sandstorm with the tide coming in. In the end, a Ponzi scheme has only two possible outcomes: you run; or you do time. Though I messed around with them in early youth, I quickly realized that to embark upon a Ponzi scheme is to plot your own demise. Not my cup of chai.

Hines, though, had a plan B, and this one at least showed some ginger. "Have you ever heard of rhodium?" he asked.

"Of course," I said. "Most expensive metal in the world. Trades for thousands an ounce."

"That's right. How about palladium? Platinum?"

"Both reasonably pricey. What's your point?"

"My point," said Hines, with again that naughty schoolboy grin, "is that some metals are precious, but some just *sound* precious. Suppose we set up shop selling titanium or tungsten or something. We hire some salesmen, pay them on commission, and move a little metal. We can even provide what we promise—a ton of tungsten delivered straight to your door! It just so happens that what we promise isn't worth exactly what they pay. Which, I don't need to tell you, happens every day in the world of sales." He spread his hands expressively. "Look, you're the expert, not me, but frankly, I don't see the downside."

"Neither did the Adelaide Street Boys," I replied.

"The who, now?"

"Bunch of Canadians. Tried that trick with germanium." I gave him a sly smile. "In fact, that's where you got the idea, isn't it?" I tapped the computer monitor on his desk. "Good ol' internet."

"Well, look, if it worked for them —"

"It *didn't* work. Most everyone involved with the game is in jail." I paused for effect. "The rest are dead." I had no idea if this was true or not, but I'd already decided that if I was going to use Hines to help me unweave Allie's web, I needed him to do things my way. Couldn't have him thinking too freely on his own. That leads to improvising, and a mark's improv impulses can be kryptonite to a con. So I had to put the fear on him. "Let me tell you a little something about victimless crime,"

I said. "It pisses off the victims. Sometimes it pisses them all the way off. Which makes your choice of cons the second most important part of your play."

"What's the first most?" he asked in a way I found syntactically charming.

"Your exit strategy." I fixed him with a meaningful stare. "This might not be so important to you, since you see all this as your last great adventure before you get your ticket punched. But I plan to live a long time, and dumping tons of tungsten on the lawns of irate customers is not a step in, you know, the right direction."

"But how do you ever cover your tracks?" he asked. "Isn't it the nature of a sting to leave someone feeling stung?"

"Not necessarily. The true art of the con is to make a vigorous fuck feel like a gentle caress. And you don't do that with a blunt instrument like a boiler room."

Hines's look made it was clear that he didn't know what I meant by boiler room, but didn't want to admit his ignorance. In relieving him of the burden of asking, I was actually demonstrating the principle of the gentle caress: Don't make people feel stupid unless you have to.

"A boiler room," I said, "as I'm sure you know," though I was sure that he didn't, but that was the gentle caress part, "is just a bunch of guys with a bank of phones working their asses off to sell nothing for something. They do it well enough, they make a bunch of money— and a bunch of enemies. Sooner or later, they have to close up shop and open again elsewhere. It's like a mobile auto-detailing service, only instead of cleaning your car, they steal it."

"So their problem is the trail of irate customers they leave in their wake?"

"Customers. Fraud squads. U.S. attorneys. Suits. Uniforms. Tar-and-feather gangs. But that's only half the problem."

"What's the other half."

"It's damn hard work! Have you ever tried beating your head against a phone twelve hours a day selling something that only a total moron or a victim of senile dementia would buy? You know what it's like? You know what it's really, really like?"

"What?"

"A job. I was never a fan of those, and you're obviously done with yours or we wouldn't be having this conversation. So let's play a different game, shall we?"

Funny thing about honesty—sometimes it's the biggest lie of all. By telling Milval the simple truth about himself and myself and the situation we were in, I actually won his trust. From that point forward, he allowed himself to be led, which was what I needed, because I knew that no matter how many contacts he'd accumulated over the years, it wouldn't be nearly enough for our purposes. He was going to have to reach out across the length and breadth of the investment community. And he was going to have to be pretty damn devout when he did.

He had to get religion.

So I had to turn prophet.

The first order of business was to manufacture some convincing cover for Hines. He couldn't just start throwing my name around like some swami-come-lately. People get recommendations for investment counselors all the time. Sometimes they take the bait and sometimes they don't, but in any case, that's a labor-intensive enterprise, the specific labors being abundant one-on-one wooing. For what I had in mind, I needed to pitch the Merlin Game to at least a hundred thousand qualified leads all at once, without anyone looking too closely over anyone else's shoulder. Why? Obviously, if someone on the heads side of the coin flips compared notes with someone on the tails side, it wouldn't take too long for the musky scent of rodent to emerge. Fortunately, there's a time-tested method for accomplishing this sort of information isolation: It's called proprietary knowledge. You just convince the mark that he has a secret line on a huge score—but only if he can be trusted to keep the secret. Scare him with the heavy money penalty for leaving a trail of spilled beans, and his own greed will bind his silence.

Even at that, though, we'd have to move fast, because Merlin Games inevitably break down—quicker than ever in this little Information Age of ours. Between the first herd cull and the final cash call, I needed the whole thing to run no more than three weeks. That takes some tight timing and some serious buzz. With the web both an enemy and an ally to the con, I needed the right internet presence and the right viral marketing. It so happens that I'm pretty good at site design. I've also been known to launch a self-propelled fad or two. I was confident I could handle the technical end of the Merlin Game. But I'd also have my hands full with other things—for example, shape-shifting into a reasonable simulacrum of a financial wunderkind and cooking up all the imaginative coin flips upon which the game depends. That was the fun part.

Though you know what? Come to think of it, it was *all* the fun part.

cooking the frog

Names, as we know, are key to the grift. They really delimit what you can get away with. While Nat Sherman could reasonably be the roofing contractor who turns a home into a money pit, it takes something on the order of a Dunhill Davidoff to sell LLC shares in a movie called *Pigs Aloft*, which has just about that much chance of ever getting made. For the Merlin Game, though, I needed more than a name. I needed an image, backed by a set of bona fides that would organically reinforce everyone's feeling of *Hey, this guy really knows his shit!*

To build such an identity, you've got to strike a balance between believability and cliché. You have to sound credible, but not so credible as to be incredible. Plus, you need a good, solid electronic paper trail, so that anyone who opts to do some serious investigating—where "serious" is defined by most people as five minutes or less of Google-hopping—will discover that you are, indeed, who you claim to be. This strikes me as one of the more enchanting forms of human gullibility— the unstinting willingness to buy into a grifter's self-validation. Say you're a "classy dame," working that fine line between believable and cliché. You're running a sham dating service and you meet a rich mook at an upscale bar, the kind of bar you frequent because, hey, that's where the rich mooks are. What's the first thing you do? Give him your card. It's a nice one, too, with those raised letters that look so impressive and a typeface that just reeks of understated elegance. Later he goes home and decides to check out your website, LiaisonsIntimes.fr. (And isn't the French URL an elegant touch?) He remembers how you promised "the prettiest, most sophisticated, most eligible girls in the world." And son of a gun if there they aren't, in all their pretty, sophisticated, and highly eligible glory. A clutch of stock photos later and, voilà, you've got yourself a money tree. Now all you have to do is shake it at intervals. Understand: This tree *wants* to be shaken. Therefore, in his eyes, the pixel never lies. If it were otherwise, he wouldn't bother with your website in the first place. That's what we call a self-qualifying lead. In the grift, they're gold, just gold.

I thought long and hard about who I wanted to be for this snuke. The perfect profile would be something like: Beijing genius with MIT econometrics, an HBS MBA, McKinsey or BCG consulting experience, a massively successful private-equity track record, and maybe an area of esoteric high-tech expertise like deep packet inspection and carrier-grade security. If little of that means much to you, trust me, it won't mean anything to the marks. But they won't care. Once the results start rolling in, my background is merely the platform on which I stand to survey the movement of wealth over which I seem to have such effortless mastery. It's like jobs on your résumé. After the second or third, no one cares what the first one was. (Which is why I say feel free to make that shit up.)

There were, however, several parts of this front I couldn't back, the Beijing genius part being the most ethnographically notable. Maybe Allie could pass for Tokyo Pop in an orange plastic wig, but not me—my European roots show through. Plus, you never want to make your lie package too complex, or too far from plausible, for every now and then you run into someone who knows what he's talking about—and therefore knows that you don't. Not good for the gaff. Sometimes not good for your health.

Also, I had to be someone who could have reasonably entered Milval's orbit by serendipity, not by suspicious design. Where was Hines likely to have crossed paths with someone with my intended credentials? In church? It could happen.* But a mere shared acceptance of Jesus Christ as our personal lord and savior would neither validate my capability nor open enough of the right kind of doors. No, I needed both a nice, organic link to Milval Hines and a clean, simple explanation for the talent I planned to tout.

I solved the latter problem first, birthing one Ryan Reed, a geek with a strong spiritual bent who found pure art in the science of computer modeling. At first, according to his résumé (available online, of course), he (I) worked in fractal abstracts. Gorgeous shit—you could swear you saw the face of God. Next he turned his attention to financial prognostication, divining those computer models like tea leaves. Rumor has it that both the NSA and NOAA put the full-court press on his services, but he couldn't be bothered, because the challenge just wasn't there. Predicting wars and weather was nothing compared to guessing which way the win blows. Zen finance, that was his game. And (to hear him tell it) there was simply no one better at it in the world.

As for the organic link to Hines, it hit me with the force of revelation: I could be his granddaughter's boyfriend.

To pitch Allie the idea, I arranged for us to meet over steak and eggs at Rudi's Eatateria, a Hollenbeck dive short on atmosphere but long on excellent steak and eggs. We slid into opposite sides of a red

---

*It does happen. It's called affinity fraud. Shockingly easy to shear sheep of your same flock.

leatherette booth and ordered some food. She listened quietly as I outlined my plan to insinuate myself into the Hines sphere of influence.

I expected at least a little resistance, something about establishing appropriate boundaries, or not confusing a sham romance with a real one, or "*Don't go thinking this is a backdoor route to sex, mister!*" Instead, all she said was, "I don't think boyfriend is strong enough." She paused. "I think we should be engaged."

Really?

She made a good case. It's one thing, she noted, to bring a boy genius home for supper sometime, but if it's the fella you're planning on building a life with, why, who could blame a doting grandfather for doing everything in his power to give the lad a leg up?

So we got engaged.

Then came the cavalcade of backstory questions. How long had we known each other? Were we living together? Had we set a date for the wedding? Big one or small? Where did we want to settle? Did we see kids in the picture? Strictly speaking, scant aspects of this false narrative were necessary, for Hines wouldn't be doing much more than providing introductions for "my granddaughter's fiancé, a kid with some very bright ideas." But once we started spinning the yarn, we found it hard to stop. It seemed like we had a great relationship. For one that didn't exist, I mean.

We explored our first fictive encounter: where and how we had met. I proposed a bar, but Allie vetoed that. "I'd never meet the man of my dreams in a bar," she said. "We met in a bookstore."

"What was I reading?"

"Zarathustra. You have a spiritual bent, remember? And you were fascinated by the idea that good words and good deeds can keep chaos at bay."

"Is that what I told you?"

"No, that came later. You were more interested in what I was doing."

"Which was . . . ?"

"Well, you tell me."

I thought for a moment. "Researching green fashion. You want to make a career in recycled clothes."

Allie laughed. "That's so bogus," she said. "I love it."

I loved it, too. I loved the whole damn moment, in fact. Which stretched effortlessly into whole damn hours. It's funny when you start backpredicting a relationship. You get all the good stuff without any of the crap. We talked at length about our first date: the movie we saw, how we agreed that it sucked, where we went for tea after, and how cute I was about not being sure if I was going to get lucky. I tried to convince Allie that the first time we made love I rocked her world. "Not so much," she said with disarming candor of the abstract. "But it got better."

She gave me a middle name: Paradox.

"Paradox?"

"Your parents were hippies. And scientists. Where do you think you got your gift?"

Of course, no relationship is perfect, so we worked up a list of mutual pet peeves. She hated how I never picked up my clothes. I hated her damn scented candles.

"Oh, I suppose you'd rather have the place smell like old socks."

"Anything's better than . . . what?" I groped for a scent. "Key lime sandalwood."

"There's no such thing as key lime sandalwood."

"There is now."

We discussed whether we were dog people or cat people. "Dog," proclaimed Allie. "The only good cat is a doorstop." I found the image florid but didn't disagree with the sentiment.

By the time we got down to giving each other pet names, we figured we'd about milked the subject dry. Allie put her hands on the table with a satisfied smack. "This is good," she said. "I think we've made some good progress." Then her eyes clouded over, and I got one of those flashes of insight: *She's about to say something she doesn't want to.* "One last thing." She paused to draw a breath, then soldiered on. "I suppose you've figured out by now that we've met before."

I acknowledged that I had. "Orange isn't your color," I said.

"I really wasn't trying to mess with you. I was just having some fun."

"I understand," I said. "Fun is good."

"Then you forgive me? For dragging you into this?"

"Provisionally."

"Good." Big sigh. "I'm so glad I got that off my chest. Because when Grandpa came up with this craziness, I remembered you from the car show and I knew right away you were perfect for the job, but only if you could be, like, not hating me."

"How could I hate my Pookie-pie?"

"I told you," she growled, "I hate that name."

"I know. That's what makes it so cute."

We walked outside and stood between our respective cars.

"Okay, there's just one last thing we have to do," she said.

"What's that?" I asked.

"Kiss." I suppose I looked a little shocked, because her face rounded into a smirk. "Come on, you think my bridesmaids aren't going to ask if you're a good kisser?"

"Your bridesmaids don't exist," I said. "This is fiction, remember."

"Well, fiction schmiction, it's still good to know." So we kissed for a while, and it didn't seem the least bit fictive. Eventually, she broke the clinch and said, "Yeah, you'll do. I'll go tell Grandpa the good news."

And who was I going to tell? Mirplo?

As it turned out, yeah, Mirplo.

Which didn't work out at all like I thought it would.

We met up at midnight to shoot baskets under the sodium vapor

lights of a pocket park near my house. You've seen this kind of basketball court before: perforated steel backboards, iron ring hoops with no
nets, cracked and faded line paint, maybe the odd hump in the asphalt
where a nearby tree threw a root. Check out the shadows, you can see
junkies on the nod or robotrippers jitzed on a cough-syrup high. Actually, best not to check out the shadows too closely.

I told Vic what I'd cooked up for Hines, and how I'd fabricated this
relationship with Allie to hook myself into the game. I expected him to
(a) admire my moves and (2) try to deal himself in. Instead he hit me
with (!) logical negation.

"You're such a fucking tool," he said, with more honest contempt
than I thought a Mirplo could muster.

"What do you mean?"

"Look, I told you this chicklet was trouble. Went out of my *way* to
warn you." (Conveniently forgetting, of course, that it was he who led
her to me in the first place.) "Now here you're playing *house* with her?
Can't you see? She's easing you in."

I fired the basketball at him, hard, a two-handed rocket pass that he
caught in his gut with a cartoon-sounding *ooooff.* "She is *not,*" I said
truculently, "easing me in." In the slang of the grift, to ease someone in
is to draw them so artfully into a snuke that they never see it coming.
It's also known as the grease and fleece, and if you can ease them back
out again without tipping the gaff, then you know you're really on your
game. For Vic to accuse Allie of easing me in was half an insult to her
and an insult and a half to me. "You're full of shit," I said. "This whole
gag's been my idea."

"Oh, *which* part?" he sneered. "The part where you get kissy-face
with the babe who's been playing you since the minute you met? Or the
part where you go mentor to an old fart who's supposed to be a straight
but seems to know enough about the grift to pitch you both wishing
wells *and* leveraged metals?"

"That was just research."

"That's what he told you. But have you even done diligence on the dude? Do you have anyone's word but his that he's legit?" I had to admit that I had not. "Jesus fucking Christ on a bicycle, Radar. I thought *I* was the stupid one. Next thing you know, she's gonna to be cooking the frog."

Now this was really insulting. Everyone knows you can cook a frog by putting it in cool water and turning up the heat so unnoticeably slowly that it'll boil to death without a fight. A grifter who can cook the frog is regarded as a master of the trade.

The frog is held in somewhat lower esteem.

"You don't watch out, you're gonna end up in love, and then your ass'll *really* be grass."

"No way," I said. "There is *no way* I'm falling in love with—"

"With who?" he taunted. "Your Pookie-pie?"

Poor Mirplo. I had to beat him up for a while.

tequila 1, idiot 0

I don't have a lot of experience with tequila, but I know you've had too much when you go to brush something off your shoulder and it's the floor.

I passed out sometime before dawn with Mirplo's critique still turning circles in my brain and the world spinning a good deal faster—according to my subjective reality—than its normal thousand or so miles per hour. They say that alcohol cannot solve your problems, and in this they are right . . . unless the specific problem you're trying to solve is to temporarily stop feeling like an idiot, in which case alcohol works as effectively on brain cells as Windex works on windows. Better, in fact, because when you're done cleaning the windows, you still have windows, but when you're done washing your brain with high-test agave, you have appreciably less brain. So: tequila 1, idiot 0.

Some unconscious hours later, I opened one crusted eye, and there close at hand was my empty enemy, a bottle of El Blanqueo, the finest tequila that money can buy in the sort of all-night liquor store where a sad Hmong employee holes up inside a bulletproof booth reading what can only be presumed to be Lao porn. I'd like to say that getting loaded was Mirplo's idea, something on the order of, "Come on, buddy, let's drink it off. Tomorrow you can tell that skirt to take a hike." But Mirplo had long since issued his last "fuck you," put Shirley Temple into grindy gear, and driven off into the night. I couldn't blame him. I wouldn't listen to reason, and I kept trying to kill the messenger, or at least do it grievous bodily harm. Mirplo was right, undeniably: I was being eased in. But who wants to hear that from a Mirplo? So I abandoned all common sense (and ten dollars and ninety-five cents) and drank away the shank of the night.

When you drink as infrequently as I do, you almost don't know what a hangover is, but a rotgut tequila hangover has a way of expounding itself in terms of terminal thirst, mortal headache, pained sensitivity to any sound louder than the batting of butterflies' eyelids, a vampire's aversion to sunshine, and a mental state the dictionary describes as dysphoria, which really means, as if you didn't know, that you feel like seventeen different kinds of shit. I rolled over where I lay on the living room rug and stared up at the ceiling, noticing for the first time a series of termite tubes hanging down from the exposed beams. Great, I thought, first dry mouth, now dry rot.

And next: dry heaves!

By the time I got done puking, I had pretty much remembered why booze and I don't get along. A hot shower mitigated my feeling of imminent demise, but my subsequent shave brought me face-to-mirror with—let's face it—an incipient victim of the grease and fleece. I guess at this point my brain started to function again, because I couldn't help asking myself, *but fleece what?* What did I have that Allie wanted? It couldn't be just money: If the girl had enough talent to ease in an (I flattered myself enough to claim) expert grifter like me, she could painlessly bank bigger against easier marks.

This took me back to revenge, and I spent some time squeezing orange juice and mulling the possibility of a con within a con within a con, at the bottom of which downward spiral would lay yours most humbly truly, victimized by a prior victim, or said victim's proxy. But, again, I couldn't make it add up. Revenge may be a dish best served cold, but it also works best as fast food. Get in, get well, get out. If Allie was setting up a revenge tip, she was taking too long and playing too loose. Besides, she genuinely seemed to like me, and while the affectation of affection is a notable tool of the grift, this just didn't feel like that. I had to trust my judgment, and my judgment told me that, behind and beneath everything as yet both revealed and unrevealed, Allie was having as good a time with me as I with her. I felt less like a victim and more like a . . .

Partner.

Partner?

Partner!

It wasn't revenge she wanted, and it wasn't my money. It was my expertise. Somewhere beyond this current con, I was suddenly certain, lay a grander, more complex snadoodle, for which Allie was either grooming me or testing me or both. Suddenly I wasn't angry anymore, and I didn't want to tell the skirt to take a hike. I just wanted to prove myself worthy.

But how to go about this? Reveal that I've broken her code? That would only prove I was half smart: smart enough to figure out what's going on, but not smart enough to keep my trap shut. No, for the sake of appearance, I'd have to maintain the appearance of Radar Hoverlander, aka Ryan Paradox Reed, running a Merlin Game for the amusement and edification of Milval Hines, grandfather (or, now come to think of it, maybe not) to a most formidable fellow snuke.

Oh, and by the way, not fall in love.

Which might be harder than I thought, for Allie was cute and clever, an excellent liar—a trait I admire—and steps ahead of me at every turn so far. She was a puzzle. And we know how much I like those. The question was, how far was I willing to go to solve this one?

Or to put it another way, if Allie Quinn was the La Brea Tar Pits to my lumbering mastodon, how heavily could I step on the crust without tumbling into the goo?

Weirdly, my first order of business was to apologize to Mirplo, not so much because I regretted hurting his feelings (which is like hitting a dog on the skull; it really doesn't penetrate) but to make sure he didn't say the wrong thing at the wrong time. Also, let's face it, an apology was in order: Vic said I'd been sloppy, and sloppy I'd been. Was I really that ensorcelled? Or was Allie just really that good? Sure, I'd been suspicious, but not nearly suspicious enough. Radar's radar, it seemed, was on the fritz. Well . . . reboot, clean slate, fresh start. There's no room in the grift for regret. If you've made a mistake, you just try to learn from it and move on.

I called Mirplo, told him he was right. Allie was easing me in, and it was going to take a certain amount of deftness to ease myself out. Mirplo, fancying himself the Lord of the Deft, told me he'd be standing by to help out any way he could. I felt certain that the best way he could help was by standing well out of the way, but I just thanked him for being such a loyal friend. And kept it in the back of my mind that he might be useful at some point. As I said, a Mirplo is a blunt instrument, but sometimes a blunt instrument is exactly the tool you need.

Next I did what I should have done in the first place, a little research on Milval Hines. I found no damning evidence online, but I knew that didn't mean anything. Self-affirming background backups, as we've already determined, are part of a grifter's basic playbook, and radarenterprizes.com is exhibit A. So Hines was at the very least "he of whom he spoke." I hoped he was on the level, or at minimum had a level side, because for the Merlin Game to work, I'd need a broad swath of his contacts, and contacts of his contacts, and contacts of his contacts of his contacts. If he was all smoke, we were game-over before we began.

When you don't know how else to act, act like nothing's wrong. I had already put together the first layer of the Merlin Game, and with Allie posing as my betrothed, I could now reach out to Hines's clients, peers, and professional associates, spreading the pitch virally from friend to friend of friend to friend of friend of friend to the ultimate iteration of an investment pool deep and broad enough to sustain the game.

I got in touch with Hines and, still playing bent mentor, instructed him to write me a letter of introduction. I guided him to the type of language the marks respond to, phrases like "revolutionary new method," "proven track record," "earn your trust," and so on. The key to this missive was that it offered information and asked for nothing in return, which is the surest way I know to flank a mark's natural Maginot. At the end of the day, the pitch boiled down to what it always does in the Merlin Game: Watch the kid pick winners and decide for yourself if he knows his stuff.

While he worked on that, I made my first pick, a newish company called Longhorn Turbines, which went around converting West Texan landowners into wind farmers. Lots of wind in West Texas; I actually thought this company had a chance to go, but for my purposes, it didn't really matter. There's only two ways for a stock to go, up or down, and whichever way it moved, half my herd would think me a winner. Stock rise, stock fall, Radar cull herd, game go on.

I had my hands full over the next two weeks, establishing my database, picking my arbitrary winners or losers, building my fictive website, setting up the crucial endgame investment mechanism, and always selling, selling, selling. After Hines's initial letter of introduction, I took over direct communication with the mooks, defining myself as someone with a frank interest in getting stupid rich and inviting everyone along for the ride. This may strike you as a bogus pitch, and I'm sure it struck some of my marks that way, but it was nec-

essary to introduce and reinforce this element in order to prep everyone for the key moment when they put all their money in one big pot
for one big push. For some, the accuracy of my picks was enough, but
others needed the ol' VPM,[*] so that when the time came, they would
invest with 100 percent confidence. Why do you think they call it a
confidence game?

Then, one afternoon, Allie stopped by my apartment and invited
me down the hill for coffee. Of course I was wary, but of course I
cloaked this and accepted her invitation with the distracted air of a
man of my hectic agenda. We clambered down to Java Man, got hot
wet somethings, and settled in at an outdoor table shaded by a taupe
umbrella adorned with the Java Man logo, a caveman with a club in
one hand and a latte in the other.

"Radar," she said without preamble, "I'm worried."

"There's nothing to worry about," I assured her. "Everything's right
on script."

"It's not that. It's Grandpa. He's starting to freak me out. He's
become totally obsessed with the grift. He's reading all these books,"
she said. "Everything he can get his hands on. It's all he talks about, too.
'Glim dropper' this, 'barred winner' that. I don't even know what half
this stuff means." At that my "false" alarm sounded, for I was certain
she knew exactly what these scams were and how they operated. You
don't get good at the grift without first being a good and thorough student of the game, and while I sentimentally clung to the remote possibility that Allie was a true innocent, my instinct said otherwise,
especially when the very words out of her mouth rang as tinny as a toy
piano.

But I played it straight. "So he's become a buff," I said. "Wasn't that
the whole point of the exercise? Give Gramps his walk on the wild

---

[*] verbal prostate massage

side?" She nodded solemnly, or possibly mock-solemnly. "I don't think it's a problem," I continued, "unless he starts tipping his mitt." This was a risk some grifters ran, where they got so proud of their tweaks that they couldn't resist crowing or showing off. It's like a poker player showing a successful bluff. Good for the ego; bad for the bankroll. "Is he doing that?"

"No," said Allie. "He's keeping his contacts at arm's length, just like you told him to."

"That's good." I had explained to them that when we ultimately burned down the house—concluded the con, that is—Hines would have to come off as burned as everyone else. He'd have to play shocked and dismayed, and sell it well enough to convince his victims that he was a victim, too. Something on the order of "*Reed seemed like such a nice young man. I can't believe he'd do such a thing to us all.*" Innocence, in other words, was his exit strategy, and it needed protecting.

Allie took a sip of her drink. "You don't understand," she said. "He's gone all random. Know what he tried the other day? Something called the vase bump?"

I laughed out loud. She darn near got a spit take out of me.

The vase bump is one of the most basic and stupid scams there is, where you buy a cheap vase, forge a receipt from a high-end antique store, then stumble into a mark on the street and drop and break the damn thing. If you get irate enough or sorrowful enough—and I've seen both methods work—certain dimwits will pay you to replace the vase. If it's no sale, you just throw the pieces in a paper bag and try again elsewhere. As I said, it's a pretty lame game (and thus a Mirplo favorite), and the thought of Hines going around running it struck me as majorly goofy. Maybe he really *had* gone random.

But, again, Allie not knowing what a vase bump was? Did she really expect me to buy that?

"How's his mental health?" I asked.

"He's not old enough to be senile."

"Granted. It's just, over time some people sort of lose their internal editor. Stop hearing the voice that tells them not to do stupid things."

"Yeah, that sounds about right," said Allie. "Radar, I think we should pull the plug."

This genuinely surprised me. We were deep into the Merlin Game, no more than a week away from burning down the house. I'd already set up the offshore account to which we'd funnel the mooks' monies, and I'd arranged the wash-back lines that would get the cash into our hands as clean as a nun's underwear. I figured we were looking at something like a hundred grand apiece. Not bad for a few weeks' work, and also not the kind of earn you suddenly turn your back on.

Never leave money lying on the table, right?

But also: wheels within wheels within wheels. If Allie were a true innocent, it would make sense to want to bail Gramps out of his bad new hobby, but she wasn't, so it didn't. Once again, I found myself trying to decrypt her hidden agenda, my effort complicated by the fact that I really didn't know who she was and what level of deception she was operating on. Did she really want to end the gaff, or did she just want to reinforce her concerned-granddaughter image? Still, there's such a thing as oversolving the problem, so I reverted back to my default value: Play it straight. *If I were exactly who I was*, I asked myself, *how would I react right now?*

"Look," I growled, making a manifest effort to keep my voice low and under control, "just because Gramps has lost a few grapes from his vine, there's no reason to get cold feet. We pull the plug now, we lose all the front-end investment, not to mention a considerable payday. Do you know what opportunity costs are?"

"No."

"Revenues lost through wasting time."

"If you're saying you want to be paid for your time—"

"I'm saying," I said, parceling a smidge of impatience into my voice, "that we see the thing through."

She looked at me with a puppy's remorse. "I never really intended for things to go this far, Radar. I think I never thought they would. You really are good at what you do."

Smoke up the ass kind of tickles, but I kept the conversation perking along on the text level. "Look," I said, "this is the best Merlin Game I've ever run. It has everything going for it. Shaky economic times, qualified leads, and a solid insider's in. It's going to wrap with a handful of extremely live ones out there primed and ready to wire transfer their fool asses off. We can't let them off the hook now. Karma won't allow it. The universe demands that they balance their stupidity with poverty. If you and g-diddy have suddenly developed a case of the yips, that's your problem, not mine. You can run along. I'll bring the fucking game home by myself."

I was going for the tough-guy grifter thing, coming on strong enough to pop some kind of reaction out of her. Well, I got one.

She burst into tears.

Dumped her drink in my lap.

And left.

I wondered if this meant the engagement was off.

the afterparty snuke

I suppose that if I'd taken Allie's tears at (streaming down the) face value, I'd have felt bad about hurting her feelings or whatever. But just as I was capable of dialing up some fake anger, I considered Allie capable of croco-dialing in some fake tears. Was I taking a risk by causing a rift? Could she not have chosen to drop a dime on me just then— outed the Merlin Game to the SEC or whoever? Maybe . . . but only if my whole read on her was wrong and she really was a citizen. Otherwise, well, she knew I wouldn't give up the Merlin Game without a fight; ergo, a fight was what she wanted. The question was *why*—a question, I confess, I was getting kind of tired of asking. Maybe when I played the anger card it wasn't all card. If so, that was a bad sign, a sign of tilt, or loss of control. Was Allie that under my skin? Was my chosen strategy of seeming to play right into her hands really just playing right into her hands?

At least I had this going for me, that just as Allie knew I wouldn't walk away from the Merlin Game, I knew she wouldn't either. Sooner or later (and it would have to be sooner because the house was about to burn down) she'd be back on my doorstep, either with a go-along, get-along apology or her real reason for wanting to kill the gaff.

Meantime, Mirplo asked me to pitch in on one of his street plays, and I agreed because I owed him for shining the sodium vapor light on Allie and also because I needed to let my subconscious chew on the deepening mystery of Allie's self-contradictory moves, and the equal mystery of my self-contradictory feelings. As it happens, the back of my mind works better when the front of my mind is occupied. So I helped Vic stooge off some afterparty passes at a rock show at the Nokia Theatre.

The beauty of this scam is, your mark won't even know he's been snadoodled until after the show is over and he tries to get into a backstage afterparty that either won't honor his bogus credentials or doesn't exist to begin with. You, meanwhile, are gone baby gone, so there's nothing he can do at that point except swallow the loss. Hell, he probably paid too much for the tickets to begin with, so what's a little more out-of-pocket pain? Besides, he got the whole fun of anticipating the afterparty throughout the entire show, and that's not nothing, right? Or am I just rationalizing?

Vic had run this game before, and I had to admit he was pretty good at it, maybe because he could relate so effortlessly to the low-wattage rock fans he targeted. Also, he picked his spots, favoring the kind of bands whose fans favor altered states. In this case, it was a Somnifer show, Somnifer being one of these eclectic jam bands who definitely sound better if you're high.

Vic had cheesed up some phony laminates on lanyards and cooked up a story about how he worked at the William Morris Agency and had peeled off these party favors from a stack intended for the agency's A-list clients. Naturally, he would tell the marks, he couldn't go himself, lest he run into one of his bosses or the pampered elite. But there was no reason some true Somnifer fans couldn't rub shoulders with their idols, right? For a price, of course.

I know what you're thinking. Someone would have to be phenomenally stupid or astoundingly stoned to fork over good money to such a transparent scam. No shortage of stupid or stoned at a Somnifer show, but even at that it was a hard play to drive home, unless you had someone to validate your parking. Someone who reeked of undercover cop, say. That's where I came in.

I watched from a distance as Vic made his pitch to a couple of buzzed treetops in tie-dyes. The girl was a long, skinny stick of a thing; her companion the kind of guy who's in good shape now because he's young and doesn't have to work at it, but you just know that in a couple of years, the weekly game of Ultimate Frisbee will fight a fast losing battle against Kettle Chips, Entenmann's, and beer. They seemed interested but couldn't find any reason to believe that the passes were anything other than exactly what they were: total Photoshop fabricats. This was the tipping point of the grift. They *wanted* to believe. They just needed some evidence, and the flimsiest would do. But Vic couldn't provide it. As the man with the merchandise, if he insisted the passes were real that would just cast doubt into their addled minds.

So I moved in for the bust.

"Hello, girlfriend," I said, clapping my hand on the back of Vic's neck in the classic jovial-but-not-really manner of cops everywhere.

"Oh, shit," said Vic.

"What's going on?" asked the girl.

"Let's get out of here," said the guy.

"Don't move," I said, and flashed my badge.

That's right: badge. This, too, was a fabricat, or more precisely a pawn shop purchase. Close examination would have revealed it to be the hardware of a Shasta County deputy sheriff, but who had time for close examination when I shut the badge wallet with a copperly swift snap, then leaned on Vic with all the snark and sneer I could muster? "You fuckin' mook!" I said. "How many times have I told you not to scalp on my beat?"

"Scalp? Who's scalping? Do you see any tickets for sale?"

I snatched the afterparty passes from his hand. The girl tried to sidle away, but I stopped her with a snarled, "Freeze, sunshine."

"We weren't doing anything," protested the boy. "We were just looking."

"Yeah, that's what the peep-show creep said. Now plant it." They planted it. It's really an amazing thing when you think about it. A fake badge and a command voice are all it takes to put you totally in charge.

Examining the passes with a jaundiced eye, I asked Vic, "Where'd you get these?"

"You know," he shrugged. "Here and there."

"You stole 'em from your boss again, didn't you?"

"Maybe I bought 'em on eBay," he said with the right mix of fear and fierceness. "What are you gonna do? Confiscate 'em and go to the party yourself? Try and get a groupie to slurp you one? They go for rockers, you know, not undercover douchebags."

"Watch your mouth, felch." I waved the passes in his face. "Just because I can't use these doesn't mean I can't make 'em disappear."

"Sorry, officer," said Vic, changing his tune for the benefit of the spellbound stoners.

I changed mine, too: to wistful. "Wish I could go, man," I said. "I hear it's going to be off the hook. Hef is going."

"Hef goes everywhere."

"Yeah, he does." I handed the passes back to Vic. "Look," I said, "keep this shit outta my sight, will you?" I turned to walk away.

"You're letting us go?" asked the girl.

"Hey," I said, "as long as there's no price tag on the things, it's not scalping, just commerce. Tell Hef I said hi."

Sold!

We stooged off another half-dozen passes before the show got under way, then wandered down the street to a bar called Muskrat

Love. Mirplo ordered a shot and a beer, but I'd done my booze for the month, so I just sat there at the bar, playing with a beer mat. Vic counted out the night's get and passed half to me.

"Keep it," I said.

"What, you don't want it? Too chump change?"

"Yeah, no, it's not that. It's just, you need it more than I do. I'm about to score big in this Merlin Game and all . . ."

My voice trailed off into that place where all liars' voices go, a fact upon which Vic's takes-one-to-know-one sensor immediately picked up. He looked at me sideways.

"You've got the guilts," he said, as if naming a particularly virulent venereal disease. "Oh, my God, Radar, you're going soft on the mark."

"That's bullshit," I said. "What do I care if a couple of baked rockers fork over some of daddy's extra green?"

"Well, what do you?"

Good question. A question so good that it almost bought me a beer. But I knew if I went down that road I'd be waking up on the floor again tomorrow, no nearer to an answer than I was right now. I shredded the beer mat instead.

One thing you get used to in the grift is thinking in layers. Like, if the mark tells you something's bothering him about a deal you're on, you peel back the thing he thinks is bothering him and get to the one underneath. This is why their "*I'm not sure my wife will let me invest*" really means "*Please give me a reason to trust you.*" Peeling back your own layers is harder, because as a grifter you're just naturally more devious than normal people, plus, everyone tends to put up more resistance when it's them looking at them. But Mirplo had a point. If I wasn't going soft on the mark (which happens to every grifter from time to time, no matter how hard we try to keep empathy at bay), then what, really, was toasting my cheese?

Allie, of course. Allie on whom I not only *wanted* to go soft, but *had* gone soft, if you think about it: soft as runny brie, soft as a bunny's belly, soft as the downy fur I imagined lay between her . . .

Stop it, Radar! Get a fucking grip!!

Mirplo and I spent an hour backpredicting everything that had happened between Allie and me since we'd met. The results were not pretty: Radar Hoverlander, a man of independent means and ways, was being led about by the nose.

Or not exactly the nose, a point Vic underscored by shifting into his "Uncle Joe" persona, a booming sportscaster type who belted out his words a full octave lower than, and utterly unrecognizable as, Vic's normal, reedy voice.

"She's got his dick in her hand!" boomed Uncle Joe. "His pants are up, his belt is buckled, his fly is zipped, but his dick is *in her hand!*" Normally, I found Uncle Joe quite funny. Not now, though. "She shoots, she scores!"

Uncle Joe aside, the evidence was hard to refute. Just look at how I'd played every choice Allie had offered me so far: She wanted to flirt at a party; I flirted. She wanted a ride home; I drove. She wanted a meeting; we met. Mentor for Grandpa? Check. And then a big, fat, lively, major league snuke that stood to net some serious green. In the midst of which her cold feet suddenly want company.

Only they don't get it!

For the first time, Allie hears Radar say no. Result? Tears and wet violence. And how does this make Radar feel, really? Bad. Really bad. Bad enough to displace his feelings to grift guilt, which is fully ridiculous: The mark always gets what the mark deserves.

My half of the night's earn was still sitting on the bar, minus the cost of drinks, which Vic had conveniently taken from my end. I snatched up the cash and jammed it in my pocket. So much, at least, for that.

As for the rest, all I had to do was peel back the bottom layer and look at it with unblinking eyes: To say no to Allie Quinn was to feel remorse. Like Pavlov's dog ringing his own bell and kicking his own ass.

Well, that was easy enough to fix. All I had to do was stop saying no.

No, I mean *keep* saying no. (God, now I'm Freudian slipping.) Keep saying no. Just stonewall until the vexing vixen gets frustrated or bored and goes off to shop for another Hoverlander to land on. *Stop playing her game, Radar! Can't you see she's in your head?*

Just say no!

I bought Vic a beer for his road and headed home.

Where I found Allie waiting on my doorstep.

The night had turned cool, and she sat with her arms wrapped around her bare knees in a TV attempt to keep warm. It made her look about twelve years old.

She made a proposition no twelve-year-old should make.

Long story short, I found I couldn't say no.

it's tricky when grifters make love

I t's tricky when grifters make love.

Even in the best of circumstances, the sack can be a hotbed of deception. "Of course I came." I "*love* it when you do that!" "No, it wasn't too rough . . . too soft . . . too short . . . too long." "Honey, making love to you is exactly like the baby bear's porridge, just right." Oh, please: The lies we tell each other. And that's just in the name of not brutalizing one another with the truth.

Now put two notorious a prevaricators in bed together, where people are supposed to be vulnerable and real with each other, and watch the walls of false intimacy fly up. First thing you both do is buy into the useful fiction that it's just a friendly fuck, a horny idea that one of you had and the other couldn't refuse. But you both know that's not true. One has an agenda hidden so deep it may never see light of day. The other fancies himself such a cocksman that, by damn it, he can *bone* the truth out of her. (I'm laughing at myself right now. What can I tell you? Sex makes everyone stupid.) Next, deny the fact that when clothes come off, things change. And I'm not talking about the physical flaws revealed. Everyone suffers that. The mole on your ass that you hate. Your outie navel you always thought was kind of a turnoff. The Dopey tattoo that seemed like such a good idea at the time. Maybe your six-pack abs are more like a pony keg. Maybe "objects in T-shirts are smaller than they appear." Thanks to porn, we all know how gorgeous gorgeous can be. In real life, it's never that way. You con yourself that your partner will forgive a few imperfections, while secretly fearing she'll realize it's *all* imperfection. Well, buck up, bucko: She's conning herself the exact same thing about you.

When it comes to sex, rest assured, we're all in the same bed.

But for Allie and me to get naked together was to make a statement that all lovers make but grifters simply can't make and mean: "*I trust you. I trust you not to judge me, belittle me, laugh at my warts-and-all all. I trust you to gentle me if I need gentling and to reassure me with your words and not-words. I trust you to witness me at my most vulnerable and exposed and . . . approve. Just approve. And when it's over, I'll trust you yet more, trust enough to risk falling asleep beside you, nestled in connection, spooning in the cherished belief that, for once in my ragged, unworthy life, someone as gloriously approving as you could risk falling asleep beside me, too.*" For normal people, maybe this works, but for grifters, it's bad mojo. It should never be done.

All of which I forgot the instant Allie threw me down on my bed, sprawled across me and stuck a tongue of pure electric fire down my throat. My tongue fought back, and for a while it was tongue war. With no clear winner in sight, we reached a rough accommodation, taking turns taking the swirling, darting lead, while our hands went looking for something to do. At first it was all safety zones: head and neck and knee and back. Then we discovered each other's ass, and that was a party of sorts. She ground her pelvis into my groin, where, as with the tongue, she met a certain form of resistance. By mutual military maneuver, our hands soon opened a second front in front. I cupped a breast through a bra, while Allie came *this close* to touching my erection through my jeans.[*]

I rolled her over. Her cinnamon hair sprayed a halo on my pillow. Color rose along her neckline, and her lips looked bee-stung, red and full. Her eyes were likewise wide—huge, with pupils big and black enough to fall into. She wore no makeup, and the flush in her cheeks brought out freckles I hadn't noticed before. In her METRO RETRO T-shirt and kilt-style skirt, she looked so schoolgirl I suddenly felt illegal.

She read some of this in my face, and uttered the word "What?" in a manner part naïf, part tart.

"This is a bad idea," I said.

"I couldn't agree more," she murmured. Then she grabbed me and pulled me down to her, her tongue making the nonverbal statement that she could, in fact, agree a whole lot less. A stronger man than I might have found the power to resist. I'm not sure that such a man exists.

Now it was all hands on deck, a frank exploration of each other's body parts—or at least as frank an exploration as layers of fabric can allow. So then it was time for that awkward thing where you try to take off your clothes without looking awkward. Trust me, no man can pull off taking off his underwear and not be at least a little bit dorky. You're fine over the hips, maybe even the knees, but once that cotton puddle is down around your ankles, even a sexy striptease will take a turn for the self-conscious. It helps if you can both laugh then; with tension that thick, you just have to.

Allie had the sexy striptease wired, right down to the self-conscious way she laughed as she bounced up off the bed and did a little hippy-hippy shake thing at once so coy and so knowing that it made every

---

[*]In fairness to my erection, it did its best to meet her halfway.

part of me tingle. I tried to play it cool, just lying there with my hands behind my head, but my body betrayed me; I was so taut, I twanged like a bowstring. Allie pirouetted her bra off, holding it against her chest as she twirled, until centrifugal force worked its magic and I could see what I'd (recently frequently, I suddenly realized) pictured: that objects in T-shirts can be even more perfect than imagined. Her eyes reached out to mine for approval. I mustered a reverent, "Wow." Then her skirt and panties were somehow made to vanish, and she stood before me, naked, in a state of grace. Part of me recognized that she might even now still be playing me, still easing me in. But then she hopped on the bed and straddled me. Then I truly got eased in, and just didn't care.

People can fake it when they fuck. Girls fake better than boys. Grifters fake better than most. You can fake the sighs and moans, the rising crescendo of imprecations to divinities. You can even fake the sticky stuff if you're good, or at least fake the value you place on that. So, yeah, you can fake the union of bodies, sure—but not the meeting of minds. Because when the connection is there, it's *there*. Undeniably. Inarguably. And you know it is, because you hit a groove, a real one, with organic pulse and tempo. Everything works and nothing is forced. Time slows and stretches till your whole world is reduced to the metronome of your bodies in synch, a perfect human piston delivering shots of combustion over and over again until you're both dripping with sweat, slick with the glisten of it, over all the parts that pass between you. You anticipate each other's change of pace and position as if the thing that links you is not pole and hole but some laser bridge between brains. You lick the sweat off each other and the taste is at once foreign and familiar, like this is the body your body has been waiting for all its life. You sense its chemical root; on top of everything else, it just *smells* right. Then all is lost: lost in a rhythm and cadence that can't possibly be anything but the real deal, a sweet union so urgent, so unguent, that it just wants to go on and on and on but also wants to end *right fucking now!* You hear her screams, muffled by the pillow she's shouting into, and you know that the force that's overcoming you has overcome her, too: a force as old as animals, as new as ten seconds from now. Then a switch trips, and signals jet up and down the length of your spines, and the thing wells up inside you as your bodies race to keep pace, and it wells and it wells until there's no place left to hold it, and in that brief frozen moment you realize this isn't just sex, it's a line that cleaves *before* from *after*, or no, not a line, a cliff, a cliff you poise on, cling to, then joyfully leap from as everything inside both of you just suddenly unspools and you come and come till your muscles melt and your bones dissolve and your eyes roll up in your head and you drop.

And your shocked limbic systems look around themselves and ask, *What the fuck was that?*

An eternity later, I looked over at Allie. She lay on her side, asleep. A drop of sweat hung from the tip of her nose, poised to fall. My tongue flicked out and snatched it, like a hummingbird sucking up God's own nectar. In her somnolent murmur, a silent spit bubble formed and broke on her lips. *Maybe everyone is innocent when they make love*, I thought. *Maybe sex makes everyone new.* Then I was gone in sleep, too, and the night took us both away.

I woke before dawn in a panic. *What did I do?! I let the enemy inside the gates and then fell asleep!* I sat up with a start, half expecting to see burning curtains and a benzene-soaked Dear John note. Or at least Allie gone, vanished into the night, off somewhere laughing at my pliancy and plotting her next duplicitous move.

But no, there she was. Still in bed, still asleep, her deep, regular breathing punctuated at odd intervals by tiny, adorable snerks. I reached out to stroke her breast through the sheet. She took my hand and rolled with it, pulling me down in behind her. With my nose against her neck, I inhaled the scent of her shampoo and fell asleep again.

Next thing I knew, it was full daylight and Allie was blowing coffee steam across my face. I opened my eyes to see her perched on the bed beside me, fully clothed, two hot Java Mans in her hands.

"Drink," she said. "We need to talk, and I bet you're witless before coffee."

I have to admit this was true, and would admit also to a frisson of disappointment at seeing her so up and about, so manifestly *dressed*. What, no second act? No morning after the night before? Was I really just a horny idea she had? Was it really just *that's that with that*?

I sat up and started to get out of bed but, weirdly, bashfulness balked me. Allie shot me a smirky look, like, *really?* and averted her eyes. I jammed to the can, relieved myself, brushed away morning mouth, then returned to the sanctuary of my blankets, huddling there with the modesty of a Hasid on honeymoon, swigging my coffee and waiting for the caffeine to kick in.

"Okay," Allie said at last. "Cards-on-the-table time." I held my breath. Half of me anticipated just additional Allie Quinn Brand Quality White Noise®. The other half dared to dream that her decision to sleep with me had somehow erased her insidity and rendered her real. The other *other* half of me just wanted to drag her back under the covers and screw the day away. I told that part to shut up. Such thoughts at this time could only be distracting at best, counterproductive at worst. Though I noticed Allie making no effort to deny me the view up her skirt. Was this a bit of Lorelei bait or the careless immodesty of a newly minted fuck buddy? It's a measure of exactly how twisted up I was that I couldn't even begin to guess. "You know how I told you we have to stop the Merlin Game?" she asked.

"Yes," I said, mime-wiping remembered hot coffee from my lap. "Seems we had some disagreement there."

"And do we still?"

"It's risk versus benefit," I said. "I look at this play, I see plenty of benefit, not much risk. Tell me where I'm wrong."

She sighed what I at that moment mentally dubbed the Allie Sigh, so rich with regret you could almost taste it. "Radar," she said, "I haven't been entirely honest with you." Now *there's* a news flash. Seriously, did she not think I knew? "And," she added, "I know you know it, too."

Oh.

She shifted on the bed, and the upskirt shot went away. I felt an immediate nostalgia for it but forced that from my head. "The truth is, my grandfather's not really the problem."

"He's not freaking out about the grift?"

"It doesn't matter whether he is or isn't," she said testily. It was the first time she'd acknowledged the slightest seam in her story, and it came off like a crack in her cool. "You speak of risk versus benefit. Okay, let me spell out the risk. I think we've been pinged." Her use of this word was another revelation, for *pinged* is grifter code for "discovered" or "found out," like a submarine will ping another sub with its sonar. In saying we'd been pinged, she confessed at last, and in a way she knew I could not fail to understand, to being in the game. This was not news, but her admission of it was. Maybe our roll in the hay had kicked her candor into a slightly higher orbit after all. In any event, I let the lingo pass unremarked. There would be time for going back over who knew what when. Right then I just wanted to know who she thought had made us and why that was a big deal.

Allie explained (and I use the word *explain* advisedly, since all or part of this alleged explanation may have been pure isinglass) that some suit-and-sedan types had visited Milval's office, asking pointed questions that pointed, well, right at me.

"You think they're closing in?" I asked.

"I think they've closed. I think they're just waiting for you to burn down the house before they make their move. Radar," she said, "so far, we haven't crossed the line. We've sent a lot of unsolicited investment advice to people who may or may not have forwarded it to authorities. But we haven't taken a penny yet. We can still walk away."

"Walk how, exactly?" I asked.

"Just part company." She patted my knee through the sheet. "Part friends, of course."

"Of course," I said, patting her knee in kind. Meanwhile, I mentally replayed her recent plays, fiddling with the pieces till they clicked. First had come the false negative, delivered the other day outside Java Man: *We have to quit for dotty Granddad's good.* That dog didn't hunt, but she knew it wouldn't. She was just softening me up for the next lie in her lineup—a lie she had to believe I'd believe, given that she'd given me "a woman's ultimate gift" and all. (Could she really go so far as to bed me, just to validate her words the next morning? Of course she could; that's how grifters roll.) Now she was playing the threat card, trying to scare me out of the picture with her "honest" admission that the feds or whoever were after me. Why? Simple. So that she and Hines could burn down the house without me and keep all the earn for themselves. It was, I had to admit, a pretty play: Ease me in, squeeze my expertise, spook me, then ease me out.

But would it work? After all, I'd been running tech on the project from the start. All the false webworks, the offshore accounts, the laundry line back to the States—all that stuff was on my computer and in my head. They couldn't trigger the burn without me, could they?

Well, could they?

"Allie," I asked, "who is your grandfather, really?" This was a fairly risky card to play, as it openly accused her of lying. After all, if Milval Hines wasn't her eccentric gramps, then who could he possibly be but an ally in the grift? Maybe someone ghosting my tech, ready to take over in case I bailed. I didn't really expect Allie to tell me the truth. I just wanted to see if she'd stick to her story or shift to a different line of defense.

She nodded, her lips tightly pursed, as if to cop to my unstated charge. "I told you: Cards on the table," she said. "He's the mark."

The mark? Now that *was* an imaginative inveracity. In order for Hines to be the mark, he'd have to be a completely guileless but exceedingly rich investment counselor that she'd found and mooked into playing a role. But to what end? To weevil into his bank account? Then why did she need me? Perhaps she'd promised that they'd burn down the house without me, but now she's changing teams.

"The mark, huh?" I said. "Okay. How do we flip him?"

"No, no, no, Radar, you're not paying attention. I told you: The heat is on. We've got to shade and fade."

"You'll forgive me," I said dryly, "if I don't share your sense of crisis."

"What do you mean?"

"Let's just say your credibility's not at an all-time high."

"Oh, you stupid ass, why do you think I slept with you?"

"To get me to believe you."

"So why don't you believe me?"

"Because I'm a stupid ass?"

This earned me another coffee bath, plus a rant of some substance. "Radar Hoverlander," she said, "if that's even vaguely your real name, which I doubt to several orders of magnitude, you're so far gone in the grift that you can't even see the truth anymore through your paranoid haze. You think I screwed you to *mook* you? God! I screwed you because I don't want to see you get hurt and I couldn't think of any other way to get over that moat you've dug around yourself.

"How long have you been alone, Radar? When was the last time

you ever actually let someone *in*? I'm talking about really in. In here."
She patted her chest, twice, with the flat of her hand. "Not just the . . ."
she groped for a phrase, and arrived at (the admirable, I thought),
"penumbra of persiflage you call the real you!" By now Allie was really
worked up. She stormed around my bedroom, hands and arms flying.
She looked like an actress going over the top on an audition piece, and
I wondered if that's what this was: her audition for the part of Radar's
girlfriend. Suddenly I wanted to believe her. Not only that, I wanted to
unwind her, backpredict her, find out who she was, how she got here,
and where she got that tremendous talent of hers. In the moment, I
dared to dream that we could actually get down to the place where
maybe we could trust each other, if not as lovers, then at least as partners in the grift. And if I was wrong? If she really was using me to serve
some other end, so what? The Merlin Game was just about money. But
Allie was one of a kind. Lies and all, she was a keeper; I wanted to
keep her.

Instead, I stepped on a land mine.

"Look," I said, "first of all, my name is my name. It says so right on
my driver's license." She snorted; I'd have snorted, too. "Second, where
do you get off slagging me for being a closed shop? You haven't been
a paragon of honesty yourself. Now, suddenly you're telling me the
truth?"

The trouble with too far . . .

"Why should I believe you?"

. . . is you never know you're going . . .

"Up till now, the only thing open about you—"

. . . till you've gone.

"—was your legs."

"Fuck you," she spat. "Just fucking, fucking fuck you." She snatched
up her shoes and ran out into the living room. I heard her fussing with
them out there. Then I heard the front door slam, then silence.

I lay in bed a long time, inhaling the oddly conflagrant mixture of coffee and sex that lingered in the sheets. Was she right? Was I really nothing but a penumbra of persiflage? More to the point, had I just driven off the sexiest, most intelligent, most exciting woman I'd ever met? Worse, had I driven off the only woman with whom, against all foreseeable odds, I could be open and honest and true?

The tap of regret opened, and the moat that Allie'd spoken of filled pretty damn quick.

Eventually I got up and got dressed. I went out into the living room, hoping that somehow Allie's earlier door-slam had been a bluff, that I'd find her sitting on my couch, arms crossed in silent fury, waiting for me to come to my senses.

Nope. No Allie. Allie was gone.

As was my laptop.

Replaced by a scrap of paper with a scrawled address.

Good times.

allie's allies

*B*am! Bam! Bam!

Thirty minutes later I'm pounding on the door of Allie's high-rise Hollywood apartment. I didn't bother trying to disguise my rage. Couldn't have if I'd wanted to, I was that irate. Allie had stolen from me. *Stolen!* She'd taken *private property* and just walked off! Who *does* such a thing? Not that it'd do her any good, apart from dissecting my browser history to see how my taste in online porn runs. It's not like I'm likely to leave passwords cached. At the end of the day, all she pinched was a giant paperweight.

I know what you're thinking: I've got a lot of nerve getting huffed over theft when theft, in a sense, is my line of work. To which I say: Yes, but no. Grifters have honor. We finesse our earn. We use guile and cunning, like wolves, and we take advantage of the weak (-minded) members of the herd, just like any wolf would. But we don't steal. That's just low. We're artists. It's con *art.* You take pride in your work. Even a Mirplo knows the difference between sticking someone up and romancing his cash. The latter takes expertise; the former, just a gun. And if Mirplo would know this, then Allie would know it in spades. That's what made me so mad. To stoop to a snatch and grab was so far beneath her. Where was her self-respect?

Uhm . . .

Right where it always is, Radar. Spang blam in the middle of her self-interest.

For a moment, the fog of my fury lifted and I saw things from Allie's point of view. She had to know that I wouldn't leave the keys to the burn just lying in a temp file on my laptop. Which meant it wasn't the computer she wanted.

Well, what *did* she want?

The scrawled address had said it all.

More Radar. More me.

She knew she couldn't burn down the house with my computer, but also that I couldn't burn down the house without it. Therefore, she hadn't stolen it, just taken it hostage. In a weird way, this made me feel better. The suppositive girl of my dreams was duplicitous, yes, but not dumb, and not low. She had me chasing my laptop across town like some ridiculous numpty chasing a gaffed dollar bill down the sidewalk while hidden kids tug it along on a string and just laugh. And she got what she wanted, Radar Hoverlander, utterly sans cool, bamming away on her door like a lunatic.

I stopped in mid-bam. Pulled out a pen. Wrote "I get it" on the back of the address scrap and slid it under the door. Then I waited. After a few moments, I heard a muffled rustling inside, and the rasp of a security chain being set. Allie opened the door as far as the chain would allow. I guess she assumed—rightly—that I wasn't the type to try shouldering my way in, and that in any case—again rightly—I didn't have near enough shoulder.

"Do you get it?" she asked. "Do you really?"

I sighed in conscious imitation of the patented Allie Sigh. "I get that this isn't about the Merlin Game," I said. "I get that you wanted me over here for a reason. And I get," I said, pointing past her to the rooms within, "that the reason's in there, not out here."

"Are you calm?" she asked. "Are you cool? Radar, there are people inside. I can't have you going all apeshit in here."

"I'm cool," I said. "Stable as a table." And in fact I found I was. I think it had something to do with surrender. Allie had proven herself capable of jugging me around like a piece on a chessboard. In a sense, the sooner the poor pawn admits it's a pawn, the happier it is. (But did she have to sleep with it? In retrospect, that was just cruel.) "It's your move," I said with a shrug. "Just like always."

Allie closed the door and undid the chain, then opened the door again just wide enough to slip out into the hallway with me. She put her hand on my arm. "You know," she said, "I could've gotten you here other ways. I didn't have to sleep with you. That was by choice."

"Yeah, I'm gonna take cold comfort in that right now."

"Oh, come on, Radar. Was it really that bad?" *No, it was really that good. That's the problem.* Still, no use crying over spilt whatever. Time to man up. I mentally straightened my shoulders and slipped into grift mode. At this I felt a certain pride rise. After all, Allie's allies had gone to some lengths to set this all up. That showed they valued my talent. Which gave me some leverage going in. And when you're flying blind through a situation, leverage is handy to have.

"Okay," I said, "let's see what's behind door number three." We went inside.

My first impression of the apartment was: *movie set.* Everything seemed studied and sterile. Worse, it all matched. The generic abstract art prints on the walls picked up color from the carpet. The plates, cups, and saucers in the china hutch bore mutually complementary floral designs—but no indication that they'd ever been, or ever would be, used for food or drink. More like a set of display dishes at Ikea. A ridiculously overchromed bookcase featured racks of classics with rich leather bindings that had likewise clearly never been cracked. Magazines fanned on a teak sideboard bore boring titles like *Coastal Living* and *Decor,* and like the books, they looked utterly unread. I wondered if they even had text inside; they could be just dummies. The dining table was artfully made up with a fake fruit display, place mats, and neatly rolled cloth napkins in stainless steel holders. Even the view out the window looked fake. Behind the figure sitting on the couch, a set of silk drapes framed a postcard-perfect view of the Capitol Records Building, and the HOLLYWOOD sign beyond.

Wait . . . the figure sitting on the couch?

I recognized him in an instant, but he seemed so out of place in this pristine realm that it took me a moment to shake off cognitive dissonance and accept the evidence of my eyes.

Finally I said, "Hello, Vic."

Mirplo squirmed. "This isn't what it looks like."

"No? That's good. 'Cause it looks like a sellout."

"It's not that simple," he protested.

"It never is."

"No," agreed a voice from over my shoulder. "It really never is." Out of the bedroom strode the player I'd expected to find here, Milval Hines.

He had changed. Where before he carried himself with the larking naughtiness of a truant schoolboy, he now oozed arrogance and sense of purpose. He seemed to have shed years from his age, but that may have been nothing more than a matter of standing up straight and switching out of retiree drag and into something more of a businessman mode. So radical was his character shift that I knew in an instant what he was—a Jake, a cherry top, practiced at undercover work—and I mentally kicked myself for not seeing it sooner.

Beside him stood a brusque young woman in a stolid polyester suit. She, too, had the look of law enforcement, from the top of her manic-repressive brunette bun, down the front of her department-store blouse and skirt, all the way to the tips of her sensible shoes. In other clothes and circumstances you'd have judged her as hot. Here, she just came off as academy-graduate gray, but I'm sure that was by design. She had my computer tucked under her arm. Jacked into one of the USB ports was a device I didn't immediately recognize.

"I believe this is yours," she said, handing me the laptop. There was something not exactly American in her English. Kiwi? South Africa? Likely Australia. Or maybe just voice paint. In this crowd, you never can tell.

"It is," I agreed. I tinked the unfamiliar peripheral with a fingernail. "But I can't place this bad boy."

"We'll get to that in a minute," said Hines. "Let's sit down. Get familiar." He gestured toward the dining table, and we all took seats. I glanced at the fake fruit. Did it come with fake fruit flies? I decided to treat the entire conversation as bugged.

"So," I said to Hines, just for shits and giggles, "which branch of law enforcement are you with?" This wasn't necessarily the best opening move, since it demonstrated that I had him pegged. But in the name of grabbing status, I wanted the opening move to be mine.

"No need to show off, Radar," said Hines. "We know you know what you know. Your bona fides are not at issue here."

"You mean I've been vetted." The closet hottie pulled a breath to reply, but I held up my hand. "Wait," I said, "let me answer for you." I put an antipodean gloss on my voice, as close a match to hers as I could manage at first pass, and said, " 'Of course you've been vetted, Mr. Hoverlander. What do you think this whole episode has been about?' " In a sense I was pinging her, trying to determine how she liked me aping her accent and also jumping her lines. To her credit, she maintained a face of utmost poker. I thought I might have to ping a little harder next time.

"Well," asked Hines, "what *do* you think it's been about?"

"I'll reserve judgment on that." I eyed Mirplo. "Since it's not that simple and all."

"I swear to God, Radar, I didn't tell them anything they didn't already know."

"Whatever," I whatevered. To Hines I said, "It's your meeting, Gramps. You've got the floor."

"Fine. Let's start with introductions." He gestured toward his colleague. "This is Detective Constable Claire Scovil. She's with the Australian High Tech Crime Centre."

"Really?" I cocked a brow. "You're a long way from home."

"It's not so far to Toluca Lake."

"She's on detachment," said Hines.

For the sum of two odd reasons, I decided that this had a better than even chance of being true. First, I happened to know that there was a furnished-apartment complex in Toluca Lake, popular with visitors "on detachment." Second, she said Toluca Lake like it was a toy she liked to play with. Like the way people can't get enough of saying Cahuenga Boulevard once they get that it's ka-WAYNE-guh, not ka-HUN-guh.

"Detached to whom?" I asked. Seemed like the logical next question.

But what happened next was not logical—and just a little bit scary. Hines and Allie exchanged looks. Not long, just a glance. But enough to let me know that they both knew the answer to my logical next question. Which meant—God, dare I believe it?—that Allie could be a cherry top, too. Trust me, there's nothing a grifter likes less than learning that one of his kind has been flipped. Or not even flipped? Perhaps she'd been law all along. Was there a police department training program somewhere good enough to spit out faux grifters of Allie's skillful ilk? The thought sent a shudder through me. If they had that level of countermeasure, I might as well hang up my fake passport and bogus notary stamp, because the grift as I knew it was done.

But that was a contemplation for later. Just then, I was still in the moment, still trying to wrest control. "Look," I said, spreading my hands. "I get that the Merlin Game has been rained out. And I get that you think you have me by the short hairs. Who knows? Maybe you do. I haven't seen all the cards in your deck. But the dramatics. This"—I gestured around the room—"bourgeois safe-house thing you've got going here. It really doesn't work for me. Can we just skip to the Cliffs Notes version of what's what?"

"Short attention span, Radar?" mocked Hines. "That doesn't seem like you."

I just glared at him. "Let's start with your real name."

"Let's start with yours."

"Radar Hoverlander," I said evenly.

"Milval Hines," he replied, even more evenly.

Okay, well, that didn't go anywhere.

I shut my yap. I'd done too much talking anyhow. Mostly when people prattle on, it's a sign of nervousness. I'd been far too chatty for my own good. Plus, I reminded myself, this was Hines's show. He'd tell me at his leisure what he wanted me to know. I could decide at mine what to believe.

Silence took its toll. Mirplo was the first to get fidgety. He plucked a fake apple from the bowl and rolled it back and forth on the tabletop between his hands. Claire Scovil looked at her nails with studied disinterest. Allie and Hines again exchanged looks. I couldn't tell from the exchange which of them had the power to change the talk/don't talk signal from red to green, but it's not uncommon in the grift for a team's real authority to rest with someone who looks like a lackey. I'd played that role many times myself: the numbnuts in the background who's really pulling the strings. I knew from adversarial experience that undercover law often worked the same way. Therefore, this could very possibly be her show, not his.

Hines spoke. "I'm with a federal fraud task force." Was there a hitch in his *I'm*, like it wanted to come out *we're*, but caught itself in time? Or was I once again oversolving the problem? Hard to tell.

"But that's not your day job," I said.

"Normally I'm FBI."

"Fibbie," I said. "Okay, well, everyone's got to earn a living." I looked at Allie and Mirplo. "Any other fibbers here?" They didn't respond, and once again I chided myself for talking too much. Like the sign says, "It's better to keep your mouth closed and let people think you're a fool than to open it and remove all doubt."

Mouth shut, ears peeled, I finally got this gist: that Detective Scovil had followed the trail of some Aussie cyberperp to L.A., where said trail had then gone cold. In concert with the fibbies, and operating under the old takes-a-thief-to-catch-a-thief paradigm, she hoped to have me warm it up again.

"In exchange," said Hines, "we're prepared to forgive your . . . transgressions up till now."

"Which transgressions are those? The ones you entrapped me into?"

With a thin smile, Hines got up from the table and went into the bedroom for a moment. When he returned, he had a manila folder. This he slapped like a summons on the table before me. I opened it and skimmed its contents.

Wow.

Holy shit.

There, in pleonastic detail, was a greatest hits version of every significant scam I'd run in the past five years. Anything that had had the slightest internet vector—and what didn't these days?—had apparently been cracked like a coconut and stored in some devious database somewhere. Plus bank records, onshore and offshore transactions, and bogus documentation of every stripe. A whole damn damning (and highly indictable) paper trail wending back through Radar's sordid adventures on what some call the wrong side of the law.

Want to know how I felt? Violated, that's how.

But I didn't let that show. Instead I just whistled a respectful low whistle. "I have to admit," I said, "I didn't think you fibbies had it in you."

"It's easy when you have one of those," said Hines, indicating the device still jacked into my computer. "You'd be surprised what this baby can do." I would be surprised. It looked not much different from a normal data stick.

"Why all the hanky-panky?" I asked. "Why didn't you just call me into your field office or whatever, and make your pitch?"

"As you said, you had to be vetted. People in your line of work talk a good game. They can't always back up their claims."

I turned to Allie. "And you trying to pull the plug?"

"For my benefit," said Claire. "To see how much bottle you had."

"Enough?" I asked.

She nodded. "You seem to have the requisite stick-to-itiveness."

"Do you talk like that at home? Do you compliment your boyfriend on his stick-to-itiveness?" I was pinging her again, on a more personal level. I didn't get much of a hit, just a hint of rising color at her collarbone, but it was enough to know two things—no boyfriend, and she felt the lack.

As for the rest of it, truth to tell, I had no idea. They could be who they said they were, or this could be just the next level of noise. Frankly, I was getting tired of shoveling such smoke. I needed some tangible facts.

Time to ping the whole joint.

I closed the file and placed both hands on the cover. "Look," I said, "this is crackerjack work, really. When I think of all the hours of research, the wiretaps, the passwords axed, well, it just puts me in awe of my mighty tax dollars at work. Either that or it's not tax dollars. For all I know, you're all on the razzle and just head and shoulders better at it than me." I looked at Vic. "Except you, Mirplo. I'm guessing that you've been played like I've been played." To Allie and Hines I said, "As for you two, you've fed me nothing but horseshit since the moment we met. Can you forgive me for not wanting to swallow some more?" Next I addressed the notional Aussie. "You I don't know," I said. "But I'm gonna go with 'guilty by association.' You look nice, though. Bet you look great in a wet T-shirt." I don't know why I said that. It was unnecessarily provocative. But something about the woman just rankled me, and I couldn't resist rankling back. I was rewarded with a look sour enough to curdle milk.

I stood up. Grabbed my computer. Popped out their peripheral and dropped it in the bowl of wax fruit. "Now then: If you've got uniformed Jakes downstairs waiting to arrest me, so be it. I've been busted before. It's not the end of the world. But I have a feeling there are no waiting Jakes, just like I've got a feeling there's no Australian High Tech Crime Centre, or federal fraud task force, and the closest you, Hines, have been to the FBI is a true-crime show you saw on the Discovery channel once. This is all just bogus bogosity, and I am out of here."

I can play ball with cops. I can. But you have to know it's cops you're dealing with, and there was just no way I could trust any answer I got from this crew. It was like Mirplo swearing by the authenticity of his Photoshop fakes. How are you going to believe the guy with the manifest reason to lie? So I forced their hand. I had to. If they did have Jakes downstairs, it would at least verify their bona fides, and then we could do business. If they were just a bunch of big lying liars, I figured they'd be so stunned by my declarative exit that I could get in the wind before they had a chance to react. I knew I'd be putting some things behind me, notably one lame friendship and one abortive love affair (and the Merlin Game, but that's just money). Plus also I'd have to vacate L.A., which was a shame, but unavoidable. Part of successfully cutting your losses is knowing when to cut and run. Which you do without ego and without stopping to measure anyone's dicks. Considering how well they'd played me so far, I had to tip my hat to their superior skill—a hat I intended to tip from the safe distant bunker of anonymity.

Okay, I was wrong about one thing.

The cops weren't waiting downstairs.

They were right outside the door.

the grifter of oz

The Jakes hustled me back inside. They did it right, too: professionally, and with respect. No attitude or guns, just, "We're going to need you to step back into the room, sir." This is how you like your cops to behave. Just because you're doing your job and they're doing theirs, there's no reason for everyone to get all hostile with each other. For the many times I've been busted, I've always admired the Jakes who had the common courtesy to treat me like a human being. All the same, though, I could see the steel in these two. I could tell I was only one gratuitous "Bite me" away from being facedown on the carpet with a knee in my back.

More to the point, I could tell they were the real deal. Not fabricats, not even rent-a-cops. You can argue chicken and egg about cop attitude—does their hard-ass nature inform their career choice, or do they osmose it on the job?—but either way, true cop mojo is impossible to fake. Grifters can't do it, except in circumstances like the afterparty snuke, where you don't have to be particularly convincing, just snarky and loud, less true cop than cop cartoon. I'm saying: See a man in officer kit, you can tell whether it's a uniform or a costume. While I couldn't completely discount the possibility of above-the-rim role playing, I felt I could trust that these Jakes *were* Jakes. On the present shifting sands of bafflegab, that wasn't much, but at least it was something.

In any case, a moment later, I found myself right back in the chair I'd vacated a moment before. While Hines walked the cops to the door, I picked up a wax apple and feinted it at Mirplo's head. He flinched.

Hines came back and sat down. He leafed through my file, then set it aside. "So far," he said in measured tones, "nothing has happened that can't unhappen. But I need to know you're on board."

I sighed—a real sigh this time. "Appreciate my position," I said. "If you're who you say you are, then of course I'm happy to help the cause of international law and order, homeland security, save the whales, what have you. Not to mention my personal passionate cause of staying before bars. But if you're not who you say you are, then I'm just a chump who's getting rechumped. How'm I supposed to know which?"

"The officers didn't convince you?"

"They convinced me a little," I granted. "But you need to convince me a lot."

Hines and Scovil took their time and did it right: a thorough and plausible job of introducing me to the Grifter of Oz and the threat he posed. If they were to be believed, he was quite an extraordinary dude.

If they were to be believed.

William Yuan was born in Sydney of Chinese parents at roughly the same time I was born wherever of whomever. Like me, Yuan was a young achiever who got admitted to, and kicked out of, college at a precociously early age. Also like me, he found it pleasing to work on the fringes of legitimacy. He made much of the internet heyday by launching websites that had great commercial promise—though no particular basis in fact—and then gulling private-equity guys into hefty buys. Really, who wouldn't take a flier on www.unearthme.com, once they learned of Billy Yuan's revolutionary new technique for scanning satellite photos of Earth to locate previously hidden mineral deposits? Gold! Silver! Rhodium! Too good to be true?

Of course!

Any knowledgeable grifter would have instantly recognized the scam as an updated version of dowsing or water witching. But the PE guys weren't that knowledgeable, and Yuan made a killing. Only, he tried to sell his vaporware to the government, and that bought him eighteen months in Mount Gambier, Australia's first privately run prison. By the time he finished his bid, he was consulting to prison management on how to make much more money by selling prisons they had no intent to build. Really, the kid had a cat's knack for landing on his feet.

And what was he up to now? Why did he beat cheeks out of Australia, and why was Australia going to such lengths to hunt him down? Here the story starts to get a little murky. In gist, Yuan had been caught sniffing around the software of the Reserve Bank of Australia. Or not caught, exactly: detected; surprised in the act of the hack. But apparently in pinging him, the authorities had pinged themselves as well. Yuan shut down his operation and hopped the first Qantas out of town.

"Our concern," said Scovil, "is that Yuan has found a way to compromise the bank's security and will, at a later time, attempt penetration."

"I love it when you say *penetration*," I said, again yielding to the urge to provoke her. Some people you just don't like. Her eyes clouded over in anger, but she swiftly regained her dark poise. It was clear that she wouldn't let herself be baited by the likes of little me. Which, of course, just made the likes of little me want to bait her all the more.

And don't think I wasn't mentally looking over my shoulder at Allie during all this. I had no idea what I was to her just then, although the word *tool*, in all its manifestations, sprang to mind. In any case, I wanted her to know that as far as I was concerned, she wasn't the only woman in the room, and I hoped that pissed her off. I also wanted very much to know what her role was here, but that wasn't the sort of question I could just come right out and ask. I'd have to nibble away at its edges, just like Billy Yuan had, seemingly, nibbled away at the bank.

"How did he get so good?" I asked.

"What do you mean?" asked Hines.

"You're telling me he's a top-flight grifter *and* a world-class hacker? That's a rare combination."

"He's a man of many talents, Radar. Just like you."

"Not like me. I can guess a password in a pinch, but I couldn't hack bank security. Hell, I can't hack a piggy bank without a hammer. So I ask again: How did he get so good?"

Scovil looked unhappy. "We trained him," she said at last.

I laughed. "You what?"

"After he got out of prison, we, ah, persuaded him that there was more benefit in working with us than against us."

"So you taught him everything he needed to know to go after your own national bank. That is rich." No one else seemed to find it particularly rich. Mirplo had gone all mopey, perhaps feeling overlooked, his ego underfed. Hines seemed worried that I wasn't buying all of this. Allie was where Allie was. And Scovil had just made an embarrassing admission. So, yeah, everyone in the room was unhappy but me. In the spirit of Schadenfreude, I decided to turn the screw. "So what's his real name?" I asked.

"What do you mean 'real name'?" asked Scovil. "It's William Yuan." I snickered. "What's so funny?" she demanded.

"The yuan is the currency of China, yeah?"

"So? It's also a very common name."

"Yes, it is. And how does it translate into English?"

"I don't know. 'Dollar,' I suppose."

"There you go," I said. "Billy Yuan. Dollar Bill. A grifter's inside joke to himself if ever there was one. He might as well have called himself Billy the Kid."

Hines looked altogether too pleased with this. "You see?" he told the others. "This is why we need Radar. He thinks just like Yuan, or whatever his name is. They're going to get along great."

"Yeah, we will," I said. "Once I find him. Anyone know how I should go about that?"

"Oh, we know where he is," said Hines. "That is, Allie does."

"Well, if she knows," I couldn't help asking, "why doesn't just she go after him? I'm sure they'll get along famously, too."

"Not so much," said Allie, and I thought I heard a piece of her past in her voice. What was there? Wistfulness? Regret?

"Oh, my God," I said. "You dated him." I didn't know if this was true or not, but looking at Allie, I could see that she didn't much like being the object of my inspection. *Okay,* I thought, *that's a card I can probably play again. But save it. Don't overuse it.*

They told me where I could find Yuan and gave me a generous forty-eight hours to make contact. With that, the meeting started to wind down. I could tell that from Hines's and Scovil's point of view, it was all mission accomplished. Allie looked less smug—in fact, it seemed to me that her smug was at its lowest ebb since the moment we'd met. Clearly the notion of me hooking up with Billy Yuan was stirring some ambivalence in her. And that only left . . .

"Mirplo," I said. "How do you figure in?"

"Mr. Mirplo," said Hines, "has worked for our organization on a . . . contract basis for some time."

"In other words, he's a snitch."

"Eyes and ears, Radar," protested Vic. "Come on."

"Why is he here now?" I asked. "Haven't you sort of blown his cover?"

"We don't need him undercover anymore. As of today, he's your partner."

"My what, now?"

"Radar," said Hines, "I know how much you love puzzles, and I have every confidence that you'll help us unravel this one. However, having confidence in a confidence man is a bit like . . . well, the metaphor escapes me. The point is, we need to make sure you don't wander off the path. With Vic at your side," he said with a smile, "you'll never walk alone."

"Great," I muttered. "The world's greatest fuckwit is my chaperone."

So the meeting broke up. Vic was now my appendage, like a prehensile tail I could neither hang from a tree with nor wag at pretty girls. I had been co-opted into law enforcement. It wasn't the first time, but still it was a suit that didn't hang well on my frame. Some people don't look good in plaid; I don't look good in narc.

A question nagged at me like a sore tooth, and that was one of motivation. If these good citizens were just out to bust Dollar Bill, then fine. Let them have their bust, and I'll be on my way. But why all the levels of subterfuge? Why not just use the same tools on him that they'd used on me: surveillance and bugs, tracks, hacks, and password cracks? Certainly that would produce enough hard evidence to present in a court of law. But perhaps a court of law was not to be the final disposition of this case. After all, they'd manipulated me to serve certain ends. Who's to say they wouldn't manipulate him the same way, once I'd helped them catch and compromise him? Even with all the what and where of things being handed out like Easter treats, I still didn't have a firm handle on the why. And without the why, I was just as lost as I'd been going in. I was, I suddenly realized, still playing the same game, just at a different level. And in order to figure out what was really going on, I'd have to keep playing, keep riding the levels, adapting to circumstances as circumstances demanded or allowed. I'm here to tell you that this is no way to run a respectable snuke. A grifter likes to be holding all the cards—or at least marking the ones he's not holding. Here my hand was limited to, well, my skill set and my healthy skepticism. I really didn't have anything else going for me: no insight, no hidden tricks, no trustworthy chums, no exit strategy.

I was, in short, in shit.

Still, not inextricably. After all, once I agreed to work the gaff, they had to give me some kind of room to move. They couldn't crowd me too close, or what I was working on wouldn't work. And with only the vaunted (which is to say nonexistent) guardian skills of a Mirplo standing between me and freedom, there was no reason to believe I couldn't shade and fade whenever I wanted. No doubt they knew this, and it distressed me that they didn't work visibly hard to prevent it. Were there invisible strings attached? Perhaps all my aliases were compromised, even the virgin ones. This meant that someone would have worked over my apartment, my storage unit, and my safe deposit boxes, and certainly that was within the realm of possibility. Still, it didn't seem like enough to glue me to the grift. If I really wanted to get gone, I could get gone. So why did they think I'd stay?

It's what Hines said: "I know how much you like puzzles."

In this, alas, he was right. Unknown people for unknown reasons had decided to fuck up my life. I was determined not to quit until I had not only unupfucked it, but gotten to the bottom of why. What can I tell you? Sometimes your pride will take you places your common sense wouldn't go.

Like, for example, to the Blue Magoon.

the blue magoon

I met a Swede once on a flight from London to Los Angeles, a two-pack-a-day man, jonesing hard for a cigarette almost before we went wheels up. At one point, he asked me, "When we land in Los Angeles, where is the soonest I can smoke? Do they have special areas, or will I have to wait till I get outside?"

"Oh, you can't smoke in California," I said.

"In the terminal in general, yes, I understand."

"No, no, anywhere; from border to border, it's been banned. They passed a law." You should have seen the color drain from his face. "I'm just messing with you, man. You can smoke outside."

But as the saying goes, "Your jokes will become your reality." Over the years, California's smoke-free airspace expanded to encompass beaches, parks, playgrounds, stadiums, even sidewalks in certain cities. It reached the point that about the only place you *could* smoke was in the privacy of your own home. Or at the Blue Magoon.

The Blue Magoon was a dive bar on Santa Monica Boulevard in the borderland between Hollywood and West Hollywood, with an oliated clientele of gay, straight, biker, junkie, and pure Monday morning drunk. The place reeked perpetually of vomit and stale beer. Also of cigarette smoke, for the Blue Magoon, its own little outlaw corner of the world, was one spot in L.A. where you could still spark up with impunity. The owner of the Magoon had been fined 267 times for violating state smoking bans. He'd been threatened with loss of license, even sued. He didn't give a rat's ass. With the ferocity of a mama lion defending her cubs, he fought every fine, every suit, every attempt to shut him down. The funny thing is, the guy didn't even smoke. He just had this libertarian streak in him—his daddy had run the bar before him and had died from secondhand smoke, and by damn, he was gonna do the same.

With its off-the-reservation reputation, the Magoon attracted just a raft of slackers, spivs, angle shooters, hucksters, mooks, art fraudists, pill pushers, franchise capitalists, and sundry other denizens of the demimonde. People would meet there to arrange alliances, pimp their sisters, sell contraband, buy counterfeits and chemicals, trade illegal aliens, and make record deals. I myself had only been there once. Walked in, turned up my nose and walked back out. Decided if that's what it took to hook up with L.A. hustlers, I'd just as soon fly solo. I'm not a snob, but honestly, to call the place a shithole makes shitholes shine.

Mirplo, of course, loved it, and when Allie told us that Billy Yuan had become a habitué, Vic nearly wet his pants. I think he thought it was some kind of Disneyland for people like us: "The crookedest place on Earth." Still, it was an iffy proposition. Here was a known grifter in a known grifters' lair. Anyone walking in the door was assumed to be on the razzle, and who extends the hand of trust to someone on the razzle? No intelligent grifter, that's for sure, and you had to believe that Yuan was *molto intelligente*, else he wouldn't have made it this far nor strewn such heat in his wake. So how do I penetrate the Magoon without looking like a guy in the game? Like I said, iffy proposition. Oddly, it was Hines who pointed me toward the angle to shoot, for it occurred to me that just as he had sold himself to me as a citizen, I might could vend myself to Yuan the same way. Of course, for a citizen to wander unsuspectingly into a place like the Magoon would be a bad mistake.

But hey, people make mistakes every day.

For what I had in mind, it wouldn't do for me to be there waiting, so I sent Vic in to loiter and let me know when Yuan showed up. He whined a little about his assignment. "What I'm gonna do all day just sitting there?"

"Do a crossword," I said. "It's good for you. It'll stretch your brain." I gave him a copy of *People* magazine (home of the world's most cretinous crossword), opened to the puzzle page. "Here," I said, "I'll get you started. One across: five-letter word for Academy Award."

He thought long and hard before barfing out, "Statue?"

"How many letters in statue?"

He counted them on his fingers and concluded, "Oh."

"Yeah, oh. Try again."

"Ah . . . award?"

"Oscar, you nimrod. Look, just go in there, stay cool, lay low, and text me when Yuan rolls in."

"What if he doesn't?"

"Then we'll come back tomorrow."

"That could get old real fast."

"You should've thought about that before you sold me out to the fibbies."

Oddly, this got Mirplo's back up. "Man, Radar," he said, "you're just gonna hafta get over that, you know? I didn't sell you out, I hooked you up, at least that's how it looked to me at the time. And if you want to kick my ass, I wish you'd just kick it and get the kicking over with, but this passive-aggressive resentment bullshit is pissing me off, so just take it, and your crappy crossword puzzle"—he slapped the magazine against my chest—"and shove 'em up your ass. Okay?" He spun on his heel and, with the hauteur of a dowager aunt, sailed off toward the Magoon.

"You sure you don't want the magazine?" I called after him.

Vic bellowed back in the third person as Uncle Joe. "He'll watch Judge Judy!"

I sure as hell wasn't going to watch Judge Judy. I killed my idle hours at a nearby bookstore, one of those giant ones with seventeen different histories of the Peloponnesian Wars and whole shelves devoted to the art of cooking with cheese. The bookstore is the library of the modern age, which you can tell just by looking around at the earnest students sitting cross-legged on the floor of the test prep section or the stinky homeless leafing through magazines and trying desperately not to fall asleep and, therefore, down.

I looked around for something to read up on, but I really couldn't concentrate. I kept thinking about how Allie and my alter ego Ryan Reed had supposedly met in a bookstore. I imagined it was one of those cute meets, where you stalk each other flirtily through the stacks, eventually simultaneously confronting each other with, "Why are you following me?" and "I wasn't following you, you were following me," prelude to an exchange of random banter, then coffee, a leisurely stroll, and a good-night kiss.

I'm not that old. Actuarially speaking, I've got like three quarters of a century to go. But as I wandered around that bookstore, waxing nostalgic for a love affair that never existed except as a fleeting figment of Allie's and my coagent imagination, I felt prohibitively removed from the snowiness you need to just plunge yourself into another person's life. Had I ever been that unguarded, that free? I didn't think so, and in that moment I felt the loss, like if you had a major league fastball but never yanked yourself away from your studies long enough to try out for a team. That was me: so caught in the grift net that I let the best of my youth pass by. You could argue that I wasn't all that innocent to

begin with, but I would argue back that even if you've never had innocence, you can lose it just the same. Let's call it the potential for innocence—in my case squandered on commerce. What was I doing when
I should have been picking up girls in bookstores? Selling artificial
gold. Lots of it, yay me. I typically had all the money I needed to take a
nice lady out to lunch but, alas, no lady, no lunch.

I buried myself in a copy of *Guns and Ammo* magazine, read up on
Finland's new Sako rifles, and tried to forget all about it, the Allie and
the innocence and all.

Some indeterminate time later, my cell phone alerted me to an
incoming text message:

    the pigeon poop is on the windshield

What passed for Mirplovian wit informing me that Yuan had
arrived. It was time for me to get into character. I quick-scanned the
shelves for the right props and found what I was looking for in *A Guide
to American Graduate Schools* and a laminated map of Los Angeles. I
paid for these things, broke the spine of the book and riffled its pages
to give it a thumbed feel, and headed out.

I was making much of this up as I went along, for I have found that
my own gift for the grift is largely improvisational. When I grab a good
idea and run with it, things usually work out, but when I try to over-
solve the problem . . . well, we've already seen how well *that's* gone.
Anyway, in Yuan's case, I really didn't want to know too much, for
when you "meet" a well-researched mark, there's always the chance
that some of your research will accidentally dribble out.

Twenty minutes later, I stood in the doorway of the Blue Magoon
letting my eyes adjust to the gloom and my lungs to oxygen debt. The
bartender squinted at me and gave the barest grunt of greeting. Mirplo
had cleared out. Of the half-dozen people drinking their day away, the
only Asian in the bar was not hard to spot. He occupied the last booth

before the bathrooms, where he sat hunched over a newspaper. His lank black hair fell down over his eyes and he pushed it away at intervals, only to have it fall back down and occlude his vision once again.

I walked to the bar, spread out my laminated map, and asked the bartender, "If I were UCLA, where would I be?"

"Nowhere near here," he said.

"That's what I was afraid of," I said. "Did I make a wrong turn off Cahuenga?" I pronounced it ka-HUN-guh.

"Man, that's the least of your wrong turns," said the bartender. He took my map and traced a route with his finger. "Go down to Holloway, shoot up to Sunset, and take that out to Westwood. UCLA's on your left."

"Thanks," I said. "Mind if I use your can?"

"Knock yourself out." I walked toward the bathroom. As I drew abreast of Yuan's booth, my cell phone rang. I broke stride to answer it.

"Hello," I said.

"It's me calling you," said Mirplo. "How's my timing?"

"Hi, Dad," I said with an edge of irritation in my voice.

"Blee blee blah blah bloo bloo," said Mirplo, carrying on his part of the conversation as he saw fit.

Now I really sounded irked. "Dad, I told you, nothing's been decided yet. I'm just having a look around."

"Ape ledger legions toothy flak offer hew knighted snakes over marigolds."

"Yeah, well it's my money, isn't it?"

"Money schmoney, honey bunny."

"Dad," I said severely, "I'm not having this conversation. That's why it's called a trust, remember? Because people trust you with it."

"There once was a girl from Cadiz, whose hooters hung down to her knees. She spread her vagina from here to Regina . . ."

"Nothing's been decided! I'll call you later."

". . . and buttered her butt crack with cheese."

I closed the phone with an angry snap.

"Trouble?" asked Yuan, not looking up from the paper. I heard the flattened vowels of his Australian accent.

"Family," I said with a shrug, and went into the can.

When I came back out, Yuan had changed position. He now leaned casually against the wall of the booth, his pipe-stem legs stretched out across the red vinyl bench. "So," he asked as I passed, "what do you want to study?"

"I'm sorry?" I said.

"Correct me if I'm wrong, but it seems you're scouting schools."

"I am." I let my voice betray my surprise. "How did you know?"

He cocked a slender finger at my book. "Between that and . . . 'Dad, it's my money,' I'd say . . . gonna take a lark here . . ." He furrowed his brow in ponder. "Something impractical. Art?"

"Worse. Philosophy."

"And father doesn't like it?"

"He's an idiot. He thinks I should study business."

"Because you have all this money to manage."

"Wow, you don't miss much, do you."

"I have a practiced ear." He leaned forward and extended a hand. "Rick Chen."

I shook his hand. "Chad Thurston," I said, then added self-consciously, "the third."

"So, family money. Have a seat."

I slid into the booth opposite, dropping my book and my map on the table between us. Yuan noted the map and asked, "Where are you from?"

"Kensington, Maryland."

"Nice place?"

"Not bad if you own it. You're from England, right?" This was a gentle ping, to see if Yuan carried the Aussie pride gene and its concordant annoyance at American provincialism.

He merely smiled indulgently and said, "Australia."

"Sorry," I said. "The accent . . ."

"Common duff. No worries."

We fell into an affable conversation ranging across topics from how my family made its money (textiles and banking) to why "Rick Chen" was in L.A. (internship), and thus traded lies for a while. And though mine was a willing surrender to the snuke, nevertheless I could feel the textured smoothness with which Yuan eased me in. Watching us over my own shoulder, as it were, I thought, *Damn, this guy is good.*

At last I said, "I better get going. I have a meeting with the department head."

"In philosophy."

"Yeah."

"What is it?" he asked.

"What is what?"

"Your philosophy. In a nutshell."

"I'm sorry?"

"You must have some sort of belief orientation, mate. I mean, you don't just go into the study of philosophy flying blind, right?"

"Well, kind of the point is to learn."

"Still, you must have some platform."

"It's really unformed."

He smiled expansively. "In a nutshell."

"Okay," I said. "Let me see . . ." I rifled through the files of my brain, looking for "my philosophy in a nutshell." "How about this?" I said at last. "The universe loves us. All we have to do is love it back."

Yuan nodded. "That's beautiful, mate. Mind if I podge it?"

"I . . . don't know what that means."

"Never mind. Give us your handy."

"Handy?"

"The phone, mate."

I slid my phone across the table. It wasn't *my* phone, of course, but one I'd dummied up for Chad Thurston. He flipped it open and punched in some digits. In a second, his own phone rang. "There," he said, "now you have my number. Call before you leave town," he said. "I'll shout you a beer."

"Wow, that's really nice of you."

"Not that nice," he said. "I kind of daylight as an investment manager. I'd like to pitch your business."

"Sounds good," I said. I picked up my stuff and headed for the door. I couldn't help smiling. But as I caught a glimpse of Yuan in the back-bar mirror, I noticed that he was smiling, too.

open kimonos

I went for a run. I only ever run occasionally, when I need to clear the cobwebs from my brain. The health aspect doesn't interest me at all because, really, what's the point? You exercise, eat right, take care of your body, you might live an extra ten years, right? But which ten years are we talking about? Ninety to one hundred? If I could have my twenties over again, then maybe, but an extra decade of decrepitude? *Nej tak.* I swear to God, before senility sweeps over me, I'm going to put together a lethal dose of sleeping pills and keep them by my bed with a note that reads, "When you forget what these are for, take them."

It pays to plan ahead.

I guess you could say that I was running for the sake of forward planning. In all my years on the razzle, I'd never been so deeply enmeshed in a play over which I had so little control. And while I was pleased with the outcome of my meeting with Yuan, at the same time, I couldn't help thinking that maybe the meeting went a little too well. I mean, I'm good at the grift and all, but did I really sell my philosopher-prince persona that convincingly? If Yuan was good at the grift, too, and it struck me that he was, then why did he bite so hard? Maybe grifters in Australia just aren't that cunning.

Maybe.

But the more I ran, the more convinced I became that Yuan was acting his role as thoroughly as I was acting mine. We were two sharp cookies grinding against each other and making a bunch of crumbs. So then, what should I tell Hines and the others? That he's not onto me but he is? Or would that be just another case of dueling fictions, with everyone lying and everyone else trying to unpry the lie? Tired of that shit. And the more I ran, the more tired of it I got.

I ran the back trail of Elysian Park, the one overlooking the Golden State Freeway, then crossed over and plunged into the acreage south of Stadium Way. Running a tangent past the grounds of the Los Angeles Police Academy, I could hear the echoing rattle of gunfire from the shooting range. That got me thinking about guns. So far, I mused, everyone's coercive intent had been backed by nothing more than words and threats, plus the usual grifter's manipulation of desire, fact, and fear. Could things escalate to gun violence? Of course they could. The thought did nothing to calm my jangled nerves. It's not that I'm afraid of guns, but I don't trust them. They lull you into a false sense of security. You think that just because you're on the right end of one you've got everything under control. In my experience, by the time the guns come out, control is a thing of the past.

The trail became steep and overgrown, and running it was less a matter of keeping stride than of bushwhacking and leaping over bracken like a kangaroo. I started to feel good, like you will when the endorphin kicks in. Just for the hell of it, I left the trail and went straight up the side of a tough hill, lunging upward from toehold to toehold, leaving little spurts of dislodged dirt in my wake. I charged all the way uphill until I burst out of the brush at the top, where I stopped to catch my breath. All of Los Angeles spread out before me, rather like a trinket I owned. I could feel my pulse pounding in a ring around my skull, from my forehead through my temples and around to the back of my neck. *I am crowned,* I thought, and it occurred to me to wonder whether every crown reference in our history and literature was just a metaphor for the buzz of hard exercise. *Jesus runs the 440.*

I heard a rustle from some bushes nearby and turned toward the sound, half expecting to see a deer or coyote or some other exotic L.A. fauna. Instead, two men emerged, one young and cut and the other, well, markedly less so. *Ah,* I realized, *they use this part of the park for that.* Talk about your multipurpose recreational resource. Just then I heard another sound, the metallic clang of chains. Not far away, a disc golfer pulled his disc from a pole-mounted basket while his buddy lined up a putt. The second shooter eyed his line, rocked gently at the knees to find his rhythm, then sent his disc on a wobbly but straight flight to the pin. It hit the hanging ropes of chain and fell into the basket. The shooter allowed himself a breathy "Yes!" and a fist-pump, then picked up his bag of golf discs and his beer and headed for the next tee.

I was overcome. It was such a prosaic moment—the intersection of gay cruisers and disc golfers—but for some reason it filled me with ineffable sadness. Perhaps it was the fact that the moment was so prosaic, so normal . . . just everyday people pursuing their everyday hobbies, habits, or sins. You think you're just in a park, but really you're standing in a place overhung with invisible nets: nets of use, nets of purpose. Open your eyes, you see them all laid bare before you. The gay cruisers and disc golfers, the couple arguing in the parked car on the access road, the sad schizophrenic mumbler sitting on a stump beneath a blue vinyl tarp, two girls in spandex walking their dogs. They're all living so unself-consciously in the now. As a grifter, you can't afford the luxury of now. You have to be thinking ahead, weighing outcomes, measuring risk. It's a high-wire life, not long on second chances. I'd always felt at home in the life and always felt free, no more aware of my constraints than a fish is aware of the ocean. Suddenly I was like, *Where did this ocean come from? Was it here all along?*

So what did I want? Off the razzle? A suburban home life? Soccer camp for the kids and martinis for dinner for Dad? Wise investments? Hawaiian vacations? Or did I just want relief from the pressure I was always (putting myself) under? A chance to relax, like a normal person. Shoot a round of disc golf. Argue in a car. Walk a dog.

Or was I doing that now? After all, if I were me looking at me, what would I see? A guy in his prime, more or less, out running the day away in track shoes and bandanna. I'd seem normal enough, wouldn't I? But if I were me looking at me, I'd know I was seething inside. I would see me questing ahead in my mind to the next move, the next snuke, the next piece of the puzzle that never seems to solve because after every piece there's another piece, and another piece and a half after that. And who's putting the pieces in play? Me. Just me. Hooked-on-calculation me.

All this hard thinking. It makes a man want to rest. Or at least find someone to unbundle to. But who can a confidence man confide in? No one I knew would treat my confession as anything but more smoke, more mirror, and how could I prove them wrong?

I didn't run back to my apartment. I walked the whole way, lost in revelation. I suddenly saw a different arc for my life, one where I didn't always have to live in such a heightened state of intensity. I could learn to relax. I could take yoga. Hell, I could *teach* yoga. It wouldn't be bad to have peace.

By the time I got home, I of course recognized this for the hogwash it was. I didn't want off the grift. I just wanted out of the present snarl.

Which snarl promised to get a little more snarly with Detective Constable Scovil waiting for me at my door.

She wasn't flying the bitch flag, exactly, but took pains to let me vibe that this wasn't a social call and we weren't about to become NBFs, new best friends. I invited her in and took her out on my deck, just large enough for two to sit comfortably and watch the sun settle into the west, casting an orange-into-red glow on the boulevard below and the wall behind us. Film directors call this the golden hour. It makes everyone look good.

For a while, we exchanged null signals, the kind of empty pleasantries you'd expect in such a situation. At last she half-turned in her seat, sending off the body tell that here came the serious shit. "Radar," she said, "we have to open our kimonos."

"Is that as good as it sounds?"

"Shut up and listen," she said, and I did.

To open one's kimono, it turns out, means to exchange data with a prospective business partner, like if you want to build WiMax power amplifiers and I've got the GaN power FETs you need, and we have to know if my devices will give your amplifiers sufficient linearity,[*] but without giving away all our trade secrets. In the business world, they underclothe their kimonos with noncompete this and nondisclose that. Out here on the rim of respectability, such niceties don't exist. You just have the other person's word for it. Sometimes you don't even have that. This is where Scovil was. She needed to open her kimono, but what promise of my discretion could she trust or believe? There was nothing for it but to drop the obi and hope for the best. "I'm not here to catch William Yuan," she said.

"No?"

"I'm here to catch Hines."

And the none-too-firm sand of reality shifted beneath my feet once again. Which was really disappointing, because I'd pretty much decided that I could make Hines authentically as a fibbie with a hard-on for fraudsters. After all, he had all that documentary evidence of my . . . let's call them adventures. For this reason, and by the sharp logic of Occam's razor, I had decided that the simplest explanation was

---

[*]Some people know what all this means; I personally do not.

likeliest to be true: With legitimate access to official records, he'd put together a blackmail package sufficient to bag a Hoverlander. But if he was working my side of the street, then how . . . ? Wait, maybe he's working both sides of the street.

I said, "You mean he's not a cop?"

"Oh, he's a cop. He's just . . ."

I filled in the blank. "Dirty." She nodded. Yep, both sides of the street. "So where does that leave Allie?" I asked.

Scovil smiled, revealing what she thought she knew about my Allie pangs. "She works with Hines," said Scovil. "We have to assume she's crooked as well."

"Well, who isn't?"

Scovil fixed me with a glare, bricking up her tough gal demeanor with the mortar of self-righteousness. "I'm not," she said.

"Oh *you're* the honest cop," I deadpanned. "I always thought that was a myth, like Bigfoot."

What happened next, I have to admit, surprised even me. In the time it took me to chuckle at my own bon mot, Scovil was out of her chair and straddling mine. With swift, practiced moves, she collected my wrists in one hand and pinned them against the wall above my head. The other hand she clamped ungently on my windpipe, to which my windpipe replied, "Ack."

She leaned in close, like she was about to kiss me, but no smooch forthcame. "I know your type," she hissed. "Don't think I don't. You skate through life on charm and think you just ooze irresistibility. Well, I'm here to tell you, this is one gal who finds you completely resistible, sooky bub. And another thing: You're working for me now. You report to me, you do what I tell you, and you always tell me the bloody truth." She squeezed my windpipe a little harder to underscore the point— not, I confess, that it needed much further emphasis. "I own you, bitch. And if you don't think I do, please consider that I'm fully capable of putting you in the ground." And here I'd been wondering if things could escalate to violence. "Get me, mate?"

I nodded to the extent that her grip on my throat would allow.

She shook her head with a look of disgust. I think she was actually hoping I'd show her some of that vaunted Hoverlander bottle so she could go on choking me, or maybe toss me off the deck and see if she could hit the Java Man from here. (I've tried it with rocks; it can be done.) Instead, she let go of my throat, though continued to hold my hands in her grasp. She ground them into the wall, I think as sort of a consolation prize to herself for not getting to kill me and such. In any event, it was clear I wasn't going anywhere until I convinced her I had religion.

Let's be clear about one thing: I'm not a coward, but I am a practical man. I'm able to discern an empty threat from a genuine one, and there was no doubt in my mind that Scovil's was the real deal. Moreover, the puzzle of her personality was clicking into place for me. She'd rubbed me the wrong way from the moment we met. Why? Because she rubs everyone the wrong way. It's what she likes to do: to define herself in enmity. In that sense, she was like the antigrifter. Where a grifter is all verbal prostate massage, she was a shaft up the ass. And, I feared, not just in a metaphorical sense.

So I caved. I caved completely and sincerely and, I confess, a bit cravenly. Not my finest hour, but what are you going to do? I had no intention of being collateral damage to a grudge match between a bent fibbie and a self-righteous Aussie cop with blood lust. And if it cost me a little pride, a little dignity, I figured that was a better deal than the whole ectoplasmic package that was Radar Hoverlander.

Which I basically conveyed to Scovil in the vernacular of "You say jump, me say how high?" Problem was, the abject capitulation of a con man gets taken with the same giant lump of salt as everything else he says. How could I convince Scovil that she did, in fact, have a broken

Radar on her hands? By playing the only card in my deck with any tex-
ture, my doubts about Billy Yuan.

I told Scovil how I'd eased myself into Yuan's acquaintance. "He's
playing me for a mark," I said, "but I'm not sure he buys it."

"Why, Radar," she offered sardonically, "you're not smart enough
to play dumb?"

"I can play dumb," I said. "I can play anything." Man, she raised my
hackles. "But there's a certain balance of power at work here. As a top
grifter, I can convince him of anything, but as a top grifter, too, he's
probably not convinced."

"Clash of the bloody titans," she said. And then slapped me.

Slapped me!

Sheesh, what'd *I* do?

"Right," she continued, "here's what you'll do. First, obviously, you
will keep this conversation to yourself."

"Obviously."

"You'll continue to work Yuan. Don't admit anything. You're
selling a fiction; so is he. That can be useful. Meantime, you report to
Hines that the meeting went well, no problems." She grabbed my
cheeks and chin, and squeezed hard. "You're on probation, mate. You
keep your nose clean, do exactly as I tell you, and never so much as
shade the truth to me, then Bob's your uncle. But if anything goes
wrong, whether it's your fault or not, I will end you. Understand?" I
nodded to the extent that my squeezed cheeks would allow. Scovil
seemed satisfied. She got up off me and, without ceremony, left my
place.

As I rubbed blood back into my hands, I wondered why, and by
whose authority, an Australian copper was after a bent Yank fibbie. But
it was one of those "Reply hazy, ask again later" questions, so I stashed
it for future contemplation. Meanwhile, I couldn't help noting how
my earlier existential crisis had been overtaken—swamped, really—by

events. No time for existential crises now. At some point in the future, I might decide that grifting for money wasn't where I wanted to be, but just then I was grifting for my life, and while I'd always managed a success rate that anyone might envy, in this case I simply couldn't afford to fail. I'd need all my judgment, guile, and skill just to tap dance through.

Plus a healthy dose of think-on-your-feet.

Starting, as it happens, almost at once.

Because fifteen minutes after Scovil left, Hines showed up.

Not in what you'd call a perky mood.

name that religion

The trouble with having a Mirplo for a chaperone is he's such a fucking blabbermouth. I should have known he would report back to Hines about my hookup with Yuan—did know it, in fact, but figured he'd be his usual slack self about checking in. But that was before I learned Hines was dirty. Or rather, *alleged* to be. In this soap-bubble world of mine, the only fact I felt I could completely trust was Scovil's death threat. Everything else was suspect. Still, if Hines was bent, then he'd be leaning hard on poor Mirplo. It's what you do when you're playing both sides against the middle—that, plus fret about running out of middle.

Thus I had barely come down from my last adrenaline spike when an ungentle pounding on my front door triggered my fight-or-flight response again. One thing was for sure: Once I got through all this (*if* I got through all this), I would definitely have to move. Too many people knew where I lived now, and seemed to have no compunction about dropping in unannounced. I felt like I was identified on Maps to the Stars' Homes.

My apartment had one of those old-school peepholes, a tiny door covered by a wrought-iron grill. I unlatched it and peered out to find

Milval Hines shifting nervously from foot to foot on my doorstep. I had seen Hines wearing all sorts of attitude masks, from clueless wannabe grifter to able investment banker to hard-nosed Jake. I had never seen him all twitchy and itchy like he was just then. It didn't strike me as a mask.

"Open up," he demanded.

"Not sure that's a good idea," I said. "You seem a little edgy right now."

"Want edgy? I'll give you edgy." He snaked his hand under his suit coat and whipped out a coal-black service automatic, which he leveled at the peephole. *Oh, this just gets better and better,* I thought. I pondered whether a bullet fired at that range would blast through the grill or bounce off, but decided not to push the experiment to the testing stage. I opened the door and let Hines in. Good news: He put his gun away.

"I need a drink," he said, exactly like a man who, well, needed a drink.

"So do I," I replied, "but this is a dry house."

He looked at me like I had syphilis. "Jesus fucking Christ," he said, "you don't even drink?"

"I drink," I said. "Just not at home." Flashing back to my recent one-man tequila fiesta, I mentally added, *at least not when I can help it.*

Hines paced anxiously back and forth, his eyes darting everywhere as if looking for lurking monsters. What could have turned him upside down so fast?

"You met Yuan," he said suddenly.

"Yep."

"How'd that go?"

"I eased him in. He thinks I'm a trust-fund baby with more money than common sense." Hines eyed me suspiciously. I suppose he was measuring my expression for some sign of a lie, but the day has not yet dawned that a fibbie, bent or straight, can read me that well. All the same, he didn't seem satisfied with my report.

"So he makes you for a mark," Hines said. "How's that gonna help?"

"See it from his point of view," I vamped. "A free fish jumps into your boat. No matter what else you've got going on, you don't throw it back. Never leave money lying on the table, right? Besides, he's lonely. Far from home. Might want someone to talk to. I'll take an interest in his investment strategies. People like it when you let them teach." This last comment was a none-too-veiled reference to Hines's playacting back in the pigeon-drop phase of all this. I half wanted him to take it as a compliment, like I'd borrowed a page from his playbook.

If he was flattered, he didn't let on. "Any way he's onto you?"

"Nope."

"Mirplo says he looks like a smart cookie."

"Mirplo's about as good a judge of character as Eva Braun. You want to take his word for it, you put him in charge. Otherwise, man, back off. I've got to have room to move."

"You should've reported in as soon as your meeting was done."

"I should've gone into sports medicine," I answered. "But we all make mistakes. Don't dwell, that's what I say."

"You've got a smart mouth, kid."

"I know," I said. "It gets me into trouble. But also out. It's about a wash."

"I don't think you appreciate how much trouble you're in right now."

"What do you want from me?" I asked. "My career's on the line. My freedom." I waved vaguely toward his hidden shoulder holster. "Maybe more. Like I said, I should've gone into sports medicine. What's done is done. I'm not going to have a bad day just because you say so. To an asshole, the whole world looks dark."

"What's that supposed to mean?"

"Nothing. It's just a saying."

"Are you calling me an asshole?"

"Never to your face, uhm . . . detective? Commander? I don't know your rank."

"Don't worry about my fucking rank," said Hines.

"Fine," I shrugged. "Then what should I worry about?"

"Cracking Yuan like an egg, and fast." There it was. The source of his urgency. Hines was putting the pressure of a deadline on me. I wondered who was putting the pressure of a deadline on him, and what would transpire if he didn't meet it. Not, I suspected, a party with cake. Then, from out of nowhere, he hit me with, "The Merlin Game, is it still set to go?"

"Cocked and locked," I said. "Unless you screwed it up."

"I haven't touched it."

"Well, assuming your list of leads was good . . ."

"It is," he snapped.

Now that I knew Hines wasn't an investment counselor, I wondered how he got his hands on such a list, but as he seemed in no mood to play twenty questions, I let it go for now. "Then I'm saying there's probably around three hundred grand worth of candy apples just waiting to drop off the tree."

"Shake it," he said.

"What?"

"Shake the tree. Get the money. Launch the fucking game."

"You know that's illegal," I said.

"I'll worry about the law. You worry about your ass." He didn't have to spell it out for me—I was reasonably confident I'd received my second coy death threat of the day, a personal best. Hines dug around in his pocket and pulled out a piece of paper. "Ship the money here," he said. "All of it." I looked at the paper. It was a bank routing slip. Destination Liechtenstein, as far as I could tell.

"That wasn't what we agreed," I said.

"New agreement," he said. "I get the money. You get your life." Okay, well, there wasn't even anything coy about that.

"What about Allie?"

For some reason he punched me. I really don't know why. He decked me good, though. Spun me around like a piñata and laid me out on the floor.

Where I figured, *You know what? As long as I'm already down here and all, I might as well just sleep.*

Then I passed out a little.

When I awoke, Hines was gone and the phone was ringing. I answered with a groggy, "Hello?"

It was Hines. "You still alive?"

"I guess."

"Do you want to stay that way?" Dumb question. I didn't even answer. "Then three things: Burn down the fucking house; flip Yuan; and if that cunt Scovil asks, we never talked." *Great,* I thought, *another sub rosa alliance.* "And by the way," added Hines, "you will."

"Will what?"

"Have a bad day if I say so. Think about that next time you call someone an asshole." He hung up.

I got up, rocky on my feet. Went into the bathroom and checked myself out. I hadn't showered since coming back from my run, and I stank. Plus my jaw was swollen. I touched it, then wished I hadn't.

After a shower I felt better, or at least clean. I chunked back some ibuprofens, then fixed myself something to eat. Every few seconds, I caught myself glancing at the front door as if I next expected, I don't know, a SWAT team, maybe. Hines was right about one thing: I was definitely having a bad day.

Could it get worse? Sure it could . . . for I suddenly realized that I'd practically handed Billy Yuan my identity on a covered silver serving tray. Would he be smart enough to lift the lid? I had to think, *yeah.*

See, back when the internet was everyone's new toy, I'd taken it into my head to found my own online religion and launch it at www.namethatreligion.com. It was more of a lark than anything else, an experiment to see if I could cook up a belief system that welcomed all ideas with equal equanimity, and made room for every notion of a supreme being, all the way from *the Alpha and the Omega no doubt* to *just an idea some people have.* The site was a moneymaker of sorts, thanks to a fee-based ordination service, but it never really caught fire. Turns out that people who have a deep interest in religion rarely have deep pockets, and I soon turned my attention elsewhere—to the Jovian Flywheel, if memory serves, a perpetual-motion machine that allegedly harvested energy from the differential between the Earth's and Jupiter's gravitational fields. Like all perpetual-motion machines, it was gogglebox nonsense, and only worked so long as the mark didn't notice the plug. You'd think after all this time—here's another scam with centuries of pedigree—nobody would fall for it, but I made some decent coin. I did.

Now here was the problem. Name That Religion had had a banner with the exact quote I'd given Yuan: "The universe loves us. All we have to do is love it back." More gogglebox nonsense, if you ask me, but people seemed to respond to it. It struck a chord. Of course I erased all the page files in the end; if you're running a medicine show, you always cover your tracks when you blow town. But the site had its fans, a small, rabid claque that spread NTR far and wide through copy/pasted progeny. Could there be a paperless paper trail leading back to a clone of the original site, buried on some server like an archaeological ruin? If so, my fingerprints would be all over it. Say Yuan followed the trail. Would he conclude that philosophy student Chad Thurston had cribbed his core belief from some fringe ism, or would he see a grifter's early attempt to use the internet for ill-gotten whatever?

I went online to see how bad the damage was.

Bad.

The banner phrase got Google hits from all over the place. The religious commentary sites weren't bad. Some people called me a "closet Unitarian," but I could live with that. The real problem was the antifraud sites. Apparently someone had long ago declared Name That Religion a scam. Well, in fairness, it was. But that sort of label haunts you. Worse, they mentioned me by name. What the hell had I been thinking, using my own name? I should've called myself Moses McCultycult or something. And while I like to think that over the years I'd grown in the grift, I had to rate my current play as no less sloppy. You don't recycle material, ever. That was just lazy of me. I kicked myself for not taking the time to make up something new for Yuan. Instead, I'd practically walked in wearing a nametag, which sucked; and now both Scovil and Hines had Damoclean hardware hanging over me, which sucked worse. And all because I met Allie Quinn and saw in her a reflection of myself, the sort of flirty, tarty, smarty grifter that only a grifter could love. The worst sort of narcissism, it had literally rendered me blind.

Well, crap.

I had to be done with it, that's all. I had to be in the wind, and I had to be there now. This was not the best of exit strategies, not the kind where everyone smiles and shakes hands when they part, but I knew we were way past that point. So let's call it my "emergency exit" strategy: the one where I throw the kitchen sink in the car and get the hell gone. Now, tonight. Before any other of my manifold miscues could catch up with me and punish me more. I wasn't worried about anything I had to leave behind. It's called cutting your losses, and the first thing you do in cutting them is admit they *are* losses. It's not heroic and it's not fun, but sometimes you just have to shade and fade.

I went outside to open my garage. It was cool out now, with the night deepening toward dawn. The darkness put a monochrome cast on everything in sight: the palm trees and jacarandas; mailboxes and trashcans; Mirplo.

Mirplo?

He stepped out of the shadows wearing his signature goofy smile and carrying something steel and compact in the palm of his hand. "Hey look, Radar," he said brightly. "Hines gave me a gun." Then his voice turned cold. "He told me to use it if you went rabbit."

Like I said: well, crap.

the prisoner's whaddyacallit

I have to tell you, when I saw Mirplo with a gun, inside me a switch flipped. Maybe my sense of outrage overcame reason, or maybe I just started to see weakness in the other players. After all, if they thought that arming a Mirplo was a good idea, they couldn't be thinking completely exactly clearly. Anyway, at that moment, all thought of bailing left my mind. This was a snuke, after all, a deep and complex one, the sort of game I'm supposedly particularly good at. There had to be moves I could make.

Not that I could make moves of any sort until I got this gun shit sorted out. Betraying no particular sense of purpose, I started shuffling in a lazy circle toward the far side of the street, where a narrow concrete stairway ascended beside a stucco garage to a hillside home whose owner, I knew, had lately gone on a security jag. "A gun, Vic?" I said. "Seriously?"

"What, you don't think I can handle a gun?"

I shrugged. "I think you can handle whatever you want to handle. I just don't think it's necessary, that's all. Do I look like I'm going anywhere?"

"Well, what are you doing out here, then?"

"Looking for the cat."

"Bullshit. You don't have a cat."

"It's not mine, nimrod. It belongs to the ovarians downstairs. They're in Guatemala, adopting a baby."

"And you're taking care of their cat? I gotta say that doesn't sound like you."

"I owe 'em. They take my trashcans up to the street. They're stronger than I am."

"Well, whatever. Let's go inside. I'm your babysitter now."

"I have to find the cat, man. Coyotes get 'er, those ovarians'll kick my ass." I turned and called into a random quadrant of night. "Pickle! Come here, girl!"

The night didn't answer. Mirplo said, "Screw the cat, man. Get in the house." He waved the gun in what I suppose he thought was a menacing fashion, but betrayed an understanding of firearms so flawed that probably local windows (or nonexistent cats) had a better shot at getting shot than I did. Still, a Mirplo with a gun. That offended my sensibilities. I continued to call for the cat, all the while edging closer to the stairway.

"Pickle! Come to Uncle Radar right now!"

"Radar—"

I looked past Mirplo. "There you are, you rascal!" Vic turned. I knew he would. It was the oldest trick in the book, of course, a variation on Mirplo's own "Look, Halley's Comet!" Still, it worked. In the second it took Vic to swivel his glance away, I darted within range of the neighbor's prophylactic motion sensor at the base of his stairs, triggering the world's brightest halogen spotlights. As they popped on, I launched myself at Mirplo, who momentarily lost me in the glare. I'm crap at violence, I know I am, but I can throw a head butt to the stomach when the situation demands, and that's what the situation demanded here. Next thing Vic knew, he was on his back, with my knees on his chest and the gun probing his nose like an otoscope.

"Shit, Radar," said Vic, his voice falling. "No cat?"

"No cat."

I took Mirplo inside and sat him down on the couch. I didn't quite know what to do with the gun. As I've said, I'm no fan of firearms. In my world, if you can't do the job through talking and planning, you're just not very good at the game. So I told Vic, "I'm gonna go put this away. You stay here." I knew he would. I could see that shock had rubberized his legs. He was probably trying to figure out how much shit he'd be in with Hines for letting me flip him. Enough, I hoped, that he might be in a mood to stay flipped.

I stashed the gun in my bedroom, amid the junk in the closet, and came back out to find Vic where I'd left him: sitting on the couch, staring into nothing with a glazed gaze. "I'm fucked," he said. "I'm so totally fucking fucked."

"Why is that?"

He looked at me and allowed a sour grin to pass across his face. "You know why," he said. "Hines is gonna kill me."

"Vic, I would hate to see that happen."

"Like hell you would. Dude, I totally betrayed you."

"Well, betrayed. The jury's still out on that. Why don't you fill in some blanks for me, let's see where we really stand."

"No, I can't."

"Okay," I said brightly. "Then go see Hines and tell him he can have his gun back anytime he wants to come get it."

"Radar, I can't."

"Well, you're kind of stuck between can'ts."

Mirplo buried his head in his hands.

"But I think we can get you unstuck."

He looked up, a glimmer of hope shining in his black eyes. "How?"

How, indeed? Against honest cops, I'd have been in a much dicier spot, but all the deception and extravagant ill-truth floating around made for ample wiggle room here. So I told Vic about Scovil's and Hines's crossed purposes and hoped he'd see the benefit of defecting to Team Hoverlander. "We can't protect ourselves," I said, "but we might could protect each other."

Vic's brow furrowed as his brain worked at max amps. "We're in the whaddyacallit," he said at last, "that prisoner's thingie." I knew what he was groping for: the Prisoner's Dilemma, the classic game-theory problem where two crooks will prosper if they cooperate, but each can rationally (though mistakenly) conclude that they'll do better by betraying the other. "If we screw each other, we're both screwed, right?"

I'd heard many more sophisticated analyses of the dilemma, but never one more trenchant. I said, "Vic, how did you get mixed up with these dillweeds in the first place?"

He took a beat before answering. I could see he was weighing his commitment to the prisoner's whaddyacallit. At last he let go, and his story came spilling out. "So last March," he said, "this wedge comes to see me. Says he's got some off-license credit cards going moldy in Louisiana. Tried to move 'em during Mardi Gras, didn't work out. But if I go mule 'em back, he'll deal me in for a nice chunk of change. So I make the New Orleans turnaround, and when I land back at LAX, they've got, like, the whole Seventh Cavalry waiting to drop my noggin." I did a quick reductive adjustment to the Mirplovian math: If he said it was the Seventh Cavalry, it was probably one overweight Jake and a crippled crime dog. "Next thing I know, I'm in some FBI lockup at the airport, and Hines is there, telling me what a world of hurt I'm in."

"You crossed state lines with counterfeit credit cards. That's a federal beef."

"Oh, intuitive grasp of the obvious, Brain Boy. But Hines offered to kick me if I agreed to stool out for him."

"You know you were stung, right?"

"Stung?"

"You think they picked you at random? They entrapped your ass."

"The motherfuckers," he said indignantly.

"Yeah, the motherfuckers."

"Damn, that'd never've held up in court!"

"Hines never intended it to get that far. What happened next?"

"I was drowning, Radar. He threw me a rope. What could I do but grab it?"

"So what'd they have you do?"

"At first nothing. Just check in every now and then and, you know, shout if something sketchy was going down."

"And who all did you rat out?"

"Nobody!" protested Vic. I barely rolled my eyes. "Okay, one or two guys. Clumsy mooks they'd have caught anyway."

"Plus me."

"You they knew about. But they were psyched to know more. How you operate, what snukes you liked to play. They said they were gonna offer you a job. Honest to God, Radar, I thought I was hooking you up."

"Yeah, Merry Christmas."

"I'm really sorry I put you on their map."

"You still don't get it, do you, Vic?" He gave me this blank look like *Get what?* "I was on their map all along. You were just their GPS."

Vic mulled this. "Oh," he said at last.

"Though it would've been better if you'd given me the high sign when you saw Hines in the Java Man that day."

"Oh, yeah, that. My bad."

"Yeah, your bad. How did Allie fit in?"

"Fuckin' Allie," muttered Vic.

"What do you mean?"

"She had in mind that the more I warned you against her, the more tied up in her you'd get. Ridiculous, right?"

Right. Ridiculous.

"She was like my acting coach and shit. Very heavy. Very serious pain in the ass." Vic's face brightened. "But I did a good job, though, didn't I? Really had you convinced she was stinky cheese."

"Yeah, thanks for that." This raised a question I didn't think Vic could answer, but I asked it just the same, for sometimes he had an idiot savant's knack for clarity. "Is she in on it?"

"Duh, of course she is."

"No, I mean as a cherry top. Or is she just pimped in like us?"

"Wow, that's a good question." Vic mused for a moment. "You know, the truth is, I've never smelled cop on her."

"Yeah, me neither. Doesn't mean it's not there. Maybe she just cleans up nice."

"There is one thing . . ."

"What's that?"

"Early in October, before you two met, she was pumping me for all your 411 and this was, like, the middle of the afternoon, but she could barely stay awake. I asked her what's the matter. She said jet lag."

"Jet lag? Really?"

"Uh-huh. And right now I'm thinking Australia."

"You know what, Vic? So am I."

"You think she went there hunting Yuan?"

"Hunting? I don't know." Back in Allie's apartment—or safe house—when I'd guessed that she and Yuan had dated, Hines as much as admitted I was right and Allie didn't say no. Granted, she might have gone to Australia "in hot pursuit" and whatnot, but Mirplo was right: she didn't smell cop. Which maybe put her on Yuan's side of the street. Maybe her business was more partnership than pleasure.

Maybe, maybe, maybe. A whole big stack of maybe just waiting for syrup and jam. Another question crossed my mind. "What was Allie doing at the car show last year? Was that coincidence, or was she already scouting me out?"

Vic just shrugged. "I don't know," he said. "You could ask her friend."

"Friend?"

"The Asian honey she was with that day. I chatted her up. Her name was . . ." he mused for a moment. "Kyoko Kaneko."

"You remember that?"

"I told you, man, I have a pornographic memory."

"I wonder if we can track her down." I grabbed my laptop and popped it open—then popped it right back closed. As it had been in fibbie hands, I had no reason to believe it wasn't completely compromised, with a buried keystroke worm to track every move I made. "We need a public terminal," I said. "What's open this time of night?"

Half an hour later, we were in a cyber café called Sunset Jackson, where, amid the Second Lifers, overseas Skypers and intellectual homeless, we searched for Kyoko Kaneko. The usual channels bore no fruit, nor did some of my more esoteric approaches—though I was reluctant to track too close to certain government databases for fear that Hines had stationed lookout bots, which I know sounds pretty far-fetched, but by this point I was putting nothing past anyone. After endless permutations, combinations, alternate spellings, and grabass guesses, I asked Vic if he was sure he had the name right. You'd think I had called his mother ugly or something. The offended dignity of a Mirplo notwithstanding, I was starting to think I was digging a hole in the wrong place, when suddenly I had a thought.

"Vic," I asked, "do you suppose this chick's an FOB?"

"FOB?"

"Fresh off the boat. First-generation American."

"Could be," said Vic. "Her English wasn't too good."

"As evidenced by the fact that she suffered a conversation with you." Weirdly, this insult pleased Vic. He seemed to take it as a measure of apology accepted, and I honestly couldn't say he was wrong. It's hard to stay mad at a Mirplo. "Okay, let's try a different approach."

I pried open an INS database and got a hit on the first try: There was a Kyoko Kaneko with a student visa that let her attend film school at UCLA, and an address in an area that the real estate agents like to call "Beverly Hills adjacent," but really it's just L.A. I jotted down the address on the back of Hines's bank routing slip, the irony of which was not lost on me.

We still had a few minutes' credit left, and Vic wanted to surf porn. I looked over my shoulder, where an African woman with toddler in arms was on a headset talking to, I guess, her husband back home. "Yeah, let's not," I said. Before Vic could protest, I had cleared my cache, closed the browser and logged off. Actually, the woman put me in mind of a phrase I'd heard long ago: luxury crisis. So much of what we go through around here, so many of the things that make us feel sorry for ourselves, are the artifacts of prosperity—say your BMW breaks down. Almost every mess you find yourself in would be an enviable mess to, say, the twelve-year-old stitcher of your Honduran *camisa*. It was something to think about—but later. Right now, my mess was my mess, and I'd do well to stick to the matter at hand.

Vic and I walked outside and stood together on the street. "Vic," I said, "you know I can't give you that gun back."

He nodded, and said solemnly, "Trust can't be granted. Earned it must be."

"What are you, now, fucking Yoda?"

We shared a laugh, and something lifted off me. Every since Allie Quinn had come into my life, I'd felt like a resistance fighter stranded alone behind enemy lines. Now at least I wasn't alone. A Mirplo's not much of an ally, but he's better than a sharp stick in the eye, which is a useful way to measure many things.

"I'm supposed to see Hines in the morning," said Vic. "What'll I tell him?"

"Tell him you lost it."

Vic pursed his lips thoughtfully. "Yeah," he said, "that sounds like something I'd do."

He started away. "Vic," I said, and he turned back. "I don't need to tell you what's at stake here."

"Nah, the gun sort of spelled that out."

"We're in this together now. If either of us fucks up, we're both going down."

He mused for a moment. "Then try not to fuck up," he said, and sloped off into the night.

don't be cool

I went home and went to bed. Later, I had a dream. I was driving a 1959 Cadillac convertible across the Mojave Desert. Elvis Presley sat in the passenger seat, singing incorrect lyrics to his own songs. "Don't be cool," he crooned softly, "to a heartless Jew."

The car was gorgeous, the color of smoke, with fins that stretched to the heavens. The air suspension made the ride so smooth I thought I was flying. Then I glanced down (through, oddly, glass bottom floorboards) and realized that I *was* flying, flashing along a hundred feet off the desert floor. The King reached over and gave me a reassuring pat on the knee. "The rules don't confine," he growled gently, "they define. True genius works within form."

Before I could *huh* a huh, I was back in my bedroom, buried nosedown in a pillow that still smelled like Allie, which was strange, because I'd for certain changed the sheets. Then I realized that the thing that smelled like Allie *was* Allie, lying beside me in bed, propped up on one elbow, and watching me with eyes as big as a Walter Keane kitten's.

"How'd you get in?" I asked. "I know I locked the door."

"Silly," she said. "I told you, I teleport."

"What else do you do?"

"Thought you'd never ask." She yanked back the covers and dove on my gear like a diabetic diving on a Dove bar.

This, alas, was a dream as well.

When I woke for real, I got my day moving fast. I wanted to be out of the house ahead of any unwelcome visitors. Climbing behind the wheel of my vintage Volvo, I headed west on Beverly Boulevard, and within half an hour was in Kyoko Kaneka's neighborhood. I parked down the street from her red adobe four-plex. Outfitting myself with some props from my trunk, including a clipboard, tie and jacket, zero-lens glasses, and sundry identifying documents, I walked to her address and rapped on the door.

A shadow passed over the peep hole, and I knew she was checking me out. "Who is it?" a lilting voice asked.

"My name is Taft Hartley, ma'am" I said, in a civil servant's neutral tones. "I'm with the county health department."

"The landlord handles the—"

"Ma'am, it's not that kind of issue. I'm looking for . . ." I flipped through some blank pages on the clipboard, then made eye contact with the peep hole. ". . . an Allison Quinn."

"You mean Allie?"

"I suppose so, ma'am. It's very important that I talk to her. Her health may be at risk."

"Why are you looking here? She doesn't live here." Interesting: I could almost hear an *anymore* in her voice.

"I see." I sounded weary, disappointed. "Ma'am, could I come in, please? I need to ask you some questions."

"Can I see some ID?" I held up my credentials. Why people think a piece of paper makes you something you aren't, I'll never understand. After a moment, the door opened, and a barefoot Japanese girl let me into her immaculate apartment. I didn't really recognize her from the car show, and assumed that she wouldn't remember me, either. Apart from the getup I wore, just think of the thousands of people you meet whose faces never register. Unless you're a freak like Mirplo.

She told me her name. I repeated it, stumbling expressively over the pronunciation. Then I said, "Allison Quinn, ma'am—"

"Would you stop calling me ma'am, please? I'm no older than you." Her English wasn't as bad as Mirplo's pornographic memory made it out to be, but it sounded studied, like she'd been working hard to Americanize her persona. I'm just wondering: Is there not a little grifter in all of us?

"Sorry," I said with a shrug. "It's how they train us." Once again I referred to my phantom notes. "Anyway, she listed you as a character reference on an application to teach in the L.A. schools." At that, Kyoko broke into a high giggle, her eyes shining. "Is something funny?" I asked.

"Allie teaching school. Tell the children to guard their lunch money."

I looked at her blankly, then pushed on. "She took a tuberculosis test. It's just routine, part of the application process, but it came back positive. We need to retest her, treat her if necessary, see if we can figure out where she got it. Do you know if she's been out of the country recently? Say in the past year or so?"

"She was always coming and going somewhere. She said she had international business. Truthfully, I think she was a hooker."

"Do you know if she went any place tropical? Africa, say, or South America."

"No. Australia, I think. Didn't even bring me back a boomerang."

"If I may say, ma—" I caught myself, "miss, it doesn't seem as though there's much love lost between you two."

"Allie Quinn is a liar and a cheat. She lived here for six months and never paid a cent of rent. It was always, 'The money's coming in,' or she had an emergency or something." Kyoko made a moue. "She said she could get my screenplay produced, but that was bullshit, too."

There it is, I thought. *Hell hath no fury like a writer scorned.*

We talked awhile longer. Kyoko was generous with information, the way people will be when they feel needed or important. From what she said, I was able to construct a picture of Allie as a transplant from somewhere, working solo grifts and just trying to get by. Though Kyoko occasionally joined Allie on bizarre adventures, like her masquerade at the car show, they never were close. They started to fall out over rent, but before that could come to a head, Allie simply disappeared. "I think she got in trouble," said Kyoko. "Some men came and took all her things away."

"Men?"

"Policemen."

"And when was that?"

"Summer sometime. Before Labor Day."

"I see." I tucked my clipboard under my arm. "Well, if you see her, please tell her to contact County Health immediately." I handed Kyoko a bogus business card. "And if I were you, I would avoid close contact."

"Trust me," she said, "I won't be kissing her anytime soon."

I cleared out. When I got back to my car, the Chad Thurston phone was ringing. I let it go to voice mail. I wasn't ready to talk to Yuan yet. I had some new information to process.

So Allie came and went. In the country, out of the country, with no real job and not a lot of cash. Thanks to Kyoko, I could reasonably place her in Australia, and though I couldn't place her exactly next to Billy Yuan, it didn't seem that far a fetch. But what was she doing down under? Sightseeing? Or setting something up? Suppose Hines had caught her with her fingers in the honeypot and flipped her like he flipped Mirplo. Unlike Mirplo, she'd be light enough on her feet to feed Hines a consistent false narrative. Maybe that narrative was one of feminine weakness—unlikely, given Allie, but still—and inability to help Hines catch Yuan without outside agency, said agency being *moi.* She'd met Mirplo and me last year at the car show. Let's say she'd intuited (or researched—I wouldn't put anything past her) that I was a good enough grifter to be represented as world class. Then she led Hines to Mirplo, and through him to me. In that case, I wasn't the source of some extravagant, sought-after skill package, but just an elaborate stall.

That explained a lot, but it didn't explain everything.

Like: why did she sleep with me?

I drove around for a while, mulling my hypothesis, testing it from different angles, seeing how other pieces fit. Could Scovil have picked up Allie's scent in Australia, either before or after Scovil made Hines for bent? Was Allie secretly (or additionally) working for Scovil? Did Hines thus feel a certain noose tightening around his neck? He wanted me to button up the Merlin Game, with himself as offshore beneficiary. Was that money intended to grease his getaway? If so, when was getaway day?

Once again, I had too many questions and not enough answers, which was really starting to get on my nerves.

Or was it?

I caught a glimpse of myself in the rearview mirror. If I didn't know me better, I'd say I looked happy. This puzzle was proving satisfyingly difficult to solve. I felt alive in my mind. Apart from the risk of getting dead in my body, I was having a high old time.

But that risk of getting dead was not negligible. I couldn't overlook it.

Now my own phone rang. I ignored it, but a moment later pulled into the parking lot of a mini-mart to check both phones and play back my messages.

Mirplo had called. "Hey, Blue Leader," he chirped, in what I suppose he supposed to be code, "Big Bird is getting testy. Wants to know if you've forgotten about the thing with the thing. I played dumb." (A Mirplovian gift, that.) "But you'd better do the thing with the thing today, or Big Bird's gonna shit on you." Threats aside, the thing with the thing—the Merlin Game—needed triggering soon, or it would lose the heat of its momentum and fall apart. This thought filled me with a strange indifference, and it felt weird to think of a $300,000 snadoodle as a distracting aside, but that's what it had become. I sent Mirplo a text telling him to assure Hines it would be done today.

Not, perhaps, the way he anticipated, but hell, you can't have everything.

I played back the message on the other phone. "Hey, Chad," Billy Yuan began, "how's that ol' universe treating you?" Man, you didn't need a subtext detector to hear the *busted!* in Billy's voice. He was on to me, and letting me know it. "Listen, mate," he continued, "two questions for you: Why did Willy Sutton rob banks? And where is the money now? Call me when you know. I fancy we can do business."

So I'd been made. Made by an arrogant prick who wouldn't even let me play his reindeer games till I passed a little test first. It put me in mind of Allie and the whole Cinderfuckingella thing. Sometimes we grifters are too cute for our own good. Anyway, the first question was easy. Willie Sutton robbed banks because, as he famously (though apocryphally) put it, "That's where the money is." But where was the money now? Was Yuan referring to the Merlin Game, trying to get me to out myself about that? I didn't think so. He might know about it, of course, from several different sources, but I didn't think that was the money he was referring to. Why? Hard to say. A gut feeling. Something from his tone of voice that said the question was more about him than about me. Like an SAT analogy, almost: *Willie Sutton is to banks as Billy Yuan is to what?*

Well, what?

I cast my mind back to Willie Sutton's days. The Great Depression.

When what money there was was in banks and almost nowhere else. Okay, if Yuan was using analogy, maybe I could, too. Great Depression is to banks as today is to . . .

Is to . . .

Nothing. My gears ground on the question, and I got nowhere.

Broaden the search, Radar, I thought. *Forget about "where is money?" Think "what is money?"* And what is money, really, but an assignment of value, a promise to pay? Wait, *promise to pay.* That tickled something in my brain. If you think of it, money stored in a bank, say, is just a representation of debt. Someone owes someone something, and the sum of that something is a bank's bottom line.

Okay, then. Who holds all the debt right now?

Got it!

I scrolled to Billy's phone number and hit *dial.* After two rings, Billy answered, "G'day, Radar."

Not even any Chadouflage. I decided to go shields-down, too. "Hello, Billy," I said. "I know where the money is."

"And that would be?"

"China."

"Excellent," said Yuan. "You got it in one."

"So I did," I said. "So now what?"

"Now we meet and discuss our plan."

"What plan is that?"

"You already know it," he said. "We're going to rob China."

the california roll

It took us a little while to work out where to meet: someplace public but cloistered, where two grifters could size each other up with appropriate discretion and wary circumspection. We settled on the Brentwood Country Mart, an open-air warren of shops on the eastern edge of Santa Monica. There was a fake-wood fire pit in the center of the mart, surrounded by fast-food joints, but originals, not franchise. It was the sort of place where people sat around tête-à-tête in conversations covering everything from real estate deals to demands for divorce. It met our needs; plus, if we got hungry, the chimichangas there were dandy.

I arrived first, and killed some time studying the window display of a specialty food store where a pyramid of elegantly labeled wine bottles pronounced themselves AcquaViva, which as near as I could tell was not wine but a fortified fruit drink that retailed for an incredible fifty bucks a bottle. A shopgirl noticed me and came out to hand me a brochure. I read it with, I guess you'd say, professional interest, as it touted the benefits of AcquaViva's "proprietary blend of 23 fruit juices and extracts, including the life-giving açaí berry, one of Mother Nature's greatest gifts."

Really?

Reading on, I learned that AcquaViva was a bona fide superfood, packed to the rafters with flavonoids, phytonutrients, antioxidants, esterified fatty acids, and just a splash, it would seem, of Ponce de León's original fountain of youth. It promised to boost energy, reduce muscle fatigue, arm the immune system, and bind free radicals. While the studies that backed these claims were suspiciously vague in provenance and methodology, they did have impressive-sounding names, such as "Double Blind Matrix Match of Antioxidant Versus Placebo Benefit-Vectors." Better still, for the professionally athletically inclined, AcquaViva had been certified by the Global Anti-Doping Association as 100 percent free of all banned substances—though in fairness, the same could be said of an empty bottle. More good news: Lucrative distributorships were available now. I marveled at the sheer chutzpah of selling, basically, grape juice at half a yard a pop. It tickled me to think that snake oil, yet another venerable and storied snuke, was still alive and well in this modern world. Truly, nothing beautiful dies.

"Why didn't *we* think of that, eh?" I turned to see Billy Yuan standing beside me. "Low overhead, high markup, sexy product." He shot me a wink. "Bit too much like real work, though, yeh?" In the light of day, outside the smoky confines of the Blue Magoon, I was able to get a better look at him. He was rather shorter than me, with a thin, wiry frame that suggested agility. I put him on yoga, or perhaps qigong. His features were so purely Chinese that it kicked up puffs of cognitive dissonance every time he opened his mouth and that flat Aussie accent poured out. I'm sure it made him good in the grift, for he was a walking cloud of deception, just by being who he was.

"Ever work an MLM?" he asked.

I gave him my best blank look. "MLM?" I don't know why I prevaricated, since we'd both already shed our fabricat identities. I guess lying has its own inertia.

Billy called me on it, though. "It would be better for us both, I think, if you stopped playing dumb. You know what MLMs are as well as you know that I'm not Rick Chen, and you're not Chad Thurston, the first, second, or third."

"Have it your way," I shrugged. "MLMs, or multi-level marketing, are tiered participation vending schemes. They differ from pyramids in the sense that there's always an actual product for sale, but the principle remains the same: get in early, get rich; get in late, get reamed. You've got breakaway plans, binary plans, stairsteps, power legs, profit legs, and base shop overrides. Me personally, I've started . . ." I paused to do a rough count, "something like two dozen MLMs, selling everything from cell-phone accessories to weight-loss products. The profit's always in the distributor fees. The most successful MLMs are the ones that push prosperity consciousness to the point of cult frenzy. They also work best when they burn hot. None of mine has lasted more than sixteen weeks."

"Ever been dobbed in?"

"Busted? For an MLM? Now who's playing dumb? They're legal as church if you set 'em up right."

Yuan smiled. "Fair go," he said. "Let's sit down."

We walked to one of the small wooden tables near the fake fire. At adjacent tables sat some skate rats munching French fries, a pair of speed-chess players with a small retinue of lookers-on, and a junior high school couple holding hands and pretending to be on a real date. On the principle of hiding in plain sight, this was the sort of place you could discuss the particulars of a murder for hire and raise not so much as an eyebrow from those nearby. They'd assume it was a movie pitch, anyway.

"So," he said.

"So," I replied.

"The Church of the Orthodox Paradox."

. "Come again?"

"Your religion. That's what I'd name it."

"I always favored 'absolute relativism.'"

Yuan nodded. "I could buy that."

Weirdly, we then talked religion for a while, and once again I found Billy Yuan easy to relax with, even in the current context. Perhaps it was a case of like minds, or just of being with someone who could keep pace in a conversation that hoboed to Nietzsche, n-space, and the Coptic Gospel of Thomas. Eventually, kind of as a game, I started searching for topics to stump him with, but finding holes in Yuan's knowledge was tough. This guy was easily as polymathically perverse as I was. And, like me, he had a knack for sounding like he knew what he was talking about even when he didn't. I think we enjoyed that about each other, like when two specialists in a really obscure medical field get together and *at last* have someone they can talk to.

"*Pemphigus foliaceus?*"

"As if! *Pemphigus vulgaris!*"

"*Ha, ha, ha!*"

But even *at last* can't last forever. Ultimately we'd have to get down to the matter at hand, or else why had we bothered to meet? Being the first to raise the subject was touchy, though, a bit like those junior romantics at the next table jockeying not to be the first to admit that they like each other, not just *like*, ya know, but really *like* like. I thought that as it was Billy's meeting, it was Billy's move. He may have thought the same of me, since I'd fronted him first at the Blue Magoon. So we reached a certain impasse, which Billy broke obliquely with a rhetorical question.

"In your opinion," he asked, "what makes a perfect grift?"

I thought about it for a moment before I answered. "No trail, no trace, no taste."

"Trail and trace I understand," said Yuan, "but taste?"

"In the mouth. No bad taste in anyone's mouth. In my opinion—

since you asked—I should be able to fleece the mark completely on Monday and have drinks with him on Friday, no hard feelings."

"That's a big ask."

"You said a perfect grift, not an easy one."

"True." Yuan lapsed into a thoughtful silence. I joined him there, for he had taken the lead and I was content to let him have it. "Would not the perfect grift," he asked at last, "be one after which you never had to run another one again?"

"Ah, the big one. The getaway grift. Around here we call it the California Roll."

"Because it sets you up in sushi for life?"

"Something like that." I paused then to consider his question. At last I said, "Can I be honest?"

Billy laughed. "I don't know, mate. Can you?"

I laughed back. "Let's pretend I can. I'm not so sure I'm interested in a California Roll. What would I do with tomorrow?"

"I agree it's a problem. For blokes like you and me, there's the risk of . . ."

He groped for the phrase. I found it first. "Chronic understimulation."

"Indeed. It's not as if we can write our memoirs. I doubt we're qualified for much of anything else."

"I thought I might study philosophy."

Yuan chuckled. "Did you now, Chad? But there comes a point, wouldn't you say, when your ambition is such that any grift you bestir yourself to run has the potential to be a California Roll?"

"If you're any good at the game, I suppose. I mean, you're not going to be satisfied selling overpriced fruit juice forever, right?"

"Right. Exactly and precisely right." From that point forward, and by halting degrees, Yuan outlined his grift. The more details he revealed, the lower my jaw dropped, for this was truly a visionary snuke.

As all the evidence indicates, in the world of larceny, there's simply nothing new under the sun, so this scam, like all scams, had historic antecedent. Back in the early days of minted silver and gold currency, it was common practice to "clip" coins; that is, shave off some unnoticeable part of them and put them back into circulation. Clip enough coins, you eventually accrue a convertible pile of precious metal. Meanwhile, the coins still trade at full value, and no one's the wiser—until everyone starts clipping, that is, and then you have all sorts of nasty problems like currency devaluation, inflation, and loss of faith in the coin of the realm. Left unchecked, clipped coins can actually tank an economy, but that's someone else's troubles, right? And if you've ever wondered why modern coins have milled or serrated edges, it's because milling makes clipping hard to hide. Not that minting matters much anymore. After all, cash was never anything but a conveniently portable metaphor for the things it might buy: corn, cows, chickens, land, salt, wine, whatever. These days, we have even more abstract metaphors, such as ATMs, EFTs, direct deposit, debit cards, credit cards, electronic checks, even microchip transceivers that let you charge what you want to your cell phone. Someone sufficiently wired into the virtual money motif could go weeks or months without handling any actual cash, and only know his worth for sure by dint of his bank statement. And if the bank isn't telling the truth? If the bank shaves a cent off his total every month, how will he ever know? He won't—no more than the guy you hand a clipped coin to can tell it's been clipped.* Thus we have an updated version of a venerable snadoodle called the Penny Skim, a scam predicated on the fact that it's impossible to go broke a penny at a time—but quite possible to get rich that way. Especially if you're working the Penny Skim on as vast a revenue pool as, say, the People's Republic of China, where all the money is.

---

*In 1559, that is, before milling.

Fun? Oh, hell, yeah. Catnip to a grifter. And when Yuan invited me to be part of it, I didn't think twice. Sure there were questions of feasibility, risk, and especially trust, but if Neil Armstrong offered you a ride to the moon, wouldn't you strap in first and ask questions later?

I had some trouble grasping the magnitude of the grift. Of course I was familiar with the concept: If you think about it, anytime anyone shortchanges someone, it's a penny skim of a sort. The last time I'd worked this snuke, I'd been . . . let's see . . . treasurer of the Oconomowoc Businessmen's Association. I moved their money through so many different accounts—applying the tiniest financial friction to each transaction—that by the time I retired from my post and repaired to sunnier climes, I'd cleaned them out six times over—and they still didn't know, because you can't go broke a penny at a time. Don't lose sleep; the organization was nothing more than a strip-club slush fund to begin with.

But what Yuan contemplated was so audacious that it stretched my imagination to the snapping point. Could you really skim an entire nation's economy? Billy seemed to think so.

All banks, he explained, need centralized operations in order to function efficiently. You certainly see it in a piggy bank—without the deposit slot, it's just a ceramic pig. At a neighborhood bank, it's the president or one of his minions who stands over the shutoff valve. Even your local loan shark will vest decision-making authority in someone's hands—perhaps those hands will be holding a baseball bat and squaring up on your kneecaps. As banks grow in size and complexity, the need for centralization grows accordingly, so that every financial institution, even (or especially) a national one, has some sort of organizational choke point. That's what Billy had been looking for when Scovil and her pals caught him hacking into the Reserve Bank.

"That were never a hack, though," he said. "I was just having a squiz."

"Squiz?"

"A look around."

And his investigation led him to two new thoughts. First, though a national bank is orders of magnitude larger than local banks, it's not orders of magnitude more sophisticated or secure—less, in fact, because the need for centralized operation makes the choke point that much larger and easier to spot. Second, free societies have *way* too much transparency. If you want to steal without being seen, you're better off working in a secret system, where such theft is already institutionalized as graft and corruption.

"Think about it," said Billy. "If you're skimming from your people (and don't tell me in China they're not) the last thing you want is easy accountability, yeh? So all we need is a way into the tent." He smiled fiendishly. "It's already nice and dark in there."

I was, of course, interested in what Billy fancied as a way in, but something else caught my ear, a certain spasm of enthusiasm in his voice that went beyond mere avarice. Why was he so keen to rob China in particular? This needed exploring, but tangentially. "How do you know?" I asked. "Spend a lot of time there?"

"Never set foot there in my life," he said. Nor, he added, did he want to. And here Billy made a kind of mistake: he overanswered the question. Told me how his industrious parents' prosperity had been destroyed by greedy Party officials, who picked them clean and drove them from the country. He didn't come right out and say it, but I vibed it; this was a revenge tip. After all, they're plenty rich in Qatar, right? Switzerland. The Vatican. And equally cloaked in secrecy. So why make China the target? Not just because that's where the money was—that's where his hate lay. I wondered if this would be a problem. Hate can make a man lose focus.

And if you're planning to rob an entire country, the last thing you want to lose is focus.

2 1.

the bite and the bark

When two grifters commit to a common con, there's no paperwork, no handshake, barely even acknowledgement that agreement has been reached. You just move smoothly and seamlessly from proposal to planning, with the understanding that task, command, risk, and reward will all be equally shared. I'm not saying that such partnerships are arrived at lightly; given the bedrock mendacity of the trade, you've never met such a look-before-leap crowd in your life. But we know there's no point in saying anything or signing anything, since the whole model for our business is the subversion of that which is said or signed. So we make no effort to spell shit out. We just have faith. If you can't have faith, you don't team up.

And if your faith is betrayed? I suppose the unspoken assumption is there's always some way to make your partner get dead.

I had no trouble having faith. That may seem shocking, considering all the ridiculous funhouse mirrors I'd been looking in lately. But of everyone I'd met from Allie forward, I felt I could trust Billy Yuan. He had that light in his eyes: a total commitment to the con. I knew he would see this thing through.

I knew also that he needed me, which made a huge difference and gave me huge leverage, for he was the bite and I was the bark.

In grifter slang, the bite is the person who works behind the scenes to set everything up, and the bark is the face of the con. To take a low-tech example, if you're working a driveway resealing scam, the bark will be schmoozing the mark while the bite is off preparing the bogus hot-mix asphalt, a slurry of oil and water that will wash off in the first good rain. A top grifter, of course, can work both the bark and the bite, but let's face it, everyone has their strengths. While I know my way around a website, there's no way I can climb walls of data security like Billy. By the same token, though Billy had a certain gift of gab, he couldn't do what I can do: sell you Ebola virus and do repeat business while you're coughing up blood. So we yinned each other's yangs. We both knew it, too. Looking back, it was mutual admiration at first sight.

Which didn't in any way reduce the number of hazardous land mines. Despite Billy's confidence that "all we need is a way into the tent," there was no guarantee that he could find the Chinese choke point, nor that I could talk us past it. It would take a ton of work and a ton of luck just to put the major pieces of the snuke into play. Nor did we have entire freedom of movement. With Scovil thinking Billy had made me and Hines thinking I was Billy's mark, our every step would have to pass two separate and largely contradictory sniff tests. Could Mirplo help? He'd been flipped, but would he stay flipped? Or would he have to be kept in his own little circle of dark?

And what about the elephant in the living room? It was time for some straight talk about her.

We discussed Allie at length. I mean serious length. Before we were done, the skate rats had skated off, the chess players had packed up their board and gone home, and the junior lovers had had a fight and broken up. Day turned to dusk, leaving the only light the cheesy glow of the artificial fire in the fire pit. And still we were no closer to getting Allie than we'd been at the start. Was she straight or bent? A grifter? A Jake? Both? Neither? We couldn't tell. No matter how we counted her, she didn't add up. In this, at least, she earned our awe, for she'd addled the brains of top grifters on two continents, and that's certainly not nothing.

They'd met outside a pub, Billy's local in a backwater part of Sydney, though what Allie had been doing so far off the tourist track had never been adequately explained. Their meeting seemed innocent enough—she'd asked him to take her picture—but in retrospect, Billy felt that they'd met rather more by design than by accident.

Yeah, that rang a bell.

"She had this ridiculous hat," said Billy. "An outback hat with corks hanging all around the rim. The tourists buy them. She posed with it on and then made me pose with it on. I felt a right fool." *Steal status,* I thought. She'd probably readjusted the hat *just so,* and then told him how cute he looked. "We shouted each other some drinks and got to talking. She asked what I did for work. Mostly when people ask that, I tell them 'consultant.' "

"But Allie got the truth out of you?"

"Yeh, she did."

"Yeah, she does."

"And I can tell you she nearly wet her knickers when I told her. Wanted to know all about it. There didn't seem any harm in telling her. She was just this sugary tourist, yeh?"

"She put you up on an outlaw pedestal."

"And looked right up my fucking skirt." I was sure Billy didn't tell Allie anything about the grift that she didn't already know. He had come to suspect the same thing, for they soon started working some yaks together. "And she was just amazingly good. To the manner born."

"A natural bark," I agreed. "What kind of jobs did you pull?"

"Sidewalk cons. Day entertainment. Aussies are a credulous lot. They can be had pretty regularly for small sums."

"Did she ever suggest stepping up?"

"No, that was my idea."

"You wanted her help with the Penny Skim."

"I did. It needs an American face."

"Was she game?"

"Not at all. She said that grifting was good holiday fun, but she couldn't see doing it full-time."

"And yet," I said, "it's what she does. Full-time."

"So she lied."

"News flash. Allie lies. Film at eleven."

"Too right." Billy essayed a wry smile. "Anyway, then she was gone, you know? Just one day gone." He paused, looking wistful. "Do you know, I think I was half glad when I had to leave Oz. I thought I might look her up over here. Instead I get you."

"Sorry about that."

"Well, whatever."

We parted company around eight, arranging to communicate from that point forward through anonymous e-mail drop boxes and throwaway cell phones. There was, of course, the possibility that our phones were tapped, in which case Tweedledee and Tweedlestupid (Scovil and Hines) were already onto us, or soon would be. About that there was nothing we could do, but why give them further easy targets to hit? And if they busted us on it, we'd both insist that each was just easing the other in.

We also worked out a verbal code, in case we happened to need to communicate meaningfully with each other in front of others. This entailed embedding some no-means-yes switches in our speech, so that we could stay on the same page no matter how convoluted our explanations or prevarications became. In addition, we compared our respective cryptolects, the natural dialect that develops among thieves, grifters, or any underground affinity group. Here in America, grifter slang is much the bastard child of carny talk, while in Australia it has many roots: Gypsy jargon, rhyming slang, convict cant. For example, my word for an easy mark was *mook*, while Billy's was *gudgeon*, a type of fish. Slang provides an organic sort of code, but it would take some doing to harmonize ours.

Of rather more pressing urgency was the need to burn down the house for Hines. The safe move, of course, was simply to do it and be done with it, let Hines have his own little offshore 401(k). Yet it kind of offended my sensibilities to just hand over the spoils of my grift. After all, what had Hines done apart from providing a list of qualified leads? And while we're on that subject, how did a bent fibbie gain access to so juicy a pool of mooks? Was there a master government list of major fraud victims somewhere? Every grifter knows that chronic dupes make the best customers; presumably the feds know this, too. Still the problem remained, how could I balk burning down the house without— possibly homicidally—pissing him off?

The answer lay in Billy's ambition to rob China. An operation like that needs seed money. What better source of funds than a simple rollover of the Merlin Game? Hines wouldn't like it but perhaps could be made to like it if he saw it as an investment in an even bigger payout. In a sense, I'd be holding his money hostage to his greater greed. This appealed to me, for it kept the cash in my pocket, and rather kept Hines there too. He might be a fibbie, but he was also a mark, and the classic strategy for holding the mark is equal parts promise and threat. As long as I had the money, Hines had to fear that he might not get it. But the promise of a mind-numbingly huge payday . . . yeah, that felt like a carrot I could dangle.

I went home and crashed for a few hours, then woke up and started

pushing the many buttons to close out the Merlin Game. My ripe targets got urgent instructions to act now or risk missing out on "the
biggest score in the history of ever." I knew they wouldn't all come
across—marks get cold feet—but statistic history taught that enough
of them would jump in to make the play pay. I told them where to wire
their instruments of deposit, and it was not to Hines's little Liechtenstein S&L. I launched everything from my laptop, which I still assumed
was gaffed, but now that was okay. Let Hines discover for himself that
his money had gone walkabout, and let him stew in his own self-
righteous juices till his anger boiled over. It was all part of the plan.

Not part of the plan was the predawn instant message I got from
Allie. How did she know my IM handle? I didn't even bother to ask. By
now she probably knew my shoe size.

My computer booped its signal for incoming traffic, and a message
popped up in a box.

```
Hola paco. Que tal?
```

I checked for the sender's name, and typed back,

```
Miss Terious? Is that the best you can do?
- Wanted u to know it was me. What r u doing?
- Playing cribbage.
- Who with?
- No one.
- Solo cribbage? Sounds dull.
- Gets me through the night.
- Well, then, "fifteen two and the rest won't do."
- u play cribbage?
- strip cribbage. Great game.
```

It went on like that for a while. Then the subject of pancakes came
up, one thing led to another, and we ended up meeting at Rudi's

Eatateria, the place we'd first gone to parse the engagement of Allie Quinn and Ryan Paradox Reed. That seemed long ago now.

I got to the restaurant first and waited outside, watching the passing industrious dawn patrol: fruit and vegetable trucks, delivery vans, and workers of all color of collar getting a jump on their long morning drives. God, I'd hate to be a citizen. The commute alone would kill me.

When Allie walked up, I looked past her for signs of company known or unknown.

"There's no one with me, Radar," she said—wearily, I thought. "We don't work like that." I shrugged and opened the door for her.

Allie didn't look great. Maybe it was the waxy light of Rudi's washing her face gray, but I swear she looked like she'd aged. I took this on board. She was showing signs of stress, and stress is pretty hard to fake. You might grimace instead of grin, but how do you forge the furrow of a brow?

We slid into a booth. Not the same one where we'd concocted our faux romance; that would've been too much irony. But I could look across the diner and see the ghost of that earlier conversation. I wondered if Allie saw it too. I wondered if it sprayed her with the same wistful mist.

We ordered pancake stacks and questionable coffee, and chitchatted while we waited to be served. For some reason, Allie insisted on deconstructing a movie she'd seen recently, a nitwit legal comedy called *Trial by Jerry.* It seemed like she was trying to establish her bona fides as a normal person. She must've caught my eyes glazing over, because she stopped herself in mid-review and said, "You don't really give a rat's ass, do you?"

"I'm not much for movies," I admitted. "Real life is strange enough."

"Yours is."

"Yours isn't?"

She chewed on her lower lip, lost in thought, as if the question had never crossed her mind. As the waitress delivered our order, I could see her looking at the pair of us, measuring us, fitting us into her pantheon of customers. Were we lovers, junkies, late-nighters or early risers? And how did any of that stack up against her own sense of self: hardworking, long-suffering eternal denizen of the graveyard shift? It reminded me once again that the view from inside our own skin is everybody's baseline. It may never have occurred to Allie that her life was at all strange. Or maybe she was just setting me up for another misdirectomy. At last she said, "Radar, can I tell you the truth?"

"Would this be the true truth or just the current version?"

"I understand that you can't trust me. Maybe if you knew what I'd been through, you'd know why I've done what I've done."

"So tell me." I took a sip of bad coffee. "I'm all ears."

Skeptical ears, but ears just the same.

queen of the motel 6

Allie Quinn was born during the trickle-down years of the Reagan presidency. Her father, an aging Vietnam vet with undiagnosed post-traumatic stress syndrome, aggressively self-medicated with alcohol. Her mother was a classic codependent who enabled daddy's drinking through sunny denial and periodic off-label pharma binges of her own. As neither was terribly adept at getting or holding jobs, they turned to such career builders as shoplifting, check kiting, and serial bankruptcy. This led to short stints in jail or, more commonly, hasty midnight departures for parts unknown. As some children will in such circumstances, Allie became self-sufficient, tough, and capable, a parent to her increasingly disabled parents. Though she attended school only sporadically, she read like a mad fiend and trained herself up in matters both esoteric (planetary astronomy) and practical (how to drive a car when both parents are too fucked up to move). She became comfortable with the dysfunctional family's nomadic ways and even crowned herself Queen of the Motel 6, complete with a self-mocking tiara made of aluminum foil and a robe stitched together from motel towels.

The grim fairy-tale phase of her life ended on her tenth birthday when her dad got macho at a railroad crossing and discovered the hard way that trains don't give a damn about macho. Mother and daughter soldiered bravely on for a short while until Mother, who felt lonely and edgy and itchy, made the spectacularly bad choice of hooking up with a cokehead in transition to crackhead and willingly went along for that ride. This left Allie navigating a whole new minefield of drug-fueled domestic violence.

On the upside, she had a nice trailer to live in.

But that didn't last long. Mommy's boyfriend decided to branch out into the exciting new world of crystal meth production (because who wouldn't naturally look to a cooked combination of ether, Drāno, and battery acid for a terrific high?). This led to Allie coming home one day to find that home had been replaced by a smoking hole in the ground.

Then began the foster-care parade, and preteen Allie learned that almost all foster dads (and not a few foster moms) considered groping their ersatz daughter to be one of the perks of the job. By the time she reached menarche, she'd been felt up so many times that it ceased to register as anything other than a natural part of the ritual of living with strangers. But when they started feeling her *down* . . .

Allie hit the road. Her innate cleverness and resourcefulness kept her from the clutches of pimps, and the memory of her mother's corkscrew descent steered her away from the insidious trap of drugs. By luck, or the affinitive attraction of like to like, Allie fell in with a reasonably competent grifter who taught her many useful short cons, the kind of street-level snukes that could keep a pretty, clever girl pretty well fed.

But then he raped her, and that kind of put a damper on that.

Allie skated America, favoring midsize cities like St. Louis, Youngstown, and New Orleans, places big enough to offer anonymity and soft targets, yet not so huge as to overwhelm a skinny, fragile thing who, despite a rapidly thickening shell, remained all brittle and broken inside. She developed the wariness of a feral cat and a jumpy instinct for self-preservation. Instinct, of course, is no match for a knife or a gun; she was assaulted and robbed more times than she could count.

Libraries were her salvation. Not only did they provide safe haven—uninterrupted hours off the street—they also let her leave her life behind. Buried in a book, whether *Treasure Island* or *Spanish for Beginners,* she disappeared from the world and entered a place with no past, no future, only the perfect floating now. Books were her drug, a fortuitously positive addiction that gave her a broad understanding of the real tools of her trade: human psychology, the romantic tug of good fiction, and sufficient general knowledge to lie plausibly in most situations.

Still, she made mistakes, bad ones, for a learning curve is yet a curve, no matter how steep. She built a fake escort ring that either ripped off the johns or blackmailed them and left her feeling as dirty as if she'd put actual dicks in her mouth. She drove a getaway car in a bank robbery in which a guard was almost killed. She had no notion of sin, for neither her parents nor the fabulous fosters had shed much spiritual light on her life, but a strong internal gyroscope told her she was spinning the wrong way.

Allie went straight for a time, scoring well enough on her high school GED to get into a community college in Gainesville, Florida. There she shared a townhouse with girls from conventional backgrounds and absorbed their ways. She got a job, a boyfriend, a car, but never held any of these things at anything less than arm's length. She seemed not to be living her life but just watching it, like a documentary on Polynesia in her Anthro 101 class.

One night, working late as a hostess at the local TGI Friday's, she fell into a lively conversation with a bright, handsome couple heading down to Miami to work a real estate scam in that city's superheated housing market. Talking with them, listening and learning, Allie felt something awaken in her: the sense of stimulation that had lately fallen out of her life. She couldn't know it, but she was hooked on that stimulation, and her cold-turkey college approach was simply not going to work. More than that, this couple infatuated her, for they were masters of infatuation, and though Allie fancied herself tough, she was yet nothing but a soft mark. Oh the promises they made! With their millennial perspective and off-the-cuff morality, they offered the best of both worlds: a life outside the square, yet squarely on the "victimless" side of crime. So Allie dropped everything—job, boyfriend, and college education—and went south with the couple to surf the land boom and make herself rich.

They betrayed her, fleeced her, and left her for broke.

After that, Allie gripped the grift with a vengeance and milked every new mark with the ferocious intensity of a woman trying to buy back a lifetime of tears and abuse one overwrought dollar at a time. She became a paragon of the con: cunning, cold, and utterly unsympathetic to the swath of destruction she left in her wake.

It was the swath of destruction that brought her to the attention of the FBI, for Allie got involved in some pretty high-level stuff: securities fraud, tax shelters, and most particularly a bogus overseas charity that tracked close enough to a front for terrorist operations to bring down the full heat of the fraud task force to which a particular fibbie had lately been attached. This was no laughing matter. Though Allie considered herself "just an innocent grifter," her enterprise fit the sort of profile that was sending people up on twenty-year bids. But Hines saw the canny ability in her and thought she'd be much more use to the cause of law enforcement as a sort of super-informant, free to use her talents as she chose, so long as Hines could pad his arrest record with her unwitting accomplices. Allie knew a deal with the devil when she saw it, but the prospect of prison left her little wiggle room.

It quickly became clear to Allie that she had merely traded one form of prison for another. As Hines's pet, she was a weird sort of kept woman, earning her keep not through sex but through the routine abuse of those who should have been her natural partners, colleagues, and peers. The real trouble was, she *liked* grifters. The more time she spent in their company, setting them up and selling them out, the more she came to feel she was working for the wrong guys. But Hines kept her on a short leash and made it clear that the second she crossed him, her official sanction would vanish and that would be the end of Allie on the street. Over time, Allie noticed, Hines managed to dip his beak in almost every bust, opportunistically diverting available cash and liquid securities from the evidence chain. He didn't much mind that Allie knew; who cares what your pet sees? Lately, though, that had started to change. Hines was a jangle of nerves, constantly looking over his own shoulder and under his own bed. Allie felt that only the prospect of nabbing two major players like Radar and Billy now kept her in the game. With presumed powers-that-be closing in on Hines, would he come to contemplate putting his pet to sleep? Was she suddenly the woman who knew too much?

Did I believe her?

I did. I thought it added up. It was Occam's razor again with this explanation the simplest one that fit the facts. In particular, it rationalized all of Allie's moves against me, and made them make sense. She'd neither been testing me nor vetting me; she'd just been stringing Hines along.

Now with this new player, Scovil, the string was running out.

I've said it's hard to forge stress. I think it's also hard to fake fear. I decided to treat Allie's as true. She was a spy coming in from the cold. Into the comforting arms of Uncle Radar. And how would Uncle Radar use this new scared and skittish ally? I hadn't worked that part out yet, but I figured that comfort, at least, was called for.

I dipped a fingertip in a puddle of maple syrup on my plate, reached across and pressed it to her forearm, then gently pulled it away. Held together by surface tension, a sugary string lifted some downy hairs. Then the surface tension broke and the hairs fell back, bedewed with syrup. I'm not sure what I expected to convey by this, but looking up I could see Allie's features soften. She recognized the tenderness there, and it became clear that if I was prepared to buy Allie's story, she was prepared to buy my acceptance. We had reached a rapprochement.

So, for the second time in two days, I made Anschluss with another practitioner of my odd craft. Each partnership was unlikely in its way. With Billy, I didn't have nearly enough history to make the judgment of trust, and with Allie, I already had way too much. But a grifter goes with his gut. If you can't do that, you end up second-guessing yourself at critical times, and then you end up dead or in jail. With Allie in particular, it was a huge relief to unload my doubt. I felt as though two irreconcilable pieces of me were suddenly in harmony. It's not just that I wanted her again, or still (I did, of course). I just much preferred to think of her as indentured to Hines rather than working willingly for him. In other words, harlot no, helot yes.

And the horrors of her past? What of them? So she was damaged goods. Who isn't? Are you telling me you escaped your childhood unscathed? I think you're forgetting your parents' casual neglect, or the tyranny of your older siblings, or rough treatment by a teacher or bully. Teenage heartbreak. Something. Maybe just the burden of self-awareness at an age when self-awareness is a tool we can't handle. Does it take a truly ruinous past to cast a grifter? Probably, but so what? Even if I think I'm normal, I don't imagine I'm the norm. At that, I'm just trying to get from one end of my life to the other with a reasonable amount of sanity and happiness, just like everybody else. If someone like Allie comes along and we can make common cause, that's great. If we can forge something more lasting, that's a damn miracle.

At that point, though, I wasn't thinking much past the necessary moves for the day ahead. Among other things, Scovil would need a report. I'd tell her that Billy had made me, rated me, and welcomed me onto his team—I was still her bitch, though, and awaiting further instructions. That was a reasonably accurate version of things, all except the me-being-her-bitch part. Hines, meanwhile, would get a different tale. Since he believed that Billy bought me as a trust fund baby, I would now tell him that Billy had offered to deal Chad Thurston into a play that would sound to Hines's jaundiced ears (though not to Thurston's innocent ones) like the Penny Skim. Thurston, the putative guileless pup, would of course have signed on, but the price of admission was a rather large wad of cash, and since real-world Radar Hoverlander wasn't well heeled like simulacrum Chad Thurston, the money would have to come from elsewhere. This would be the logic of using the take from the Merlin Game simultaneously as seed money for the Penny Skim and bait for Billy Yuan. I knew that both sides of that equation would appeal to Hines, and I would lead him to believe that he could have it both ways. He could bust Yuan and also dip his beak in an obscenely larger birdbath. That Hines knew about the Skim—had heard about it from Allie during her post-Australia debriefing—would only serve to harden the mortar around his assumptions.

Now all that had to happen was for Scovil and Hines not to compare notes. I knew they weren't best buddies, but they were still at least notionally colleagues, and they would share such information as they could safely share without giving away their own backdoor plans. What I needed was a firewall between them, a barrier of mistrust that would make them unwilling to trade secrets. That's where Allie came in. She already had Hines's ear. She would need to persuade him—not that he'd need much persuading—that Scovil was not to be trusted and must be kept in the murk.

Unfortunately, she couldn't similarly reach out to Scovil, for Scovil knew that Allie was Hines's chattel and would naturally figure she was also his mouthpiece. Okay, then, whose word would Scovil take? Not mine, for what could I possibly know about the real Milval Hines? And not Billy's—he and Scovil couldn't meet until the endgame. Well, that just left . . .

Vic Mirplo. The original blunt instrument.

Time to sharpen it up.

Allie and I stepped outside the restaurant and prepared to part company. She had to see Hines, to warn him off Scovil, and I had to go prep the world's worst liar to sell a lie, which I could only do by making him think it was truth. And yes, that meant lying to Vic, whom hadn't I brought into my confidence? But this I figured to be a necessary evil, as I rated myself more likely to lie convincingly to Vic than Vic likely to lie convincingly to a grade-schooler or a corpse. Anyway, it was for his own good. If I managed to finesse my way out of this bind, I'd be taking him with me.

Of course, that was still a fairly jumbo-size if. Well, one thing at a time. Next on the agenda was kissing Allie good-bye.

That makes it sound premeditated, but it wasn't. I just knew that the deal needed sealing. If nothing else, it would confirm that we could kiss as two (reasonably) honest people. I guess Allie had arrived at the same unpremeditated meditation, for I found her lips waiting for mine.

Kissing Allie this time was a totally different experience. Gone was the fierce erotica, replaced by the sacred grace of her chrismal tongue. Residual maple syrup lent a tacky, sweet overtone, but we really didn't need it. We kissed like a movie kiss, and like a movie kiss, it was utterly authentic because we willingly suspended our disbelief. We kissed like bubble gum, like prom night, like the top of a Ferris wheel. We kissed for the benefit of the sad commuters who passed us by in their hapless transits from heavily mortgaged homes to soul-killing dead-end jobs. We kissed for our freedom. We kissed for our lives. And by the time we were done kissing, I was about 75 percent in love.

value town

I t no longer served my purpose to work on a compromised computer, so I drove over to Value Town, a pirate electronics store that
operates out of the back of a boba tea shop in Monterey Park. Value
Town carries a line of goods you're not likely to find at Best Buy, such
as weapons-grade tasers, DV descramblers, and the thing I was after,
an aftermarket laptop tricked out with the latest anonymizers, cookie
crunchers, RPGs (random password generators), and ISP baffles. I
selected a hardware platform, then chose from a tasty menu of options,
including something I'd never seen before, a fail-safe fingerprint sensor
that would wipe the hard drive if it detected the wrong hands on the
keyboard. Wow. The owner of Value Town was a sunny Thai illegal
named Charoenrasamee—Chuck to her friends. As she spooled up the
operating system on my new laptop, my thoughts turned back to the
odd USB plug-in I'd seen at Allie's "apartment." I asked Chuck about it.
At first it rang no bell, but when I described its size, shape, and func-
tionality (according to Hines, it could do everything but slice bread),
her eyes lit up and she said, "Ah, you mean Hackmaster 6000!"

"Of course I do," I said. "What else would I mean?"

The Hackmaster 6000 turned out to be a daughter-of-necessity invention first thought up in some federal spook shop in the ugly early days after 9/11, but not actually brought online until late last year. Sort of the Swiss Army knife of wireless cards, it linked to the internet via proprietary government broadband frequencies and featured a most impressive array of AI spiders, password mimes, active and passive data traps, and inbound and outbound GPS. In the time it takes to call the play, the Hackmaster 6000 could search, cull, harvest, and rationalize every available bit or byte about you, from your high school test scores to that speeding ticket you got in Reno that time, and even the name of the hooker in the car with you when you got popped.

The government, of course, didn't call it the Hackmaster 6000. That was its street name, for no sooner had it gone into production than clones started turning up as curios in places like Value Town. It was a tough tool to use well, Chuck told me, because for all its advanced stealth technology, it left a detectable trail of electronic breadcrumbs. If you assumed that someone was watching (and it's always healthy to assume that someone is), it was likely only a matter of time before the fact of your fact-finding mission would surface some-where. For someone on the inside, like Hines, that wouldn't matter, but for me it made the Hackmaster only a hit-and-run tool at best.

Still, a tool is a tool. "You don't happen to have one?" I asked.

"I have!" said Chuck. "This Valu' Town!"

She reached under the counter and pulled out a plastic bag con-taining a matte black cartridge similar to the one Hines had had—except that this one bore the logo of a smiling, dancing tiger.

"What's with the cat?" I asked.

"Private brand," she said. "Valu' Town special. It do tricks!"

"What kind of tricks?"

"You read manual." She opened the bag and took out a hand-Xeroxed, -folded, and -stapled instruction manual written in charm-ingly fractured English. I read the first sentence—"Hackmaster 6000 are first name on digital survalence, not for childrens"—and decided to save it for later. Chuck tapped the Hackmaster with her purple lacquered fingernail. "Last one," she said brightly. "Bargain price."

Chuck's idea of a bargain price could have kept her extended family in boba tea for a year, but she bundled it together with the new computer, rounded the whole thing up to an extravagant number, then discounted it back down to a reasonable sum, and sold me the whole package for that. This was how Chuck did business. She haggled with herself, and seemed to enjoy both sides of the negotiation. "Thank you for shopping Valu' Town," she intoned in her delightful singsong as I left. "Tell your friends." *This,* I thought, *is what makes America great.*

I didn't go home. I needed to work awhile without interruption, and considering all the people who had lately made my joint their crossroads, I thought a Java Man would serve me better, so I selected the one closest to Value Town (a mere stone's throw, like they all are) and set up shop there. It took me some time to get used to the new laptop. Though sleeker and faster than my old box, it lacked my familiar shortcuts, and I really didn't feel comfortable until I had those all dialed in.

After that, I checked on how the Merlin Game was paying off, and was gratified to see returns running ahead of projection, both in absolute numbers and average handle. To tell the truth, not having run a Merlin Game in a few years, I wasn't altogether sure how it would play out. The pick trick brings them in, of course, but in the end, it's all about the bafflegab, and you like to think your pitch is still sharp, even after a long layoff. Seeing the mooks rise so avidly to the bait gave me some confidence as I looked ahead to the Penny Skim, because there the sell would be a good deal harder. It's not that you have to convince people to be greedy. The greedy ones are greedy by nature and need no convincing, and the others never even notice you, so it's kind of self-selecting. Nor was it the prospect of working in Mandarin (not my strongest language, but I muddle through, *ni hao*). The thing is, my targets would be newbies, virgins, innocent to the grift, for IT professionals high up in the Chinese central banking system had likely never been approached by a Western-style scam artist before. And while you might think this would make them soft targets, in fact the opposite was true. They wouldn't naturally recognize the benefits being offered to them, and they'd need spoon-fed assurances that the yak was plausible, profitable, doable, and safe. They'd have to learn to believe in the magic of something for nothing.

I'd have to get my teaching chops on. In Mandarin, no less.

It occurred to me that Billy might have Mandarin (though this was by no means given—who knows what immigrants teach their kids at home?), and I shot him a quick IM to find out. I used one of our agreed-upon ghost accounts, but got no response, which was odd, because I knew he'd slaved his IM to his new cash-and-carry cell phone, and we'd kind of agreed to keep those phones always on. I tried him again a little while later, but still nothing, so I dialed him up.

The phone rang about five times before Billy answered. "*Pronto,*" he said—and I nearly sprained a finger stabbing *end call*, because *pronto*, while it's how they answer a call in Italy or in certain pretentious circles of Eurotrash wannabes, was also one of our predetermined code words. In this case, the code meant *can't talk now—compromised situation.*

After a moment, my phone lit up, signaling an incoming call. Caller ID told me it was Billy calling back. Some instinct told me to just listen, and I did. Good thing, because Billy had surreptitiously managed to open the line, so that I could hear the conversation he was having. The voices were muffled—probably the phone was in his pocket—but I could easily make out the speakers. One was obviously Billy.

The other?

Sigh.

Hines.

"Are you certain you haven't seen him?" asked Hines.

"Not for a couple of days," answered Billy, in a tone of such sincere helpfulness that even I bought it—for a moment I thought I was wrong about the guy. But then he added, "I'm sorry I can't be more help, Mr. Thurston."

Mr. Thurston? *Ah-ha!* Hines was representing himself to Billy as Chad Thurston's dad, and why not? I'd told Hines about the picture of filial conflict I'd painted for Yuan. No doubt he was playing the aggrieved father come to town in search of his wayward son. Billy, of course, knew there was no Chad Thurston III. Did he know this was Hines? Probably he could guess, but in any case he'd do nothing but play it safe and play along.

"Give me your number," said Billy. "I'll call you if he gets in touch."

"You do that," said Hines. Then I heard him jack up the tenor of threat in his voice as he added, "Listen carefully, young man. My son is very impressionable, and prone to bad decisions. Under no circumstances are you to accept money from him, do you understand?"

"Why would he give me money?" asked Billy.

Hines must have realized he'd overplayed his hand. He backed and filled quickly. "He's . . . the boy's deranged," he stammered. "He likes to give money away."

I chuckled silently. What a lame cover. It showed that Hines wasn't thinking things through. Indeed, I thought, Hines's whole line of play was weak here, ill considered and rushed. How he'd managed to track down Yuan I don't know, but he did have a Hackmaster, and he also had Allie, who couldn't reasonably deny him information about Yuan without tipping her loyalty shift. Nor could I guess why Hines had decided to go this route in the first place. Did he see some hidden advantage in introducing Chad Thurston père into the mix, or was he just losing the plot? Either way, I knew I'd have to meet with him right away and chill him out. I didn't want his anger peaking too soon. He was liable to just start busting people (or heads) and queer the deal for everyone.

So I disconnected Billy's call, grabbed my other phone and punched up Hines's cell. He didn't answer—I hadn't expected him to—and the call went to voice mail. I left a message about a hiccup with the Merlin Game, something that would make it seem like the money had not gone where the money was supposed to go. I assured him that this was an accident, easily fixed, but that we should get together right away and discuss the ramifications.

Next I phoned Mirplo and fed him the mislead that Hines wasn't a bent cop after all. Rather, he was working an internal-affairs investigation on his own bureau, trying to uncover cops who *were* bent. I told Vic to contact Scovil and alert her to this. He didn't ask why, which was good, because there was no way I could make the logic of that disinformation stand up. But that's the beauty of a Mirplo: they act first and forget to ask questions later. As for Scovil, I doubted she'd fully take Mirplo's word for this, but it might cause her to break stride, which was the best I could manage for now. At a certain point in the con, your lies are like ball bearings. You just throw them all out across the floor and hope that someone slips on something.

Hines was waiting for me when I got home. I had a feeling he would be. I didn't expect him to be in exactly a Little Mary Sunshine frame of mind, nor did he disappoint. While I calmly washed, changed clothes, and fixed myself a grilled cheese sandwich, he raged around my apartment calling me unspeakable names. But I thought his rage seemed a little theatrical. He must have realized that I had (A) his money, and (2) therefore him over a certain barrel. I tried to see myself from Hines's point of view. Here was a con artist he thought he'd cowed and corralled, only to face some bullshit story about the money "accidentally" going astray. He didn't buy it but probably wondered what he could do about it. Turning up the bluster wasn't the only move that came to his mind, no doubt. He may have considered arresting me, shooting me, or just kicking my ass. But he had to save those moves for later. For now, he'd try to do the least he could do to regain control of the situation. Which meant hissing and posturing like a puff adder.

I must admit it felt good watching him go all Sturm und Drang around my apartment. What had he expected from me? Fair play? Come on—is it not my job to outthink guys like Hines? Should he not have realized that I'd have never caught his eye in the first place if I weren't damn good at what I do? In other words, the mere fact that he knew of me meant he shouldn't underestimate me.

Yeah, but that's the ego talking, isn't it? I paused to remind myself (as I flipped the grilled cheese sandwich over in the pan) that this wasn't in any sense a dick-measuring contest between us. After all, what good would it do to send him down in flames if his last, vengeful act was to take me down, too? Of this he was certainly capable, and I'd do well not to underestimate him. A puff adder might be a vicious, stupid, cowardly snake, but it's a snake just the same.

And what do you do with a snake?

Charm it.

"Grilled cheese?" I asked. Hines looked at me like I'd just landed from Mars. "Come on," I encouraged. "A man's got to eat, right?"

"Fuck food," he said. "Just tell me where's my money."

"Ah, that," I said. I didn't see any point in bothering with an "I know you don't trust me" preamble, and so instead launched straight into the bafflegab. "You understand that I couldn't send the money straight to Liechtenstein, right?"

"Why the hell not?"

"Paper trail," I said. "Think about the high rollers we're dealing with here. You think none of them have been scammed before?" Judging by Hines's reaction, I knew I'd pinged a true target—that he had, in fact, gathered his candidate list for the Merlin Game from prior victims of cons, perhaps even some of mine. "And some of those scams were likely tax dodges, no?" I could see Hines repress a nod. "Which puts at least some of our marks on IRS radar, who will then surely have sentinels monitoring their outbound transactions." I had no idea if that was true, but it sounded good. "Well, look, the bank you gave me is a known offshore larder." Again, pure fabricat, but I figured that Hines must've learned about that bank somewhere, and government lists of black banks seemed as likely a somewhere as any. "If I'd sent the money there," I continued, "it would've rung alarm bells in half a dozen watchdog agencies, not just the IRS but the SEC and your friends at Hometown Buffet Security. Is that what you wanted?"

I could see that this put him back on his heels, so I pushed ahead. Once you get going on a good run of bafflegab, you just let momentum take over. "So I washed the money some. First I sent it to a folksy little ma-and-pa bank in Altoona. I've worked with them before. They have close ties to big mutual funds, so major money flowing through them doesn't raise eyebrows." Hines gave me this "go on" glare, and I knew he was on the hook for believing me. Which is remarkable because I was literally making this up as I went along. As I said, I like to improvise. "I let the money rest there for a day—that's why you didn't hear from me—then I cut it up into parcels."

"Why?"

"To chop the trail." I raised an eyebrow. "You never heard of trail chopping?" Not likely, since I'd just that instant invented it. "Next I bounced the parcels around. They passed through a Delaware shell corporation I own." Well, in my imagination I do. "And then to a Texas credit union with a sister bank in Mexico. So . . . over the border, down to Costa Rica, then across the South Atlantic to Zimbabwe. Now the beauty of Zimbabwe is their inflation rate is so high that the banks—"

"Just cut to the fucking chase, Hoverlander. Where did my money get lost?"

"Ah. Well, that would be France. In the end it was a language problem."

"Language?"

"Yeah, I wrote all the transaction orders in English, and apparently in France these days that's a no-go. They did the same thing with Google. French only, some bullshit. So now all the funds are in impound while I get a language waiver, whatever that is." I let disgust leak into my voice. "The fucking French, right? Anyway, it shouldn't be more than a day or two. France is the final rinse. Next stop Liechten-stein, and your money, all five hundred grand of it, will be nice and clean and fresh."

"Half a million?"

"Yeah, we did a little better than expected." Hines looked pleased at this. In his mind, his runaway retirement just got a little more comfy. Maybe . . . comfy enough for two?

A chill ran down my spine I don't know how I knew, I just knew. Maybe the faraway look in his eye suggested a picture where he wasn't alone. Or maybe it was just the final cylinder of a complex lock clicking into place in my head. Whatever. In that instant, I flashed on all the times I'd seen Hines with Allie, how he'd deferred to her. I'd thought it was part of their snuke, but suddenly I knew different. He had a crush on her, and his endgame for all this involved Allie running away with him, if not for affection then as a lesser-of-evils alternative to prison. Or death.

A whole different kind of chill ran down my spine. Man, I wanted to run just then. Just . . . drop everything, grab Allie, and run. But I knew that was a fool's paradigm. Hines, I now saw, was the whole lethal package: a bent cop trying to shade and fade; plus a vengeful fuck who wanted to put the hurt on poor Radar; plus, worst, a middle-aged horndog. He wouldn't let go. He'd scorch the earth before he let go. No, the only way out of this thing for me was through it. Spang-blam straight through the middle.

I have to admit that at that moment my confidence wobbled. Since meeting Billy, I had allowed myself to believe that with the prospect of robbing China I could easily lead Hines around by the greed-shaped ring in his nose. Now I wasn't sure. Suppose he just wasn't interested. After all, half a million should be enough to meet any crooked Jake's needs, right? Suppose he gave me forty-eight hours to get my so-called language waiver and then after that, called in his markers? If I gave him the money, he'd kill me to keep me quiet. If I didn't give him the money, he'd just kill me for spite. In his panic, he'd probably kill Allie, too, and anyone else he could think of. I couldn't have that. It was too messy an endgame. Plus too lethal.

So, okay, that meant I had to chum the waters and hope he liked the taste. Really, what else could I do? Time to put Chad Thurston to rest and reveal the formidable tag-team alliance of Billy Yuan and Radar Hoverlander.

"Listen," I said, "there's something else I want to talk to you about."

I slid the grilled cheese sandwich onto a plate and handed it to Hines.

After a moment, he took it.

moiré or less

Somewhere in the bowels of the information technology depart- ment of the People's Bank of China, IT manager Zhao Guixian had just received an e-mail. The wording and syntax, plus some eso- teric insider's slang, would seek to convince Zhao that the e-mail came from his opposite number in Taiwan's Central Bank of China. In fact, it came from my laptop, but a powerful address emulator (Chuck was right—the Hackmaster did *tricks*!) said otherwise. The e-mail took pains to couch its intent in circumlocution, but the gist was this: that certain code cowboys in the Central Bank's IT section had written some skim software, "just for fun." Now they were thinking about moving it out of the fun stage and into implementation, but the regu- latory atmosphere in Taipei was not conducive (i.e., too nosy), and would Mr. Zhao be interested in speaking to the regulatory atmo- sphere in Beijing?

Billy and I had worked on the pitch day and night for a week. That is, I had worked on the pitch while Billy backstopped my language choices (it turned out that, yes, he was fluent in Mandarin) and also refined the relevant software, which intended to exploit certain book- keeping lags and inefficiencies—friction, if you will—to grift the smallest fraction from any transaction. Though the amount of each skim was negligible, when you multiplied it by billions of transactions, the sum of the get would be exactly, uhm . . . a buttload. I, meanwhile, built a moiré effect into my pitch. In graphic design, a moiré effect is created by two sets of lines or dots imperfectly aligned so that other patterns emerge. Such patterns can be beguiling or distressing, but mostly what they do is occlude: They make things fuzzy. In the grift, a moiré effect is a sorting device that presents a pitch to prospective marks in terms that can be interpreted as an offer or a threat, depending on the mark's proclivities and point of view. It's self-selecting in the sense that those who consider it an offer come after it, and those who see it as a threat (those cowering cowards we don't want anyhow) just blow it off. Naturally, I wasn't putting all my eggs in one Zhao-shaped basket. Like every other grift, you separate the qualified leads from the chaff—but you don't want the chaff going around making noise. The moiré effect, with its veiled *you might be blamed for this* warning, assures that relevant whistles go unblown.

If Zhao doesn't respond, then, someone else will. Even a centralized system like a big bank has redundancies, and like every other part of China's bloated bureaucracy, the People's Bank IT department (in both the central branch and its many lucrative regional offices) was top-heavy with earnest wage earners desperate to stay ahead of the nation's rapidly steepening prosperity curve. For some, this meant keeping up with the Jianses in the rush for more appliances, better mopeds, and— God love them that they dare to dream—two-bedroom apartments. For others, it was the pressure of grease from above. When every palm must be crossed with silver, lest hopes for advancement be dashed, silver is a never-ending need. Now here comes an offer to partake in the nation's national pastime—corruption—cottage-industry style. Accept or decline the offer, that's moiré or less up to you. But be sure that if you don't, your brother will, and there's no point in ratting him out because then you'll just be passing the benefit up the food chain to someone who, let's face it, is already sucking at the public tit too much as it is.

Thus I put my prospectus out to every midlevel brain boy with access to the big bank's mainframe. Given the size of my target market, I projected that we'd get dozens of positive responses. More than enough for our purpose.

It was Sunday evening—Monday morning in Asia. We had just unleashed the pitch on China and were kicking back, congratulating ourselves on the completion of phase one. Allie had come over to my place, where, for convenience, Billy and I had set up shop. She'd brought Chinese food, which I thought was clichéd, but she offered it with ironic intent. Allie, Billy, and I had passed pretty quickly through the whole "I know you like me, but I'm dating him now" thing. To his credit, Billy had taken it in stride, and I thought I understood why, for there's nothing like an involving snuke to take your mind off your thwarted heart.

Mirplo was there, too, trying to interest everyone in a game of shenanigans, which is not the board game you may be thinking of, or the album by Green Day, but the grifters' version, where a gang of you invade a public place and at the drop of the code word— "Shenanigans!"—all start acting in some chaotic, random fashion. This can be just for fun or to create a diversion for other endeavors, like shoplifting. Vic wanted to hit the Glendale Galleria, open late for holiday shopping, but I vetoed. Last thing we needed in the middle of a major grift was a misdemeanor theft arrest.

I figured that Hines was watching the house, or having it watched, in which case he'd know that we four were hanging out. Was he cool with that? Hard to say. Having shed the Chad Thurston identity, I was now working in diligent open partnership with Yuan, and Hines wouldn't mind that. But what about Allie? If he saw us together, would he assume she was still playing me, still easing me in? I decided not to give a rat's ass. Allie was with me now for the duration—even if that duration turned out to be only the last ten minutes before police battering rams arrived.

And Detective Constable Scovil? MIA. Completely. Which I found a tad distressing. In terms of personal appearances, this staunch Sheila was 0-for-December—odd for someone who'd previously come on so strong. What gave? Had she bought my mislead so completely that she'd had to bank her fires while confirming up her chain of command that she wasn't inadvertently stepping on another undercover operative's toes? Had she, in short, believed Vic? Impossible. Who believes a Mirplo? But if she'd doubted him, why had she not confronted me? I was still her bitch, right? Or was I? Had she changed the parameters without telling me? While I would feel affronted by such duplicity (what, she didn't trust her bitch to stay bitched?) I could certainly understand it. She'd want to keep me guessing.

I asked Vic if she'd given him any hint about how she took his news. "She told me to go fuck myself," he said, "if that's any help."

It wasn't, not really.

She was a worry, though. All week long, she'd been like a seed stuck in my tooth. What was she up to? Was she really content to let me work without her supervision? Did she really trust me that much? Unlikely.

So then, she was giving me leash, and a whole damn lot of it, too. Why?

Well, on one level you could say that while she didn't trust me, she still might have confidence in me: confidence that, via either the Penny Skim or the Merlin Game, I'd reel in Hines, the fish she wanted to land. But wait a minute, whose word did I have that he was, really, her intended catch?

Hers. Only hers.

I cast my mind back to my first encounter with Scovil, how we'd instantly rubbed each other the wrong way. I hadn't really disliked her,

I recalled—just responded to the vibe she'd given off. But where did that vibe come from? Why did she loathe me so? She didn't even know me.

Did she?

Well, did she?

"Hey, Billy," I asked. "How far back do you and Scovil go?"

"Years, mate. She recruited me out of prison for her training program."

"Yeah, that's what she told me," I mused. "That was a rather profound act of trust."

"She said she had my measure. Knew my type. Said if I so much as thought an evil thought, she'd know it."

"Knew your type, huh? I wonder how."

"Ah, well, as to that, she's had long experience with the art of the con."

"As a practitioner?"

"Nah, mate. Victim."

My ears pricked up. "Go on," I said.

"Right, well," said Billy, "you have to know she was drunk when she told me this, so it could either be true truth or only pub truth, yeh?"

"Understood."

"It was the night my training program finished."

"You'd already figured out you were going after the Reserve Bank?"

"Too right. You don't want your training to go to waste."

"So much for having your measure," said Allie.

Billy smiled. "Anyway, that night there was a bit of a piss-up down the road. We shouted rounds back and forth till closing. At which time she confided in me that her parents had been ruined by a grifter. Picked clean. They lost their home, savings, everything. That's what brought her into anti-fraud."

"Righteous indignation?" asked Allie.

"Fuckin' rage."

I rubbed the bridge of my nose with my thumb and forefinger. I had an awful premonition about what I'd hear next. "Did she say how they got snuked?"

"Mortgage fraud. They thought they were leveraging their land to buy more land. Exotic shit, too."

"A tropical island?"

Yuan's eyes widened. "How did you—?" He bit off the end of the sentence. "Oh, no. Oh, mate, you didn't."

"What?" asked Vic. "Didn't what?"

"I'm afraid I did." (Through a dummy corporation called Vala Island Holdings. Look up the latitude and longitude and you'll find it's blue water.)

"How?" asked Allie. "They were half a world away."

I shrugged. "The internet," I said. "It extends your reach."

"Wow," said Billy, reverently. "Well now, that's a coincidence."

"What's a coincidence?" asked Vic, still not catching on.

"I don't believe in coincidences," I said, and with that began to ponder the possibility that I, not Hines, had been Scovil's target all along. If so, I would now have to percolate everything through the filter of new information. Say Scovil was after me on a revenge tip and Hines was after me for pure go-to-hell. Were they after me together? Was their mutual enmity so much smoke? If yes, it meant they thought they could hustle a hustler. This outraged me some, as it showed disrespect. Then again, they had managed to get me up to my elbows in a big, muddy grift, the kind of grift that could put poor Radar in an orange jumpsuit for the rest of his natural borns.

Somehow I didn't think that was enough for them. Who goes to all the trouble—comes halfway around the world, in Scovil's case—just to make life hell for one nonviolent perp? It's not like busting me was going to bring world peace. Anyway, I knew what Hines's play was: money. Maybe that was Scovil's real play, too, and all her righteous spew was just another wheel within the endless wheels. Hmm. So now I had to ask myself whether Scovil was capable of thinking that many levels deep. Could I picture her in an Aussie public house planting the seeds of phony baloney on the outside chance of organizing a payback party for me at some point in the indeterminate future? Could she really be that devious?

"Billy," I asked, "apart from her 'fuckin' rage,' do you think Scovil's an honest cop?"

"Oh, lilywhite, mate."

"Any chance you're wrong?"

This gave Billy pause. I saw his eyes go up and to the left, which is where the eyes go when the memory files open. I imagined he was reviewing every interaction he'd ever had with Scovil, measuring them against this new possibility. Like all great grifters, he would have the ability to recall those conversations not just word for word but nuance for nuance. He would now be rethinking those nuances, looking for the telltale "rift in the fabric of space" that augers a lie. "It's possible," he said at last.

"Possible," I repeated. Possible that for Scovil, revenge meant not just getting back at the bad guys but getting her taste, too. After all, the world hadn't been fair to her family. Some people react to such circumstances by investing that much more heavily in fair. Others just say, "Screw fair." Well, if Scovil was on the "screw fair" side of things, it meant not only that she could be bought but also that ultimately she would name her price.

So: Was she giving me enough line to land a whale or enough rope to hang myself? Both, my gut told me. Really, she probably wanted both.

The evening waned. Mirplo played heads-up poker with Yuan and ended up losing everything, even the pink slip to his shitbox Song Serenade, which Billy took one look at and immediately gave back. In gratitude, Vic invited Billy out to the Broadview. I hoped Billy had money, because going to strip clubs with Mirplo is like dating the homecoming queen: Mate, you're gonna pay.

Later, Allie and I were in bed together and the subject of money came up. "Radar," she asked, "how much cash do you have?"

I thought about the steel ammo box buried in the hillside below my flat. "Maybe ten grand," I said. "It's my dash cash."

"I have about the same." She twirled an idle finger in my minimal chest hair. "You think we should?"

"What? Dash?"

"We have a bankroll. It's not a lot, but enough to get started. We could rebuild."

"And Vic and Billy?"

"They could come, too. We could be a road gang."

I had dismissed the thought of jetting before, but the metric had now shifted again, for if Scovil was as bent as Hines, then who in the picture would want to see us stand trial for our heinous crimes? The likeliest endgame any of us could anticipate involved guns and shallow graves.

If we did dash, of course, we'd have to go off the grid, which meant cash cons only—old school stings like the Texas Twist, Candle Shop, and Block Hustle. This had a certain romantic appeal. We could be like those 1930s flim-flam men, selling personalized Bibles to loved ones of the newly departed. But when you start to examine it in the cold light of reality, it quickly loses its charm, for life on the cash con is a life of small towns, hick marks, truck stops, fat cops, and grotty motels. Nor was I confident that there was any such place as "off the grid" in modern America. If we bailed on Hines, he wasn't likely to forgive or forget, not unless we left the keys to the Penny Skim just lying on the table when we ran.

And you know what? I wasn't prepared to do that. I was kind of surprised that Allie was. So I asked her about it.

"I don't want to tell you," she said in an oddly vulnerable voice. I didn't force the issue. I figured she'd tell me or not tell me as she saw fit. We passed a quiet moment together, she still worrying my chest hairs and I happily tracing the line of her cheekbone with a fingernail. At last I heard a tiny intake of breath, the kind people make before they speak. Still the words didn't come. Another moment passed. Then she murmured, "It's you, you know."

"What's me?"

"Something I've never had before." I could feel her heart beating. "Something to lose."

I blinked. "I'm something to lose?"

She buried her head in my chest. "I can't believe I said that out loud."

I stroked her cinnamon hair. "You're something to lose, too."

Allie lifted her head and looked at me with wide eyes. "Am I? Am I really?"

Listen, if you grift long enough, you're going to work every game there is, and for me that had included enough sweetheart scams to know how to sell love. But I never uttered any "I love you" with anywhere near the honesty I invested just then in a single, silent nod. I thought Allie was going to cry. Or maybe that was me. "I'll run if you want," I said. "We can be like Bonnie and Clyde, only hopefully not getting ventilated in the last reel. But I refuse to believe we can't outplay these mayonnaise motherfuckers."

Allie laughed. "Mayonnaise what—what kind of motherfuckers?"

"Mayonnaise motherfuckers. White bread, you know? Easy marks."

Allie took my arm and put it around her shoulder. She cuddled in close. "You're a strange, strange man, Radar Hoverlander. What's your real name?"

I waited a long time before I answered. "Radar Hoverlander," I said. But Allie was already asleep. I could smell General Tso's Chicken on the gingery exhalation of her breath.

dead man's switch

We already know why Willie Sutton robbed banks—'cause that's where the money was. And we know why George Mallory climbed Mount Everest—because it was there. Of more interest to me is why Picasso kept painting or Dickens kept writing long after they got so rich that they could bathe in champagne every day and still endow a trust. I'm guessing they got hooked—not on the money but on the buzz of doing what they did so well. Maybe they just wanted to prove they could still do it; unless you're Mallory, there's always a higher mountain to climb. And some people climb even though they know they're going to fall. Just ask Mallory, who vanished on Everest in 1924, or ask any air force test pilot who ends his last flight as a smudge on the desert floor.

Or maybe just ask Billy and me as we zeroed in on our California Roll. It's not like there's a hall of fame for people like us, but if there were, then pulling off this snuke would make us lock admits. I only mention this because I don't want it thought that financial edacity alone kept me in the game. The money was beside the point. I wasn't robbing China to get rich. I was robbing China because it was there.

I know, right? I'm a stupid, stubborn son of a bitch. That said, I wasn't going to give Detective Constable Claire Scovil, or Special Agent (or whatever) Milval Hines the satisfaction of moving me off my snuke. Especially when it occurred to me that being a stupid, stubborn son of a bitch was actually the perfect card to play.

So Monday morning I took a chance. I needed to know if Scovil or Hines or both were traveling dark with respect to their bosses and betters. I hoped so; I didn't think that what I had in mind would work with headquarters peering over their shoulders. I figured that Hines was well and truly off the reservation since, as Allie put it, he was getting his beak wet at every opportunity, and that's not a gag you can pull off without a lot of earned autonomy. Of Scovil I wouldn't have suspected it up till now, but after last night's conversation with Billy, and my own tranquil reflection on all my interactions with her, I became more and more convinced that she had likewise gone rogue. It wouldn't take much—a leave of absence from work and the next flight to L.A. But I needed to know for sure, so I turned to the Hackmaster, not forgetting what Chuck said about the trail of electronic breadcrumbs it could leave.

Conundrum! I had to shine a light in dark places without anyone tracing the beam back to me. So I settled down with the Hackmaster's instruction manual to see if I could find a way. Hours later, apart from some grins at crimes against syntax—"for avioding of crinminal charge use a nony mouse relay protical"—I had nothing to show for my work. The device could do what it promised, but it couldn't promise not to be seen. *Okay,* I thought, *if I'm going to be seen, let's make being seen not a problem.*

I first cooked up a new identity, that of a teenage hack hobbyist from—I picked an Eastern European country at random—Romania. I gave myself a name, Luca Durbaca, and a screen identity, Jokerman23. Then I established a loud presence on the kind of underground discussion boards routinely monitored by interested government officials.

(Taking care first, of course, to launder my posts through three or four "a nony mouse relays.") What I had in mind was to hide my efforts in plain sight. Posturing like a teenage hacker high on testosterone, I boasted that I had written slam code to breach law-enforcement databases all over the world and would post results of my work within twenty-four hours. Naturally, I had written no such code, but if the Hackmaster was everything it awkwardly expressed itself to be, that wouldn't be a problem.

I picked an international array of police departments, army intelligence bureaus, and national security agencies, including the German Bundespolizei, Tatmadaw (Burmese military), the defense intelligence services of Uruguay and Paraguay—and the Australian High Tech Crime Centre and Hines's fraud task force. See what I was getting at? If anyone in those places noticed me snooping around, they'd trace me back to these discussion boards and decide that I was on a self-indulgent because-it's-there teenage jag. They might worry about Luca Durbaca selling access to their secrets, but they wouldn't worry about Radar Hoverlander looking for the goods on Scovil and Hines.

I spent the better part of the day happily crashing the inner sancta of the world's law-enforcement agencies—and wittingly laying a breadcrumb trail back to the fictive Jokerman. I have to say that the Hackmaster worked a pip, and if I ever wanted to run, say, a friendly little blackmail game, I now knew that the finance minister for the government of Iceland favors sex-tourism excursions to Nicaragua. Merely out of hacker curiosity (or so it would appear to subsequent keystroke analysts), I checked out the operations files of both the Aussie crime center and the Fibbie task force, and found not a whisper in either place of Billy Yuan or yours most humbly truly. This indicated that Scovil and Hines were indeed running dark, so mission accomplished.

Or maybe not. Unfortunately, absence of proof is not proof. I might have been looking in the wrong place, or they might be working with wink sanction. Ah, well. I'd done the best I could to establish that their activities didn't officially exist. If I was wrong, I was wrong. I'd just have to improvise a new solution if it came to that.

There was one last search I wanted to run, to get Hines's real name, which of course I didn't have, else his FBI affiliation would've surfaced back when I first searched Grandpa's bona fides. I thought I might be able to flip that rock by running Allie through a general cross-reference matrix. I might also get independent evidence that Allie was, indeed, on board as a protected informant, which corroboration would certainly be a balm to my suspicious soul. In the end, though, I abjured the search, for going after so specific a target might belie my hacker holiday masquerade, and I couldn't take that chance. I'd just have to keep calling Hines Hines, and keep taking Allie on faith.

I *had* faith. Weirdly, I did. Confidence, too, steadying up again after its earlier wobble. After all, I held many interesting cards to play. I had half a million dirty dollars, with the prospect of a whole lot more on the way. I had friends—rare in this game. Most important, I had uncovered my adversaries' hidden agendas, which is just huge in the grift. Knowing what the other guy wants is key to getting what *you* want, and that's true whether you're talking about negotiation, poker, or the rarefied art of the con.

Also key is keeping the other guy off balance, which is why I arranged a meeting with Hines—and invited Scovil, too. This was in the Polo Lounge at the Beverly Hills Hotel for no other reason than that I'd always wanted to check it out.

You should have seen the look on each of their faces when the other arrived.

I saw. I was watching from a service alcove by the kitchen, while the Salvadoran busboys looked at me like I was some kind of eccentric, though no shortage of those in Beverly Hills, right? Hines walked in first, went straight to the bar and ordered a big double something, straight up. He snarled when the bartender asked if he wanted a menu. Scovil entered a moment later, dressed as she thought a woman going to the Polo Lounge should dress—in a black cocktail thing that she absolutely couldn't sell. When they caught sight of each other, they looked like televangelists look when the news crews are waiting outside the porno store. In this sense, I was pinging them: By their unvarnished surprise I knew that, at least, they weren't updating each other's Day Runner. In another sense, I was pinging myself, for in that instant, they both knew they'd been snuked in a minor way—two dates to the same dance, as it were. I imagine they were both quite pissed off at me, but neither could show it without raising the larger question of why each hadn't bothered to fill the other in. So they both clamped down on their expressions with, to my practiced eye, only modest success, and started looking around for me. I ducked into the kitchen, went all the way around through the back-of-house, emerged in the lobby, and sailed into the lounge like the happiest little Radar on earth.

Let's pause and review for the folks in the back row. Scovil had told me she was chasing Hines as a bent cop, though I now believed her real target was moi. Meanwhile, my story for Scovil was that Billy Yuan had made me as a grifter and wouldn't let me into his confidence, though we all know that wasn't true. Hines, on the other hand, knew that Billy and I were working the Penny Skim and therefore saw the firm of Yuan and Hoverlander as his Super Lotto Jackpot. Was he worried about Scovil? Probably not. He figured he could take the money and give her us to hang on her Sydney gibbet.

All other things being equal, I preferred to remain unhung.

In the five seconds before I made my presence known, I could see it occur to both of them that I might not show up at all—that I'd just called this meeting as a goof. While I'm certainly capable of such random acts of whimsy, that wasn't what I was about here. I was working a variation of a con called the Dead Man's Switch, which is basically just taking the other guy's opportunity and turning it into his problem.

I sauntered over, all smiles, handshakes and pats on backs. "I suppose you're both wondering why I asked you here," I said. I knew I couldn't sound more clichéd—exactly the tone I was going for. "I think it's time we cleared the air.

"Milval . . . Claire . . ." I said. "Do you mind if I call you Claire?" Scovil glared at me like I'd asked to sniff her panties. "You two haven't been entirely honest with each other." Both of their faces contorted as they essayed the impossible task of conveying devil-may-care calm and shut-your-mouth menace at the same time.

I addressed Hines first. "Milval," I said, "Claire told you she came here after Billy Yuan, right?" Hines nodded warily, wondering just how liturgically loose this canon was going to get. "She didn't. She's after . . ." Scovil took the extraordinary step of grabbing my arm. I don't think Hines saw, for he was pretty well steeped in his own dread just then. ". . . me," I finished, with a broad, cocky smile. Scovil relaxed her grip. This was interesting, because if Hines wasn't on Scovil's agenda, then why would she hate to have him think he was? I filed that contemplation for later. Time to put the fear on Hines, too.

"And Claire," I said, "Milval's not really interested in Billy either. He just wants to take . . ." the money and run? Was that what I was about to say?

Nah. ". . . me down, too." I saw Hines clench, then unclench. "I think you two are going to have a jurisdictional issue."

"You think we care about that?" growled Hines.

"No, probably not," I said. "But the fact remains that the two of you, in your ardor, have given the fox the key to the henhouse, and you'd better start figuring out what you're going to do about that, because Billy and I are about to do something that could . . ." I paused for effect ". . . kinda wreck the world's economy. And if that happens and all you have to show for it is one busted Hoverlander,[*] I don't think your bosses are going to be too damn pleased."

"What do you mean you and Billy?" asked Scovil. "I thought he didn't trust you."

"This may come as a shock to you, Constable, but people don't always tell the truth." Here was a new problem for Scovil, for she'd threatened me with death if I lied to her and must now be wondering why that threat had lost its clout.

That was just part of her emerging emotional stew which, like Hines's, was reaching a stage of redolent roil. In the few minutes since they'd arrived, they'd experienced the shock of each other's presence, the fear of being outed, and the relief of me pulling back from that brink. Now they were tied up in a snarl of feelings, including resentment, confusion, anxiety and, considering the way Hines knocked back his drink and ordered another, the first stage of spifflication. Judging them sufficiently softened up, I pushed ahead.

I gave them a full brief on the Penny Skim, noting with some amusement how hard Hines tried to make it all look like news to him. I told them it was a done deal, with confederates already in place all over the People's Bank's IT structure. For a price—a percentage of the skim—these worthies were already providing Billy and me with password hacks to their own security systems. I told them that Billy had written, and was ready to release, the go commands that would automate the process of clipping virtually every transaction into, out of, or through the Chinese banking system. What's more, the thing was designed to spread virally, so that every skim opened the door to another, geometrically. By my (admittedly impromptu) math, it would take about six hours for the bank's watchdog software to

---

[*] "The Sky Crane will fly off and crash-land a short distance away."

catch on, and who knows how long after that before someone in the chain of command had sufficient spine to call all engines stop. By the time China slammed the door, the skim would have spread to other hubs of national finance, including the Bank of England, the Central Bank of the Russian Federation, the Saudi Arabian Monetary Agency, and of course the Reserve Bank of Australia and the U.S. Federal Reserve.

You may be thinking that there's no way a skim can "spread" magically past the passwords and firewalls of other nations' banking systems. Know what? You're right. But you're not under the sort of pressure that Scovil and Hines were under, and when it comes to selling bafflegab, pressure is a grifter's best friend.

"Can you see where I'm going with this?" I asked. "In the space of a day, the global economy will come up short to the tune of . . ." I paused to pull a number out of my ass ". . . some one and a half trillion dollars. And that's not all, because every bank in the world will have to lock down to stop the process. Know what happens then? Panic. Runs on banks. Chaos. Riots. Total economic collapse."

"Bullshit," spat Hines.

"Is it?" I asked, utterly rhetorically. I then gave them a quick primer on coin clipping, how it had repeatedly devalued and destroyed strong economies down through history. Byzantium. Persia's Safavid Dynasty. I even laid the fall of the Roman Empire at the feet of unscrupulous *solidus* shavers. This was more than bafflegab; it was pure whole cloth invention. But they bought it completely.

I guess I was just on my game.

"And," I added, "that's back when they measured economic change in centuries. You know how it is these days: Someone pets a monkey in Uganda, flies to Chicago, you have Marburg all over the Midwest by midweek. Same thing with public monetary confidence. By the time it hits CNN, it'll be too late to stop.

"Like I said, your bosses aren't going to like that. Especially since your bosses have no idea what you're up to, do they?"

Hines and Scovil exchanged unhappy looks. Now to administer a tincture of panic and beat a hasty retreat. "Here's the deal," I said, "Two million dollars in twenty-four hours stops this thing in its tracks. And gives you Billy Yuan as a kind of a consolation prize."

"You'd sell out your partner?" asked Scovil.

"What partner? I've known the dude two weeks." I turned to Hines. "But Allie's mine. She walks."

"Why?" asked Scovil, which suggested that Hines hadn't clued her in on the latest state of *l'affaire Allie.*

So I jerked a thumb at Hines. "Ask him."

Hines opened and closed his mouth. More for cover than anything else, he said, "What about Mirplo?"

I smirked. "If you think you can put this all on his scrawny shoulders, be my guest. For the record, he's not as loyal a servant as you think he is." I turned to walk away, then paused, as if something very important had just occurred to me. "By the way," I said, "if you're considering some sort of preemptive strike, either legal or . . ." I fixed them both with meaningful looks ". . . extralegal, I suggest you look up 'Dead Man's Switch' on Wikipedia." Then I walked out, leaving the Polo Lounge to its standard olio of dealmakers, heartbreakers, and, I predicted, two morose cops who would run up a hefty bar tab before they stumbled out into perfect Beverly Hills.

I stopped by the Blue Magoon on the way home. The place was creepy, but somebody there had something I thought I might need.

event horizon

"You what?!" shouted Vic. "You fucking sold me out?"

Unable to stomach yet another Java Man, we were hanging at one of its one-off competitors, Sheik of Arabica, located way down Slauson and situated, we hoped, well off Hines and Scovil's map. Allie, Billy, and I were quaffing cappuccinos. Vic was throwing a bit of a fit.

"Relax, Vic," I said. "Nobody sold anybody out. It's all part of the snuke."

"Well, I like your part better than mine. Two million bucks. You'd better fucking cut me in."

"Vic, use your head. They couldn't possibly pay, even if they wanted to, which, trust me, they don't. Hines has a theoretical half million from the Merlin Game, but, what? He's gonna pry it out of me to give it back to me? And Scovil, what's she going to do? Hit an ATM for a million-dollar advance on her credit card?"

"Well, if they're not gonna pay," he asked, "what *are* they gonna do?"

"Probably try to kill me."

Allie flinched at this but recovered quickly, realizing, "That's part of the snuke, too?"

"Of course. First they'll make a separate peace with Billy, and once they've got him tucked in, they'll finish the unfinished business of me."

"That would satisfy Scovil," said Billy, "but Hines still needs a pay-day, yeh?"

"That he does," I said. "Likely before he endgames my ass, he'll try to strong-arm Allie into romancing away the Merlin stash."

"He already has," said Allie. I blinked. I had figured that my little confab with Hines and Scovil would stimulate action, but I didn't think it would come on so fast. "Though it wasn't exactly a strong-arm situation."

"What do you mean?"

"He said if I managed to get the money, he'd cleanse all my records, and I could go stroll."

"Anything else?"

"Well . . . he kind of made a pass."

"What kind of pass?"

"Oh, lifetime. He told me how great I'd look in something sexy— like a Moroccan villa."

"What did you tell him?"

Allie fixed me with a level grin. "What do you think I told him? That I can't wait to be his burka baby."

Vic snorked a laugh, but then his primeval brain returned to the subject at hand. "Still, what about me? You think I want to take the fall for this?"

"Of course not," I said. "No more than I want to get dead."

"Then why are you poking sticks in wasps' nests?"

"That's what happens at the event horizon, Vic. You've got to stir shit up. Make people make mistakes."

"So they're not going to arrest me?"

"No, yeah, they probably will."

"What?!"

"They have to arrest you, Vic. And flip you so you go Judas on me. Hines'll probably offer you immunity, witness protection, maybe a new car."

This elicited a laugh from Billy. "Take the deal, mate."

Vic glared at Billy, and in that glare I detected Vic's true love for his rattletrap. What can I tell you? The heart wants what the heart wants. He turned his attention back to me. "Dude," he said, "why would Hines think I need flipping?"

"Well . . . I might've told him."

Vic opened and closed his mouth. "Why would you do that?" he burbled. "And don't say it's part of the snuke."

"Okay, I won't. But it is. Look, Vic, Hines is a suspicious guy. I've made him more suspicious, that's all. But it's all good. This way, when he brings you in to get religion, he can feel like your conversion is legit."

"Oh, I get to get religion, do I?"

"Yeah. He might feel like he has to beat it into you, but I'm sure you'll cave before that happens."

"Fucking Radar Hoverlander," muttered Vic. "How do you know all everything about everything? Does it ever occur to you you might be wrong?"

"Of course it does. Why do you think I'm generating so much heat? Vic, look, I don't know all everything about everything, but I do know I want the other side thinking less clearly. So I'm pushing their panic buttons. It's standard endgame shit. You know that."

"But why me?" he asked, plaintively. "Why does it have to look like you're selling *me* out?"

I templed my fingers. "Vic," I said, "this is gonna sound harsh, but . . . look around." I nodded toward Billy and Allie. "Who else *would* I sell out?"

Vic didn't take that too badly. I guess when you think you're the bottom of the food chain, there's comfort in knowing that everyone else thinks so, too. All he said was, "It better be fucking worth my while. Especially if I get beat."

"Don't worry, it will be." I turned to Billy. "Speaking of which, Billy, how's plan B shaping up?"

"Oh, it's working a treat, mate."

"Good deal. ETA?"

"Basically whenever."

"Great," said Vic, "now there's a plan B. And what might plan B be?"

"Never mind about that, Vic. You can't tell Hines what you don't know."

"So just what exactly am I supposed to tell him?"

"Anything you like. It doesn't matter. He won't believe you anyhow."

"Well, if he won't believe me, then—"

"Distortion, Vic. Misdirection. We're tearing holes in his fabric of space."

"For the 'event horizon'?" he mocked.

"If you like." I threw an arm around Vic. Viewed through a certain filter, I suppose this was a patronizing gesture, but what the hell. "Things are speeding up now, acquiring their own momentum. At this point in the snuke, almost nobody knows how it's going to turn out."

"But you do."

"I have a good idea."

"An idea that involves throwing poor Mirplo to the wolves," said Vic.

"It has to be done."

"You know, Radar," he muttered, "sometimes you can be a real cheesedick." He shrugged out from under my arm. "Well, guess I'll go get me arrested now."

After he left, Allie gently suggested that I might have taken a different approach. Actually, not so gently. "He's right, you know. Sometimes you can be a real cheesedick."

"I don't even know what that means."

"Really? Radar Hoverlander, master of the neologism, at a loss for definition?"

"I . . ."

"That kid's loyal to you, Radar. Loyal like a dog. And because he's loyal, you can kick him all you want. But just because you *can* kick him doesn't mean you have to."

"It's part of the scam," I said lamely. "He knows I don't mean it."

"No, I think you do mean it. I think it makes you feel good to prove how smart you are. But why you feel like you need to prove you're smarter than a Mirplo, I do not know."

"No, I don't. I mean, why would I?"

"Well, why would you? Why don't you think about it and see if you can figure it out?"

Allie left. Billy and I went back to my place, where Billy applied the skim's finishing touches. There was little left for me to do, just wait for the event horizon to arrive. Usually I loved this part of a snuke. It's a ballet, kind of an orderly chaos, where all the setups get paid off, and if everything goes according to plan—but no, everything never goes quite according to plan, so you have to stay light on your feet, ready for anything. It's very adrenalating. It's the part that gets me high. But I didn't feel high just then. I felt . . . betrayed . . . and betraying. I took it up with Billy, leading with a "Women, huh?" point of view that gained no traction whatsoever.

All he said was, "I think you're missing the point, mate."

"Which is?"

But he offered no insight, merely put his head back down over his work. I watched him hammer away at code for a while. Soon he was lost in it, sunk down in the never-ending if/then stew, his total consciousness dedicated to solving a problem that was at once exacting in detail and overwhelming in scope. He chewed on his lower lip, brushed hair from his eyes, and cricked his neck from side to side, all utterly unself-aware. I marveled at the brain that could get so lost, and yet stay found, in the halls of such elegant abstracts. It occurred to me that if I ever wanted to get off the snuke and into something legit, that'd be a place to go: somewhere that made your whole mind bind.

I went out on the deck. The night had turned overcast and damp. Winter was coming to Los Angeles, classically defined as two months of rain between the smog season and the smog season. I loved this time of year around here. Big storms rolled in off the Pacific, arctic tempest moderated by the long trip south, resulting in daylong cleansing soaks. Just then, as if my thoughts invoked it, the rain began, first gentle, soon hard enough to kick up the pungent mix of wet asphalt, oil, and rubber smells from the boulevard below.

Was I missing the point? Was I really?

A long time later, I went back inside. Billy was crashed out on the couch, one half-curled hand still on the keyboard of his computer, the other covering his eyes against the glare of the overhead light. I switched it off, the old-fashioned pushbutton switch yielding a satisfying *ponk* as the room went dark.

Billy and Allie had mostly worked solo. They didn't get that things break down at the end of a snuke. Pressure mounts. Tempers fray. People don't act their best. Me, I'd run enough grift gangs to know that if you get through the event horizon without someone going completely off their gimbals, you're working with zombies, not humans.

Vic, though, Vic understood this. At least I hoped he did. He was going to have to sell real outrage to Hines. So maybe I helped him along by making his outrage feel real. So what? It was a move as old as any shell game, where part of getting the mark to gamble is riling his righteous ire to the point where nothing matters but screwing the devious weasel who's running the game. You've seen it on the street, maybe: Some blameless granny loses her pin money to a three-card monte man, while you stand there just knowing that the lady got cheated. Now here comes a casual third party, saying he has a surefire system for spotting the red queen or picking the pea or whatever, and you go hard for it because the three-card monte man just *deserves* to lose, for granny's sake. Then your money goes away, and you wonder how the surefire system went wrong.

What you don't see is granny and the monte man and the casual third party all meeting later to carve up your dough.

The key, the linchpin, is pissing people off, to the point where anger trumps judgment. Beneath that, though, is the hidden assumption that you have the power to piss people off . . . or charm them . . . confuse them . . . manipulate them as you see fit. Truly, if you don't rate yourself a puppet master, you don't win in the grift.

But if you're the puppet master, then everyone else is a puppet, and that can get old.

I think it was getting old for me. At a time when I should have been reveling in the snuke, delightedly planning the last cascade of dominos, all I could think about was Vic's feelings, and Allie's, even Billy's. It's one thing to objectify the mark; it's a whole other thing to objectify your friends.

Still, Vic was right in one sense: I was poking sticks in wasps' nests. Now it was just a question of how the wasps responded.

As it turned out, like wasps.

I fell asleep around dawn, though with the rain, dawn wasn't much more than a whisper of light in the sky. A couple of hours later, the phone rang. I couldn't rouse myself to answer it, but Billy did, and a moment later stuck his head in my room.

"Mirplo called," he said. "He needs a lift."

"Hines done with him already?" I mumbled into my pillow.

"So it would seem." Billy threw a piece of paper down on my bed. "Here's where."

I left Billy to button up the last of the skim code and headed out. The rain was still pouring down, turning the roads of my hillside neighborhood into rivers of water and mud. Out on the main streets it was even worse, as L.A. drivers underwent their predictable first-storm-of-the-season freakout. Some sped up, as if by driving fast they could dodge the raindrops. Others slowed down, fearful that eight months of accumulated crap on the road surface would turn to glare ice beneath their tires. In the ensuing mismatch of fast and slow, accidents broke out like acne, and getting from point A to point B became an obnoxious waiting game. Worse, point B for me was the FBI resident agency at LAX. It made sense that Vic would be there, for it was a federal hold, likely the same one Vic had visited on his return from Louisiana last year.

But it was hell to get to, a slow grind through gridlocked surface streets and up onto a freeway that was just a joke. *Honest to God, L.A. learn to drive in the damn rain, will you?* I tried to stay patient, but it was hard. I felt I was losing control.

Then I *did* lose control, and slammed into an SUV.

slickery when wet

There's nothing like a car accident to knock the arrogance out of you. One minute you're driving along, listening to some radio traffic guy describing road surfaces as "slickery," and wondering whether it's a portmanteau word or a mistake—admirable if the former, laughable if the latter—and the next thing you know, you're looking out your front windshield at the astonished face of the driver in the next lane, and you *know* that can't be right, so you crank hard on the wheel, but the harder you crank on the wheel, the more you seem to spin. You recall advice you once heard, *when you go into a skid, turn in the direction of the skid,* but it was counterintuitive then, and it's counterintuitive now, so you continue with your stupid panic response of *crank the wheel, stomp the brakes,* while your car resembles nothing so much as a whirling teacup on that ride at that place. Then you're sailing exactly backward down the freeway, and you look in your rearview (now your frontview) mirror, and see this great black wall of a Ford Destroyer or something, stopped dead ahead, and there's just no way you're not going to hit it, so you close your eyes and brace yourself and wait for the sound that everyone always describes as a sickening crunch, but it's not sickening, really, you know, it's just annoying. Because the minute your car slid sideways, your day slid sideways, too.

Bang! My car ass-ended into the SUV. My neck snapped back, then forward, and I hit my head on something, I don't know what. I immediately felt a welt rising, and my first thought was, *if there's blood, I'm screwed, because they're going to want me to get treatment, and I do* not *have time for that right now.* I glanced at myself in the mirror and saw an angry red third eye already rising in the middle of my forehead, but no break in the skin, thank God. I groped around in the space between the seats and found a baseball cap bearing the logo and slogan for Dog's Nose Beer ("When I want something cold and wet, I reach for a Dog's Nose"). Jamming it down low on my head, I stumbled out of the car and stood blinking in the downpour. I figured that the best role for me to play right now was befuddled, wet L.A. driver. It seemed like the right choice, since I was, in fact, both befuddled and wet.

I did an adequate job of holding it together as I and the other driver waited for the cops. She was a soccer mom–looking gal, with a fresh Shroud of Turin coffee stain down the front of her white cable-knit. I gave her a full blast of Hoverlander bijou, and she seemed to like it, but there was a ringing in my ears, and this silent soundtrack kept repeating over and over again the words *soccer mom, soccer mom, soccer mom, soccer mom.* It made it hard to concentrate.

A CHP cruiser arrived and ran a traffic break. We got our rigs off to the side, then stood in the rain some more, exchanging insurance information while the highway patrolman did the license and registration thing. Of course my documents came back pristine—I keep a clean set for just such occasions—but when the chipper handed me back my paperwork he looked into my eyes and asked, "Are you okay, Mr . . ." he glanced again at my license, ". . . Roykfritt?"

"Fine," I said. "A little shook up."

"Are you sure you're not hurt?"

"Not a scratch. Lucky, huh?"

He gave me a hard look, and I figured I was about fifteen seconds away from a field sobriety test. Which I'd pass, of course, but that wasn't really the point. I already realized that I probably had a concussion, but I also knew that I had to get to the airport. No way I was going to the hospital. Not if I could drive away.

I took a quick, officious walk around my Volvo, inspecting the damage with the practiced eye of an insurance adjuster (which I've been—or played anyway—on more than one occasion). The damage wasn't too bad. The trunk was somewhat crumpled, and a craze of cracked glass ran though the rear window, but the wheel wells were clear. The only real issue was the rear bumper, which clung to the car by a single bolt. There didn't seem much point in trying to refasten it, nor did I have the rope, tools, or even duct tape for the job. Opting just to set the bumper free, I grabbed the loose end with both hands and gave it a good yank, but it was so slickery that I lost my grip and fell down.

The officer helped me to my feet and asked me once again if I was all right. I simply nodded, afraid my voice would give me away. Then I grabbed the bumper again, this time cradling it like a fat toddler, and heaved with all my might. It came away in my hands. Acting as if that were the most natural, everyday occurrence for me, I opened a rear door and threw the bumper across the backseat. I climbed behind the wheel. The chipper leaned in. He looked like he was going to say something, but I offered him my biggest, glowiest smile, and I guess he bought it, because he waved me on my way.

I made it to LAX without further mishap—apart from getting lost and stopping twice at the same mini-mart to get directions. And throwing up several times, which I should have taken as clear evidence that I was in no shape to drive; however, I was also in no shape to think clearly, and when something impairs your judgment, your judgment of your judgment is the first to go. So I thought I was fine.

I parked in a short-term airport lot and made my way to 600 World Way, the United Airlines terminal, where the FBI has their resident agency. It was a surprisingly low-rent presence for a major anti-crime agency: half a dozen nondescript rooms behind a blank steel door marked FBI. I had to pass through a metal detector to reach the administration desk, and it was only the vestiges of self-preservation that kept concussed me from making some dumb gun joke. Even so, by the time I got to the desk, I was dizzy and sweating, and it took pretty much everything in my power to stay upright, and also not puke on the desk officer's desk. I may have had a cogent conversation with that man, but for the life of me, I can't remember it now.

I was made to wait on a hard plastic chair the color of burnt melon. I know there's no such color as burnt melon, but that's the way it struck me at the time. It further struck me that though that color didn't exist, it *should* exist, as should ministry, gestation, and especially oxymoron, which, to my addled mind, seemed the sort of mint-magenta color of coleus leaves. Eventually I was taken to a windowless room in back, where I waited some more, eschewing more melon chairs for the floor-bolted steel table that, for some reason, looked comfy as a feather bed. I stretched out on it and had a little snooze.

An indeterminate time later, a voice growled through my doze like a buzz saw through soft pine. "Well, well, well," said Milval Hines, "look at this mayonnaise motherfucker over here." His use of that phrase should have rung alarm bells in my head, but no bells could sound through my thick cranial batting. I rolled over and looked up. Hines was staring down at me, his misshapen (it struck me then) face silhouetted against the bare energy-saving twisty bulb overhead.

Vic was standing to his left, looking smugly flipped, which seemed according to plan.

But Allie stood to his right, which somehow did not.

You know what cognitive dissonance is, right? The grimness that grips you when you try to hold two contradictory ideas in your head at once. This wasn't that, exactly. More like just, "What's wrong with this picture?" Given my state of mind just then, all the phantom colors I was seeing, I couldn't be entirely sure she wasn't a pigment of my imagination. I tried to make eye contact with her, get some unspoken explanation, but she looked right through me. I had to check my extremities to assure myself that I had not, in fact, become transparent.

Hines placed two fingers against the knot on my forehead. I winced at the touch. "Does that hurt?" he asked. He pushed down hard with both fingers and, yeah, it did hurt. I managed to slither away, just far enough to fall to the floor.

"Gravity," intoned Vic. "Not just a good idea, it's the law." He seemed inordinately pleased with my pain.

Hines heaved me into a chair. He grabbed another one, spun it around and straddled it, facing me. I flashed back to the day we met and I'd straddled a chair exactly the same way. Odd that I could remember something from weeks ago but, suddenly, nothing from early today or yesterday. It was like my near-term memory had been whacked out of my head and replaced with a sign that read "This space intentionally left blank."

"So, Radar," he asked, "where'd you get that nasty bump?"

"Cut myself shaving," I muttered.

"You know that makes no sense," he said. I blinked at him. All six of him. "Well, whatever," said Hines. "I've been having some interesting conversations with your friends here. Seems they think you're something of a cheesedick."

"I am," I confessed. "A great hulking pepper-jack pecker." The effort of speech sent a radiating blob of pain outward from my forehead, but I kept spreading the mustard on my bravado sandwich. "What do you want me to do about it now?"

"Well, at first I was thinking of a twelve-step program: Assholes

Anonymous. Teach you to socialize like a decent human being. But then I thought, 'That's Radar Hoverlander. If he can't bluff being a decent human being, no one can.' So no rehab for you, Radar. Unlike a ham, you're incurable." He reached over and thwacked my forehead. My eyes twitched and watered uncontrollably. "This is fun," he said. "I like this."

"Go easy on him, Milval," said Allie. "Can't you see he's hurt?"

"Yes, of course I can see he's hurt. That's why I'm having so much fun." He thwacked my lump again. This time I may have whimpered. "I'm still wondering how it happened, though. What'd you do, Radar? Bang your head against your ego?"

Hines started winking in and out of view, as if someone were flipping miniblinds open and shut between us. As that seemed unlikely, I imagined that it was my own consciousness turning off and on like a light. A phrase floated up from nowhere to the top of my brain, and made it out my mouth. "The Dead Man's Switch . . ." I said.

Hines laughed. "The Dead Man's Switch is a joke," he sneered. "A pretty good one, I have to admit. You really had Scovil going. You even had me going for a little while. But I checked with some economically minded friends of mine, and they assured me that the global calamity you predict is impossible."

I tried to say, "Your friends don't know what they're talking about." I suppose I got close enough to that, because Hines laughed again. I felt like I was being a good host at a party.

"They may not," he said. "In my experience, people are idiots. But my other friends here"—he gestured toward Vic and Allie—"inform me that the whole threat is what you so charmingly call bafflegab. Just something to scare small children. Or extort FBI agents, as the case may be." He wagged a finger in my face. "Which, by the way, is a big-ass serious crime, the sort of crime that wins medals for arresting officers." He sighed. "So that's the cat out of the bag, isn't it, Radar?"

Hines patted Allie's hand. She didn't seem to mind, which I think I minded a lot.

I racked my brain for cards to play, and arrived at, "I'll drop a dime . . ."

"I'm sure you would," he said. "Therefore, much as I'd like to have that medal, I'm afraid I'm going to have to go for plan B on that. My own plan B, by the way, not the nonsense you told Vic to feed me. Honestly, Radar, you have to be more imaginative in your lies. You're getting too easy to read."

I considered this claim to be unfair, unjust, and just not true, because I uncertainly recalled telling Mirplo to make his own shit up. But I was too muzzy to voice the thought, or even be sure it was a real memory and not some post hoc backprediction. I shook my head to clear it, which only served to rattle my brain unpleasantly inside my skull. Allie looked at me with an expression of either compassion or disdain. She mouthed the words, "I'm sorry." Or maybe, "Bye, Charlie." It was hard to tell. As for Vic, he just smiled at Hines, his NBF.

Some time later, we left. I have a vague recollection of walking out of there in something of a fugue state, with Vic and Allie propping me up to keep me from planting my face. I caught the desk officer shooting a dark glance at Hines, something on the order of *There goes that crooked sumbitch I'm powerless to do anything about.* Or maybe I was projecting—my perceptual flame was guttering pretty good just then.

They poured me into the back of a black sedan. My head lolled against the window, rapping painfully on the glass every time the car took a bump. I thought about moving it, but couldn't muster the muscles. I kept my eyes closed mostly, for every time I opened them, the world flashed past in a blast of cars, billboards, storefronts, and rain, overwhelming my optic nerves and causing my gorge to rise. I tried to mentally slap my cheeks, for I knew I had never been less well equipped to enter an event horizon. You hope this part goes easy, and often it does, for you've told a story so compelling that there's only one logical conclusion. In other words, if the mook has swallowed the beginning and middle, he'll happily swallow the end. But Hines was no mook. The moment called for artful bafflegab, and I just wasn't up to it.

And Allie was back with him. How the hell did that happen? I felt a sick lurch in my stomach, as a wave of, guess you'd call it, existential vertigo washed over me. All my arrogance, my manipulative gifts, my objectification . . . all the stuff I was so good at, had seemingly had the unintended effect of driving her away. Here I thought I'd been so cagey but really I'd fallen into a classic trap of the grift, the one where you get to thinking you're so holding all the cards that you don't even have to play out the hand.

Well, fuck.

Allie was sitting beside me. With massive effort of will, I swiveled my head and looked at her, trying to read something, anything, in her expression, but it was like looking into a doll's eyes. In that moment, I was sure that whatever we had was gone, sacrificed on the altar of my vanity. I felt the loss like a shot to the gut. There went my soul mate.

And Vic? Vic was supposed to be mock-flipped, but he sure didn't look the part. From his catbird perch in the shotgun seat, he glanced over his shoulder and delivered a sardonic grin, loudly broadcasting a silent song called "The Sidekick's Revenge". Because the thing about a sidekick is, he does get kicked. Apparently I'd kicked him once too often, which was a shame because at the end of the day, I liked the mutt.

Again, fuck.

The trouble with too far is you never know you're going till you're gone.

28.

better luck next life

As we pulled up to my place, I thought about all that had gone on in and around there in the past few weeks. The many monkeyshines with Allie. Mirplo and the gun. Hard-ass confrontations with Scovil and Hines. Billy and me building the Penny Skim like a high school science project. Funny: all that traffic through my life. It made me realize how sterilely I'd lived before. You think you're so out there in the world, you know? But if all your relationships are just narrow wires of exploitation, then you're really not in the world at all, you're just taking up space. It could be my epitaph: He just took up space.

I got out of the car and went inside. My head felt less like a used piñata and the ground felt less like an ongoing aftershock, but my over-all cognitive structure still seemed cracked and shattered, jarred loose. A rough mosaic, like pixilated boobs on a tabloid TV show. This was no way to run an endgame, but what could I do? I didn't see anyone giving me the rest of the day off.

Scovil stood in the middle of my living room, arms crossed, scowl-ing down at Billy Yuan. I saw tension hanging between them like Ghostbusters slime. Literally saw it. So now my visual cortex was acting up. Terrific.

"Okay," said Hines, "let's do this by the numbers. You," he said to me, "get word to your marks that you need their pass codes now. You," he said to Yuan, "launch the skim as soon as the first codes arrive."

When you've been on the snuke as long as I have, some things are second nature, so with my volition in tatters, instinct took over. "Yeah, that's not gonna happen," I heard myself say.

"What do you mean?" asked Scovil. The fear vibe in her voice told me she had more than a rooting interest in the Penny Skim succeeding, and also that maybe my ability to read people was coming back online.

"It's going to happen," growled Hines.

"Or what?" I asked. "You'll kill me twice?" That was more like it. That old Hoverlander élan.

Hines didn't dignify my jape with a response. He just said, "Burn down the fucking house."

"Can't," I said.

"Why not?"

"It's a house of cards, you moron." I saw Scovil stifle the urge to say "What do you mean?" again. "There's no Penny Skim," I said, and then repeated for emphasis, or just because the words sounded good inside my head, "There. Is. No. Penny. Skim. Billy and I made the whole thing up. You've been mooked, you mook. Haven't you figured that out yet?" Hines's face turned red. I turned to Allie and Vic, and said, "Sorry, guys, you backed the wrong horse. Or rather, I guess you'd say, you backed a scratch." I thought that might make sense, at least on a metaphorical level, but I really wasn't sure. The air seemed to go out of Allie and Vic. Hines and Scovil looked deflated, too.

But there was Billy with a can of Fix-A-Flat. "He's lying," he said. "The Penny Skim is real," he said suddenly. "And it's already on."

"Fucking Billy," I said in a low warning voice.

He looked at me and shot me a shrug. I could see the little thought balloon popping up over his head. It said, *Every man for himself.* I had no doubt that Hines and Scovil could read it as clearly as I. "I launched it as soon as you left this morning," Billy told me. He swiveled his laptop toward Scovil and Hines. "See for yourself," he said. "The take so far is $675,000. It'll go a lot higher."

"No it won't," I countered. "That's a dummy webpage running a dummy program." I glanced at the screen. "Nice work, though. I have to admit."

"Give it up, mate," said Billy. He stood and faced Hines, carrying himself with the confident air of someone playing a long-held card. "What Radar had in mind," he said, "was to blow you off by selling the skim as a perpetual-motion gaff gone wrong. He figured you could get us for attempted something, that's all. We'd do some short time, and meanwhile the proceeds would pile up in a Manx bank, just waiting for our coming-out shindy."

"Billy," I said, "I don't know why you're doing this. You're never going to be able to show them the money."

Billy ignored me. "I knew it was only a matter of time until Radar double-crossed me." He gave me another knowing look. "New leopard, same spots, yeh?" He turned back to Hines. "Then I found his subroutine."

"My what? My sub what?"

"When it comes to computers, Radar likes to play dumb, but actually he's a bit, well, not. I don't know when he did it, but he buried some code inside my code to move the money yet again, into some Liechtenstein bank he discovered. Apparently it's quite covert."

"That's noise," I protested. "Hines, he's making it up as he goes along."

"Something he learned from you, no doubt," said Hines.

Billy pressed on. "So I talked it over with these two," he said, indicating Vic and Allie. "We decided to form our own consortium. Everybody gets a piece except this one." He jerked a thumb at me. "Frankly, we don't think he deserves it."

The moment froze. Looking around the room, I took a quick fix on everyone's emotions. Scovil looked relieved. Allie and Vic seemed to be balancing guilt against a big payday. Billy was doing a mental victory dance. And Hines had bird feathers in his mouth.

So there it was. My friends and enemies allied against me. It served me right, I supposed, for the company I chose to keep. Bunch of corrupt motherfuckers. Ah, well. The cheesedick stands alone.

But you know what? It didn't feel bad. In fact, it felt great, the lifting of a giant weight. All my life, I had snuked, mooked, cheated, stolen, and lied. And for what? Not for money, not really. Just trying to win and keep winning. Somewhere along the line, I should have realized that's a bottomless hole, because every successful scam just diminished the marks in my eyes, and who could relish such tiny triumphs over trivial foes? Now here I was, losing at last. Losing everything. Only it didn't feel like losing. It felt like a wrap-up, that's all, giving it all away. *Oh, well,* I thought, *better luck next life.*

Or was that the concussion talking?

"Hines," I said, "Billy is right. I was trying to snuke you. Really thought it would work, too. Guess I underestimated you." I smiled a self-deprecating smile. "Just one of my many mistakes." I turned to Allie. "Cinderfuckingella," I said. "So you threw in your lot with this ridiculous fibbie, after all, huh? I guess I get it. Security. A clean slate. But the grift is going to miss you, girl. You're like the Madame Curie of the thing we do." I swallowed hard. "You know I love you, right?" I saw her eyes glisten. "But your choices are your choices and I respect them. No hard feelings?"

She gave a tiny nod of assent. Blinked back some tears.

I cast my glance toward Vic, and saw him go tense, like maybe he thought I was going to go off on him. To the contrary, I wanted to throw my arm around him, but stopped myself—that condescending gesture. "Vic," I said, "the original Mirplo. Buddy, you're right. I am a cheesedick. Was from the start. Should've treated you better, brother. You've got more talent than I ever gave you credit for." I offered him a fist bump. "No hards?"

He thought about it for a moment, then knuckled my fist with his. "No hards," he agreed.

"Billy Yuan," I said next, "Dollar Bill. You're a rock star, man. How'd you manage to launch the skim without me?"

"Mate, I just opened channels to your people. I cloned your ISP so they'd—"

"Forget it," I said. "I don't want to know. It's like with a magic act. If you learn how they do the trick, it spoils the fun." I shook my head. "I would've liked to work with you some more, though. We could've torn it up."

Continuing my valedictory, I turned to Scovil. "This must be Christmas for you, huh, sugar? Got payback at last. I just hope it's worth the price."

"Price?"

"Like the sign says, 'You can't go home again.' I could see how badly you needed the Penny Skim. I didn't know why, but now I do. You burned a bridge when you let Billy leave Australia, didn't you? And fine, you used him to get to me, but now that you've got me, what next? Have fun living in exile in Java or wherever.

"For what it's worth," I continued, "I'm sorry if I screwed your family. I could say something about how only victims get victimized, but why bother? You need me to be the bad guy. Okay, I'm the bad guy. I fall on the sword of your revenge." Scovil responded by not responding. What did I expect? A prize for acuity?

I directed my attention back to Hines. "Don't let the skim go on too long," I advised. "There's a ceiling of about six million. After that, the cracks in the accounting will start to show. If you can keep your greed dialed down, you'll be fine." I nodded toward Allie. "Just treat her good, huh? She deserves it." I don't think Hines knew what to make of me, for I seemed pretty cool in my capitulation. "So what now?" I asked. "Scovil babysits the skim while you and I take a drive?"

"Something like that," he muttered. He seemed nonplussed. I suppose he'd have felt better if I'd cowered, but I had a sick headache and couldn't be bothered. Was this the most assed-up endgame I'd ever engineered? I just wanted it to be over.

"Fine," I said. "Let me get a dry jacket. It's nasty wet out there."

I went to my bedroom. It took about seven seconds for Hines to come after me. Of course he caught me palming the gun I'd taken from Mirplo, the gun he now knew hadn't been lost. But in my jacket pocket I felt the Hackmaster 6000. Did I just put it there, or had it been there all along? I was having a tough time holding a thought.

Ten minutes later, I'm back in Hines's car, handcuffed and lying down on the backseat, and he's telling me that if I so much as sit up, he'll plunk me. Honest to God, he used the word *plunk*. It was all I could do to keep from laughing, which I attribute to the existential absurdity of the situation and the lingering effects of a skull bash. I lay there, absently (and awkwardly, considering the handcuffs) fingering the Hackmaster in my pocket as I watched the trees and power poles flash past against the featureless overcast above. It felt like a self-indulgent tracking shot from some European art film. And, as self-indulgent European art films will do, it quickly put me to sleep.

When I awoke, the world was white. Snow fell through a mix of mist and fog. So okay, that put us in the San Gabriel Mountains, the nearest elevation high enough for snow. I had anticipated something like a *hole in the desert*, but Hines was apparently thinking more along the lines of *coyote food in a deep ravine*. Well, whatever. Dead is dead, right?

Hines hustled me out of the car and removed the handcuffs. This puzzled me at first, but then I realized they were probably serial numbered, and it wouldn't do for some random future hiker or mountain biker to find Hines's issued equipment on my skeletal remains. I rubbed blood back into my wrists and looked around. Tire tracks in the snow showed the way we had come: along a washboard fire road that switchbacked up from a desolate stretch of asphalt. We had arrived at the road's dead end, a heavily mudded clearing surrounded by sugar pines and thickets of sumac. On the far side, a sloppy wet trail led downhill and disappeared into a taffy pull of cloud.

Hines drew his gun and, with that flick of the barrel that gun users use, gestured me down the oozy path. I dutifully stepped off in that direction. I suppose that someone else in my situation might have made a stand right there, maybe forced Hines to use his gun, if for no other reason than to generate forensic evidence. But that's cold comfort to the dead, isn't it? To have an incriminating slug lodged in your decomposing corpse. Besides, this was the end of the endgame. I needed not to hurry it.

It was gorgeous in those woods. Ice and rime hung from the branches of the sugar pines. The air, cold and crisp, made my breath puff out before me as I walked. Snow and fog dampened all sounds: the cries of crows and the distant *thock thock* of a woodpecker. Hines walked behind me, his shoes crunching dully in the snow. I imagined that his gun was pointed at my back and felt a self-conscious tingling there, like you get at the end of your nose when someone holds a fingertip close. It didn't take a genius to figure out our destination: some suitable precipice he could throw me off.

Okay, fine.

Do I sound blasé? I know I sound pretty blasé. I wasn't feeling that way inside, trust me. I mean, look at where I was: wandering around the woods at the wrong end of a gun. When you get to that point—on the wrong end of a working firearm—it can certainly look like you've lost the plot. Granted I was impaired, but still . . . I could tell without turning around that Hines was grinning at how I'd fucked up. He was probably feeling pretty arrogant. I knew from recent experience that arrogance can make you careless.

Our angle of descent steepened, and anyone who tells you it's not hard work to climb downhill has never tried it on narrow path of mud, snow, and sodden underbrush, in totally the wrong shoes, and to the accompanying drumbeat of a head injury. My thigh muscles started to burn and, cold as it was at this elevation, I started to sweat. It became difficult to breathe. Then the clouds lifted a little, and I could see a break in the trail ahead where, five or fifty years or five hundred years ago, a furious landslide had sheared away the earth, leaving a steep scarp plunging some half a mile to a pile of granite scree. I thought of the Hackmaster in my pocket. Value Town Chuck said it did tricks. Was it doing one now? Only one way to find out.

I turned to face Hines, a look of pure panic on my face. "I don't want to die," I said. Sweat ran down my face. "Please."

"Begging, Radar?" he said. "Really?"

My breathing was now *really* labored. I could feel it coming in great, desperate, gulping gasps. My skull throbbed from where I'd been struck. "I don't feel well," I said. My eyes rolled up in my head.

I crumpled to the ground.

I felt the toe of his shoe prodding me ungently in the gut. "Get up," he said. "Get up, or I'll shoot you where you lay."

He meant *lie*, of course—shoot you where you lie—but had inadvertently shifted me into the past tense. That had ironic overtones, as did the word itself, for had not the sum of so many lies led me to where I lay?

Radar, Radar, Radar, what is this obsession you have with language? Here you are facing death with your eyes closed, and all you've done is disappear into a word game. You're stiff and fetal-curled, and is that a string of saliva dripping from your lip? You don't respond to

Hines's words or his increasingly vehement kicks. It's almost as if you're . . .

. . . playing . . .

. . . possum . . . .

I heard a leathery *snick* as Hines holstered his gun. Next thing I knew, he had grabbed me by both feet and was dragging me down the path to its bitter end. Dirt and snow smeared along the side of my face; some went up my nose. I stifled the urge to clear it. Playing dead is playing dead, after all; you don't get to choose your comfort level. As it was, I had two things working for me: (A) the high ground—Hines was dragging me from below—and (2) . . .

"You on the trail!" a sportscaster-sounding voice boomed forth from some hidden spot in the woods. "Drop that man and raise your hands!" As Hines's head swiveled toward the sound, I seized the moment to drive a cold, hard foot into his crotch. He doubled up and fell down, and with the practiced hands of a pickpocket, I located his holster and relieved him of his gun.

Like I said, I'm not a fan of guns. They're the bluntest of blunt instruments. But you know what they say about desperate times and desperate measures. I stood over Hines, holding his gun in two shaking, unpracticed hands. I looked like a bad accident waiting to happen.

I hoped it wouldn't happen to me.

shenanigans

Who was in the woods? Vic, of course, using his most intrusive Uncle Joe baritone. I presumed that Allie and Billy were with him, scoping me through the trees. In my mind's eye, I could see Billy cradling his laptop, running the application that homed in on the GPS transmitter in the Hackmaster 6000. Well, how did you think they found me? ESP? I shouted an "All clear," and the three of them emerged from the woods, grinning like Cheshire cats. It had been Vic's idea to use the ol' "Look, Halley's Comet!" I didn't think it would work on a seasoned scoundrel like Hines, but Vic said it would, because it had (as he put it) the "elephant of surprise" on its side. Well, what the hell: Even a blind pig finds an acorn in the snow.

We escorted Hines back to the clearing, where Vic's Song Serenade was parked behind Hines's GI sedan. I found Hines's handcuffs and snapped them on the wrists he obligingly stretched out to receive them. I could see the questions starting to form in his head, all of them amounting to one version or another of *What the fuck?*

"You're probably wondering, '*What the fuck,*' " I said. He didn't answer. Wouldn't give me the satisfaction.

"At the end of the day," said Allie, "it was a garden-variety snuke.

We all convinced you that we'd flipped on Radar, and you bought it because you wanted to."

"It's the sign of a good con, mate," added Billy. "Play into the mark's cherished beliefs."

I have to say that for someone held in handcuffs at gunpoint, Hines didn't look too worried. "So what now?" he asked. "Are you going to kill me? I don't think you have the stones. Allie, maybe. Not you girls."

"Murder is the last refuge of the unimaginative," I said. "So tell me if this works for you: We tie you to a tree or whatnot, pack our bags, and grab the first flight to anywhere. Our last phone call before takeoff tells someone where to find you, and you sleep in your own bed tonight."

"You'd better just kill me," he said.

"Oh, why? Because otherwise you'll track us down? Follow us to the ends of the earth?"

"You bet your ass I will."

"I'm saying that's a bad idea." I pulled out the Hackmaster and tossed it gently back and forth from hand to hand. "Your whole sordid history is right here. And here it stays unless, you know, it doesn't."

"Naked bluff," sneered Hines.

"Maybe. But you can't afford to call. So: You keep your distance, we keep ours. It's a big world. No real reasons why our paths should cross."

A shadow of doubt passed over Hines's face. "What about Scovil?" he asked, grasping at a certain straw.

"She's sorted," said Billy.

"Sorted?"

I flashed on the errand I'd run to the Blue Magoon. I hoped Scovil was okay. She was a bitch and all, but still . . .

Vic, meanwhile, had fetched from his car a padlock and a coil of braided cable. He ran the cable twice around a suitably girthy tree and prepared to lock the loop ends to Hines's handcuffs.

"We'll leave the keys over there somewhere," I said, nodding to the far side of Hines's sedan. "It'll probably be dark before help arrives. I'll tell them to bring a flashlight."

"At least let me piss first," said Hines. It seemed like a reasonable request, so I nodded my assent. Hines unzipped right there in the clearing, which seemed odd, but triggered the not-odd reaction of all of us momentarily looking away. As I studied a treetop, I had the vague sense that I was overlooking something crucial. *Did I handcuff him right? Don't they usually handcuff behind the back?* The thought lingered on the tip of my mind, then floated away. I wondered how long I would have this butterfly brain, or indeed whether I'd ever think fully straight again.

Then I suddenly remembered what I'd forgotten.

Mirplo's gun!

Too late. Hines already had it out and pressed against Allie's ear.

A frozen moment opened while the shock of the reversal settled in. Mirplo took a step forward, but a growl—literally, a growl—from Hines stopped him. Allie looked stoic. Knowing her history, I figured this wasn't the first gun she'd had held to her head. I've been there myself; needless to say, it's nothing you get used to, but if you're strong, you don't fall to pieces. I caught her eye, and she gave me a look like, *If you don't get me out of this, we are so over.* Billy, meanwhile, had taken a couple of steps to his right. For my part, I slid left, widening the angle.

This, apparently, was not an angle Hines would let us shoot. "Don't fucking move," he said. "Get down on the ground."

"Well, which is it?" I said. "Don't move or get down?"

"That's right, asshole, keep making jokes. Trust me, there's plenty of bullets to go around."

Bullets. Now why did that ring a bell? Again, I had a thought I couldn't immediately finger. I made a mental note to get a CAT scan at the first opportunity.

But you know what? If you're in the game, you play the game, even when you're not feeling game, so I struggled to view the situation from Hines's point of view. I suppose he was weighing a number of factors. Like: was the Penny Skim really real, and if it was, was there any way he could trust us to deliver a decent slice? If not, what plays did he have? He could arrest us, but then what? He'd be virtually arresting himself. No man is more dangerous than when he's drowning in bad choices. The least worst of which, unfortunately, looked like *start shooting.*

Except . . .

Bullets! Ha-ha! "Here's what's what," I said suddenly, pointing Hines's own gun at him. "You're going to let Allie go."

"Excuse me?"

"Uh-huh. And then you're going to shackle yourself to that tree like a good boy. Want to know why?"

"Why?" asked Hines, belligerently.

"Because I hate guns. I hate them so much that when I have one around—stashed in my closet, say—the first thing I do is unload it. So if you'll just be so kind as to—"

Blam! A shot whistled past my ear. It took out the windshield of Vic's car.

"Fuck, man!" shouted Vic. "Shirley Temple!"

"What the hell?" I added.

"Fucking moron," said Hines. "A gun can't be reloaded?"

Oh. Oh, I hadn't thought of that. Definitely not clicking on all cylinders.

Long story short, Hines held the gun to Allie's head till I caved in and gave up the other piece. Then he made a truss line out of Mirplo's braided cable, bound us waist and wrist, and tossed us down together in a puddle of mud and snow. A bad mix of concussion sickness and bruised regret swamped my mind. As I sat there on the ground, snow seeping through my pants, I couldn't help thinking, *This is so fucked up.* I'm not saying I made a deal with God or anything, but the thought did cross my mind that if I managed to get out of there without being dead and whatnot, I would definitely start looking for another line of work. Something that didn't involve the risk of guns or, more prosaically, the cold discomfort of a clammy ass as you sit on the ground in the mud in the woods. I knew things weren't entirely my fault. Elide the concussion from the equation and this endgame spins like a top. Ah, well. You can't unbreak an egg.

There's a certain sort of scam I've always hated, one where the grifter acts like a victim and preys on the misplaced sympathy of the mark. Admittedly, some of these can have a certain elegance, like where you call a bookstore masquerading as an author who's due in for a reading this week, only you've been robbed, mugged, whatever, and need some Western Union succor ASAP. In a typical filigree, the bad guys stole your laptop with all those pictures of your mother on the hard drive. For some reason, that detail turns the mooks' screws. At the end of the day, though, it's such a lame and needy thing. Basically, you're telling the mark that you've failed as a human being and that he, as a human being, somehow owes it to you to bail you out. Behind the whiff of faux desperation lies the whiff of real desperation. It's just too pathetic for words.

But I was feeling authentically sorry for myself just then. Besides, Hines had just relieved me of my Hackmaster and smashed it to bits with a rock. As a grifter, you pride yourself on always having other cards to play, but I was definitely running down to deuces in my deck. "Hines," I said, "can we talk for a second?"

"Kinda busy now," he said. And busy he was—siphoning gasoline into an empty soda bottle and dousing the upholstery of Vic's clunker.

I had a premonition of the four of us packed in there like flambéed sardines.

Vic saw a different sort of vehicular manslaughter. "Hey," he yelped, "leave Shirley Temple alone. She hasn't done anything to you."

Hines just sneered. "You should have thought of that before you fucked me."

"*I* didn't fuck you," protested Vic. "*He* fucked you." Meaning me. "You think I thought up any of this shit?"

Well, that was a good point, but Vic's plaintive lameness wasn't doing him any good now. I didn't see anyone passing out *get out of jail free* cards.

Which, of course, was exactly what Hines needed. But would he take one from me? This, in a nutshell, is the downside of being such a damn lying liar. By the time you're authentically ready to surrender, no one believes you anymore. Still, it was worth a shot. "Seriously," I said. "We really need to talk."

He crossed from the car and stood over me, gun in one hand, bottle of gasoline in the other. "What's on your mind now, smart guy?"

"I'm just wondering what it'll take to buy us out of this. I mean, you know that you have to run, right?"

"Well, obviously."

"You'll never see the Penny Skim. And the Merlin Game, that's gone, too."

"I have my own resources."

"I'm sure you do," I said. "But wouldn't, say, a hundred thousand, cash, improve the picture?"

Hines squatted down beside me. "And where would I find this windfall?" he asked. "Tucked inside your BVDs?"

"I have it," I said. "Buried back at my place. It's my dash cash." Okay, so I added a zero. You bait what hooks you've got.

"Your dash cash," he repeated. "You have a way with words, bub.

I'll give you that." He thought for a minute. "Maybe I'll deal," he said. "Answer one question first."

"Shoot," I said.

"What's your real name?"

I answered without hesitation, "Radar Hoverlander."

Hines stood up, accidentally baptizing me with a slosh of gas. "See, that's the problem," he said. "It might be. It might not be. You might have a hundred grand in dash cash buried in your backyard. You might have a dead goldfish." He shrugged. "There's just no way for me to know. So we'll do things my way." He walked back to the Song Serenade. "And oh, by the way, if you *had* been capable of, I don't know, thirty seconds of honesty anywhere along the way, I wouldn't have to kill you now."

See what I mean?

Anyway, Hines splattered more gas inside the car and this maddened Mirplo to the point of action. He leapt to his feet, but the steel braid connecting him to us flopped him back down. He landed in the snow and mud with a goopy sploosh. Despite everything, I had to laugh.

Hines glared at me. "What's so funny, funny boy?" Well, that made me laugh even harder. It was a syntax thing. *Funny, funny boy.* That just cracked me up.

I suppose I was becoming hysterical.

But whatever, it was contagious. First Vic got it, as he tried to wipe the mud off himself, but just succeeded in smearing it around. "I'm a mud man!" he shouted. Next Billy went off, muttering under his breath, "Shirley Temple? Shirley bloody Temple, mate?" Finally, Allie started, with a chuckle that morphed into a cackle, then unstoppable serial laughter. For no reason I can think of, she flicked some mud at me. It hit me just above the eye and resounded with a soft splat. I fell back melodramatically, as if shot. Thwacking down hard into the mud, I sent up a cratered cascade, much of which landed on Billy.

"Mate!" he howled in protest, and started flinging handfuls of mud at me. I returned fire. Allie and Vic got caught in the blowback, and soon joined in.

Pause for a moment to view this scene from above. Four young grifters are bound together by coils of cable cinched snugly at their waists and wrists. All of their actions are two-handed, and none of them can move far without moving the others. Being good grifters, they have a finely honed understanding that random times call for random actions. Being on the verge of death, they seem to have lost all sense and reason, but that's bluff. They dive on each other, hurl mud, try to stand, fall down, drag each other down, flop around like beached flounders, and generally make idiots of themselves. Off to the side stands an FBI agent with two guns but no clue. Should he fire a warning shot? Into someone's leg, maybe? Just start killing indiscriminately? He'd rather not put bullets into people if he can avoid it. Bad for the evidence trail. He can't understand how people could take so dire a moment and turn it into a mud fight. Maybe he doesn't know how to have fun. Maybe he hasn't grasped what every good grifter knows: that the best offense is a good pretense. Nor does he notice that the fight is developing its own rhythm and cadence. First one grifter is standing, then brought down. Now two are up, now down. Three get to their feet; the other drags them down, reeling them in by the fistful. They're laughing, carrying on, having a wonderful time. The fibbie yells at them to stop. His problem, he's not a whimsical person.

His other problem, he didn't hear someone call shenanigans.

We were Brownian motion, a Heisenberg uncertainty principle, bouncing and jouncing and flinging mud like chimpanzee dung. Some hurled insults with the mud. Vic seemed to have had enough of Billy's mockery. Allie aspersed my manhood. Me, I just sang. Hines thought we were nuts. It made him lower his guard.

Our random movements finally brought all four of us to our feet at the same time.

That's when we rushed him.

It was a clumsy charge, not exactly a pro blitz, but it had its desired effect. In a second we had him face down in the guck, with the weight of four bodies and a considerable quantity of mud holding him there. I saw one gun go flying, but the other was . . . where? Underneath him? Lost in the mud? And where was the key to the padlock? In his pocket, I supposed, but how to get at it without maybe giving him the chance to gun someone down? It was an odd little impasse. One that I apparently could have bought myself out of with thirty seconds of plain honesty somewhere back down the line, but the next sound you hear will be the barn door slamming behind that particular cow. I didn't even have the Hackmaster, which meant I'd lost my leverage. I supposed I could vamp about backup files on hidden hard drives, but see above: barn door; cow.

I was starting to think that honesty was a surprisingly powerful card, and one I should really try to play more often.

"So what do we do now?" asked Vic. "Just lie here till we all freeze?"

"That could take a while," a voice said. "Maybe I'll just put everyone out of their misery now."

I looked left, and there were the no-nonsense black boots of Detective Constable Claire Scovil. She bent into my field of vision and scooped Hines's pistol from the muck. "Let's see . . ." she said, brushing off the snow and mud, "Milval's gun. Milval's bullets . . . I'm thinking murder-suicide," she said. "How does everyone fancy that?"

the hot tub of truth

I'm saying I didn't fancy it at all. All my life I've tried to (well, had to) hold on to things fairly loosely. Homes, cars, possessions of all kinds. The way grifters roll, they need to be ready to drop everything and run. I thought I held on to life the same loose way. It was a fine party and all—the best I ever crashed—but every party ends, and anyone who doesn't acknowledge this is just not being realistic. You can fantasize that you're immortal. You can hold out the hope of heaven, if you like. Me, I was always just *enjoy the ride, and turn in your ticket when you're done.* But finally staring death in the face—or from this prone perspective, staring it in the chunky Doc Martens—I found that I wasn't holding on so loosely any more. Why the change of heart? My something to lose, of course, sprawled there beside me in the mud. Having finally found love, I would be royally pissed off not to get to enjoy it and cherish it for the next sixty or seventy years.

Want to hear something really weird? Much as I couldn't bear the thought of me dying and her living, I couldn't bear the thought of me living and her dying even more.

Nobility from a grifter? A genuinely selfless act? It was beginning to look that way—*if* I could pull it off.

I tried to roll over, but I was all cabled up against Billy's back and couldn't gain leverage. The mud caked on my face was starting to harden. I felt like *Quest for Fire*. "Claire," I said into Billy's shoulder blades, "you don't have to kill us all. Just kill me. I'm the one you want, right?"

Scovil settled down on her haunches and brought her eyes level with mine. "Nobility, Radar? Really?" See? She didn't buy it either.

"It happens," I said, trying but failing to shrug. "People change." She just shook her head. "Anyway, what about the money? Don't you want that, too?"

"Honey, I want it all. But first I want an explanation." She thwacked Billy on the nose. "Mate. Why was I knocked out for two hours, and why do I have such a headache?"

"Ah, that would be the flunitrazepam," he said.

"The what?"

"Roofies. Surprisingly easy to get in this country." He had that right. At the Blue Magoon, they practically sell them over the counter. "You're right lucky I only gave you a half dose."

"Thanks for that. I'll only kill you half dead."

"It was my idea," I chimed in.

"More noblesse, Hoverlander? What are you, applying for sainthood?"

"Nah, *mate*. I'm just trying to buy my friends' lives."

"Since when do you have friends?"

"I know, huh? It surprises me as much as it surprises you. But look, you know . . . the Penny Skim . . . plenty enough to share."

For reasons that beggar imagination, she kicked me quite hard in the ribs. "I don't want to hear any more about the bloody Penny Skim," she said. "I made it for woffle the first moment I heard of it."

"I don't know what woffle is," I said, gasping for breath, "but I assure you—"

And she kicked me again! Now *that* was uncalled for.

"Radar," said Allie, "let it go. You can understand why she doesn't believe you."

"Yeah, I can," I agreed. "I've learned a valuable lesson in credibility through all this, I'm telling you that right now." A thought crossed my mind. "But tell me something," I said. "How did you find us here?"

Scovil hooked a thumb at Hines. "He told me where he'd be. In case he needed backup. Which, to the look of things, he does."

"So you were in it together?"

"From the start." She smiled in mock surprise. "What? You think you're the only one who can spin a yarn?"

"And the bit about killing us all with his gun?"

"Don't tell me you can't take a joke."

"Some joke," muttered Mirplo. "I think I crapped my pants."

Scovil waved the gun lazily back and forth. "Right. Get off him now. Wrestling hour is over."

We rolled off of Hines. With a fair amount of bruised dignity, he rose to his feet, wiped off what mud he could . . .

. . . then popped Scovil in the jaw.

I'm not sure Hines could've taken Scovil in a fair fight, she was that staunch, but sucker punched as she was, she went down hard. The gun flew up out of her hand. In one smooth motion, Hines caught it on the fly by the barrel and gonked Scovil on the skull. Lights out.

"She . . ." started Allie. She didn't get any further.

"She's my partner?" mocked Hines. "Guess she's not the only one who can spin a yarn."

Yeah, I guess. In my mind I quickly restacked the facts. If Scovil and Hines weren't together (and judging from the heap of Scovil lying at his feet, I think you could take that as read), then from the start, all she was to him was a problem to solve. But which kind of problem? Honest cop or competition? Even at that moment, I couldn't confidently say, but I realized that from Hines's point of view, it wouldn't matter. He couldn't stand to let her shine a light on his operation, and as for sharing the take, well, let's just say that sharing wasn't his strong suit. Now, of course, it had all gone to hell, and Hines had the haunted look of a bunny in a leg trap wondering, *Well, how much of this will I have to gnaw off?*

Hines positioned himself near me in the mud. He picked my nose with his gun muzzle. I could smell the acrid scent of its recent discharge. I wanted to sneeze, but thought maybe I wouldn't. "This is your last chance to be honest," he said.

"I'll take it!" I cried.

"The dash cash. Is it real?"

"I . . ." I hesitated. Honesty did not come naturally to me. "I may have overstated the exact amount."

"Is there five figures?"

"Oh, definitely."

"It'll have to do."

So here was the new play. Hines and I would leave everyone here, locked up. We'd go back to my place and dig up the dash cash. If it was there—at least five figures—Hines would give me the key to the padlock, and I could come and fetch my friends at my leisure. "Or not," he said. "That'll be up to you." I have to tell you that I found this statement very offensive, which was a measure either of how far I'd come or how far gone I was. In any case, I didn't hesitate to take the deal. Anything that made space between Allie and Hines made sense to me.

Hines unlocked the padlock and extracted me from the Möbius cable. He rolled me over in the mud and held me, prone, at gunpoint, while the others locked themselves back up, adding the limp Scovil to the chain. If she ever woke up, there'd be a fourth for bridge. Then he bound me and hustled me into his car.

All the way back down the mountain, I tried to make chitchat with Hines, but he wasn't in a gabby mood. It was night now, and though

I knew vaguely where in the mountains we were (I saw a sign for Cedar Springs) I feared I'd have a bitch of a time finding the others in the dark.

Once again, and for what I hoped was the last time, I tried to play the game from Hines's side of the board. He'd be disappointed, no doubt, at finding only ten grand in dash cash, but it'd be enough at least to get him to whatever offshore nest he had undoubtedly feathered in advance. What he needed was a head start, clear transit through some airport or across some border. It wouldn't serve him for me to send up a signal flare the moment he was out of my sight. I suppose he'd feel he had to tie me up or something. I could live with that.

I know what you're thinking. I should have been thinking it, too. But every time I thought my head was starting to clear, it turned out that it wasn't.

So when we got back to my place and Hines had me dig up my ammo case from its hillside home, I stood there feeling rather grand as he counted out the money. At least I'd told the truth about that. Honesty? Best policy? Yeah!

"That's it?" asked Hines.

"It," I agreed. The rain was really pouring down again, and the hillside was shot through with rivulets of flowing debris. "I have some vintage baseball cards if you want those, too." I slipped on the slanty slope as I turned and headed back up to my place.

"Stop right there," he said.

"No baseball cards?" But before I turned around, I knew he'd pulled his stupid gun again, and speaking of stupid, I guess I get the prize for that. I should have realized on the car ride down from the mountains that Hines didn't need a short head start but a long one. Just tying me up was not going to cut it. But murdering me and leaving me on a wet hillside . . . yeah, that'd do.

"Oh, what is this?" I asked tiredly.

"What do you think it is?"

"Look," I said, "all I want is to walk away. I won't drop a dime. Really. You can trust me."

We both knew how ridiculous that sounded.

And you know what? I was kind of ready to go. After all, I'd saved Allie, right?

Right? Sure, right.

Except after he'd done me, what was to stop Hines from going back up the mountain and finishing the job? Once you get into murder, the actual body count becomes somewhat moot.

Well, that just completely and utterly burned my bacon. Here I'd made a reasonable deal with the man (giving up $10,000 is not nothing!), and he'd treated me like some kind of schoolyard mark. Which, I guess you'd have to say, I was.

So there we stood on the hillside, rain pouring down, mud covering our shoes, one guy holding a gun on the other. A real noir moment. Far below I could see the glowing lights of the Java Man. I thought of all the times I'd been up and down the hill to that place. I knew that slope pretty well. I knew how treacherous it could be, even when half of it wasn't draining away in the rain.

I also knew how many neighbors' windows looked out on that tiny slice of urban verdance.

"On your knees," hissed Hines. "Now."

"You know what? No." It was the hiss that gave him away. He wanted to keep this whole thing nice and quiet: another skull-gonk, say, then a smother in mud or similar silent demise.

Hiss notwithstanding, Hines wasn't ready to concede the point. "Do it," he said, "or I'll shoot you where you stand."

"Shoot," I said. "Go ahead. And everyone will hear, and you won't even make it out of this neighborhood, much less on the last flight to

Wherethefuckistan or whatnot." I've said it before and I'll say it again: The grift is like poker; when you're down to deuces, deuces is what you play. And when you think the other guy is bluffing, you go with your gut, and raise.

I turned and took a single step uphill.

Blam! A single shot rang out.

Okay, not bluffing.

I suppose I owed it to rain or bad light or uncertain footing that Hines didn't hit me. He came close, though; I actually felt the slug whiz through the negative space above my shoulder and beside my head. At that moment, time stood still, and it seemed like I had forever to think things through. Either that or you get so used to playing *nothing* straight that in times of stress a certain rote behavior takes over. In any case, I whirled around (as if shot), fell to the ground (as if shot), and howled bloody murder (as if—well, you get the gist).

Hines labored up the hillside to finish me off. He grunted as he neared, losing his traction in the softening earth. I rose up with a feral roar and hurled myself at him. He outweighed me by a fair amount, but I had elevation on my side, and my momentum toppled us both into the mud. Then gravity ("not just a good idea, it's the law") took over and sent us both rolling and tumbling down the hillside, clawing and kicking and punching at each other as our bodies slammed against roots and rocks and wet nasty pricker bushes. Somewhere along the way we hit something big, started cartwheeling, and didn't stop until we slammed into the back wall of the Java Man.

My head hit cinderblock with a thud that I'll just go ahead and describe as sickening. *Man,* I thought as consciousness swam, *twice in one day. That is just not fair.* But then I looked left and saw Hines crumpled at the base of the wall with his head more or less at right angles to his neck, and I thought, *Well, things could be worse.*

The Java Man's manager came running out. "What the fuck?" he asked, more or less rhetorically.

I tried to answer. Instead, I took a nap.

I woke in a hospital. A doctor stood over me, peering into my eyes. He asked me to follow his finger, which I did, and this pleased him, I thought, a good deal more than it should. He turned to the primly dressed woman standing nearby. "He's going to be fine, Mrs. . . ." He paused to consult his chart. ". . . Rook. Your husband, Geen . . ." He did a double take. "Is that correct? Geen?"

"Yes," answered Allie in a perfect South African accent. "Geen Rook. It's Afrikaans."*

"Very well," said the doc. "He should be clear in a day or two. In the meantime, he'll be well cared for here. He has excellent health insurance." Of course I do. That's what the Geen Rook identity is for. Clever of Allie to dig it out of my files, and bonus points for dealing herself in as my wife. Maybe she'd like some cosmetic surgery while she waits.

No, you know what? She's perfect how she is.

Two days later, I left the hospital with the whole welcoming committee there to greet me: Allie, Billy, and Vic. They were well, despite having spent eighteen rough hours in the elements until some hikers found them the next day. I was so happy to see them. My team . . . my friends . . . they'd executed the gaff perfectly, mooking Hines into thinking that they'd all betrayed me and, especially, staying with it when I got whacked on the head and forgot that Allie was in on the twist. Solid performers. Even Vic.

At that, I confess, I was a little surprised to see them walking

---

*For "No Smoking."

around so . . . free to be walking around. Hadn't the cops asked embarrassing questions about the whole chained-to-a-tree situation?

"What cops?" asked Allie.

"Well, I mean, didn't the hikers notify someone? That was a pretty funky state you were in."

"Too right, mate," said Billy. "So we told them it was a bondage game gone wrong, and they cleared out fast." Ah. Couldn't blame them for that. I would, too.

But what about Scovil?

Apparently, she'd come to before dawn, aching and angry, but a lot less rattled in her cage than I'd been. Her first thought had been to blow a big whistle, bust Hines, me, them, and anyone else she could think of.

They had many hours to persuade her otherwise. All it took was a little attentive listening and a whole big pile of cash.

As it turned out, Scovil's family *had* been taken in by my tropical island scam, and pretty well wrecked on it, too. This had propelled Scovil into a law enforcement career, with a particular ax to grind for the grift. But a fascination, too, the way anti-gay crusaders are sometimes the ones who end up in the men's room stalls. So she'd always had a love/hate relationship with Billy and, by distant extension, me.

Poor Scovil, so deeply conflicted. Was she a contrite law officer trying to unflaw her flawed judgment by bringing Billy to justice? The aggrieved daughter of swindled victims on a revenge tip against me? Or a formerly straight cop trying to become bent and get what the other half has? In the end, I don't think even she knew, and that's what made her play so erratic. Try to have your cake and eat it, too, you often just drop it on the floor.

But she came to see that it would do her no good to dob us in. She'd been tarred with Hines's brush. It would be a lot simpler for her to pretend that America never happened than to explain what really went on. Especially with the proceeds of the Merlin Game to help grease the skids. That was a high price to pay for our freedom, but Allie paid without a second thought, and I stand by her choice; it's hard to spend money in jail. Certain that the Penny Skim was bafflegab, Scovil had the satisfaction of taking, she supposed, pretty much everything we had.

So she took the money and ran . . . where? Back to Australia? Off to a fresh start? Or up some mountain to figure her shit out? I didn't know and didn't much care. As I'd told Hines, it's a big world. No reason why our paths should cross.

She has a quality, that one. Some day she might even make a part of a good grift team. Its muscle at least.

With Scovil sorted, it became much easier for me to deal with my own Jake issues, for now I could leave Allie, Vic, and Billy out of the equation altogether. All I had to do was backpredict a series of events that plausibly led to Hines dead at the hands of a Java Man wall. My story went something like this:

First, I admitted to a certain loose relationship with legal commerce; no secret there, just take a look at my rap sheet. This, according to my narrative, Hines had done, and decided that I'd paid sufficient debt neither to society nor to him. Then comes blackmail, my wet attempt at a payoff, and an unhappy accident at the bottom of a hill. Simple, clean, direct. Pure woffle, as Scovil would put it, but more than adequate to satisfy the LAPD, who could hardly charge me with assault with a deadly Java Man, and were warned off a wider investigation by the FBI.

As for the interrogators the fibbies sent around, I think they didn't buy my story, but didn't much care, for by dying, Hines had done them a tremendous administrative favor. Now all they had to do was keep a lid on the scandal. Did they have access to his dossier on me? If they did, they never said. I think you'll find it under the same rug where the rest of this mess got swept.

Get this: They even paid me. For my trouble? Or my silence? You make the call. They offered ten grand. I negotiated up to twenty-five. Never leave money lying on the table.

Not that twenty-five grand was anything more than a drop in the bucket (and the Merlin Game only a slightly larger drop) compared to the Penny Skim, which (A) was not the woffle Scovil supposed it to be and (2) made us all stupid rich.

The Chinese caught on quicker than I thought they would, but still we netted something like three quarters of a million each before they shut us down. I toyed briefly with the idea of not awarding Mirplo a full share, but then I thought, *What the hell.* He may not have contributed the most in terms of brains or sweat equity, but he did share the danger.

Billy took his cut and got in the wind. I told him to shout me up if he ever thought of doing something fun, like robbing Fort Knox. Allie and I, meanwhile, gathered what keepsakes we favored and headed south to a suitably banana republic. Vic rolled with; you don't like to leave the kids at home unsupervised.

The experience had greened our little Mirplo. For the first time in his life, he carried himself with the swaggering confidence of a winner. I had no idea how long the transformation would last, but for the moment at least, you could look at Vic and say, "There goes a grifter." Not the world's best, perhaps, but not a complete, well, Mirplo in the end.

As for Allie and me, we were in love, that mushy, kissy-faced ardor that everyone except a grifter knows well, but that hit two new-minted innocents with the force of revelation. And it might even last. Or maybe, like Vic's confidence, it will waft away one day on a tropical breeze, as our bedrock grifter natures reassert themselves. Well, that's for tomorrow. Tonight, we're lolling in a hot tub, beneath the swaying palm trees of a posh resort in San Somethingdor.

Allie turns and looks at me.

"What?" I ask.

"Nothing," she says. "It's just . . . I have a question to ask."

"Ask away."

"Yeah, before I do, I'm designating this here . . ." She indicates the Jacuzzi, ". . . the Hot Tub of Truth, okay?"

"Okay,"

"And you understand that when you're in the Hot Tub of Truth, you absolutely cannot lie."

"Of course," I nod. "How else could it be?"

"Okay, then. Now, tell me: What is your real name?"

"Radar Hoverlander."

"Really?"

"Really, really."

But it's not. Not really. Even in the Hot Tub of Truth, you have to hold some things back.

Acknowledgments

The author wishes to thank the two new women in his life, Betsy Amster and Sarah Knight. I never got why writers lavish such praise upon their agents and editors, but with the faith these worthies showed in this book and the care they took to make it ever better, I now understand. I also want to thank Maxx Duffy, my wife and inspiration, who tolerates my every "Listen to this" and "What do you think about that?" and keeps me tethered when I'm threatened with wafting away. Thanks to the real Radar Hoverlander. You know who you are. I also want to thank the internet for knowing everything. See you next book, everyone!

John Vorhaus has been inventing new words since third grade, when he decided that a frog should be called a flypogger and why not? His romance with language has led to one-night stands and tawdry affairs with songwriting, screenplays, nonfiction, anagrams, limericks, and haiku. He's proud to say that he's been a self-supporting writer for a quarter of a century, but this is not entirely true, for he subsidizes his habit by traveling the globe and teaching others what he knows, especially in the area of television scriptwriting. When not off "making the world safe for situation comedy," he lives in California with his wife and an endless rota of dogs. You can find him online at www.radarenterprizes.com.